FINDING HIS MARK

A STEALTH OPS NOVEL

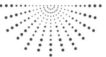

BRITTNEY SAHIN

EMKO MEDIA, LLC

Finding His Mark

By: Brittney Sahin

Published by: EmKo Media, LLC

Copyright © 2018 Brittney Sahin

This book is an original publication of Brittney Sahin.

Editor: Carol, WordsRU.com

Proofreader: Anja, HourGlass Editing

Proofreader: Judy Zweifel, Judy's Proofreading

Cover Design: LJ, Mayhem Cover Creations

ISBN: 9781720103363

❀ Created with Vellum

To the awesome ladies in my Facebook group, Brittney's Book Babes - this one is for you!

PROLOGUE: RECRUITMENT

Undisclosed location

Luke blinked, adjusting his gaze to the dimly lit room once the black bag had been removed from his head.

"Sorry I had to do that, but I can't let anyone know where we are. Not even you."

Luke cast a suspicious glance toward the man in a suit. "And binding my wrists behind my back? What was that for?"

"Had to curb your impulse to yank the bag off your head." The guy held a seven-inch, partially serrated steel blade and circled the chair to remove the flex-cuffs.

Luke eyed the weapon as he set it on the table alongside a laptop.

The man dropped his focus to Luke's shoes before his attention gathered back up to his face. "Why the hell are you in your dress blues?"

"Why else does one take a C-17 cargo plane in the middle of the night to Dover . . . unless to ID or pay respects to a serviceman lost?" Luke wasn't about to show up in cargo pants and a tee for that.

His head crooked to the side ever so slightly.

"Clearly, since men in suits bagged and cuffed me upon landing, this trip is about something else." Luke stood and hooked his thumbs in his slacks pockets, trying his best to maintain his cool. "So, you gonna tell me why your man pulled me from Jalalabad?"

The guy remained quiet for a moment, simply observing Luke as if unsure about him. The feeling was damn mutual. "Speaking of which, you didn't need to give my guy a hard time in J-Bad about leaving. Surely you have confidence in your team to handle the HVT you were recently greenlighted for."

Tension tapped at Luke's temples, pressure building there. "Who the hell are you?"

Few people were privy to commissioned ops led by the Naval Special Warfare Development Group, or more commonly known as DEVGRU or SEAL Team Six—so this man had to be high up in the chain of command.

He continued to study him, trying to gauge if he'd seen him before and just couldn't remember for some damn reason. Threads of silver darted through his black hair, and his green eyes tightened as he continued to observe Luke right back.

The guy's chin edged forward. "Your sister's been kidnapped."

An instant coolness frosted his insides as the man's words replayed in his head for a solid minute. "Who took her?"

"Kaleem Rassani."

Silence hung heavy in the windowless room, the only light coming from a low-watt bulb dangling from a thin cord at the center of the ceiling.

Was this an interrogation site?

"Why'd you bring me here?" he asked through gritted teeth, his arms hanging loosely at his sides now.

"Your sister, of course. We thought you'd want to be part of the investigation." He kept his green eyes steady on Luke's.

Neither man blinked.

"For starters, the Feds would handle a kidnapping case." Luke took one step forward. "There's no way a Tier One operative would be pulled from J-Bad to interfere with an FBI investigation." He took another step, the distance dwindling to a foot between them. "*Interfere* being the key word because I couldn't possibly remain objective. Also, if I found the cocksucker who'd taken my sister I'd slice and dice the pig. And that kind of shit might float during war, but not on U.S. soil."

The guy remained quiet and impassive, his lips a straight line, his face resolute and unreadable.

"Secondly, Kaleem Rassani's dead. I should know since I double-tapped the bastard two months ago outside Ramadi. Two kill rounds fired because the guy wouldn't put his hands behind his head."

"Anything else you want to add?" he responded with a mock of casualness in his tone.

"Actually, yeah. I'd venture to say you're not a congressman based on your cocksure attitude and posture. And given the SOG S 37-K blade you've got over there, it's safe to assume you were once a Teamguy. How long have you been out of the SEALs? And why the hell are you lying to me about my sister being kidnapped?"

The only door in the room opened a split second later. A spear of light shone through, and his sister walked in.

Luke looked back at the man, and the guy removed a

comm from his ear. He assumed his sister had been listening to the conversation.

"What the hell is going on?" Luke sidestepped him and strode across the room, embracing his sister.

It was nice to see her alive and safe, even if he'd known in his gut she hadn't been taken.

When Jessica pulled back, he realized she looked different. There was an unmistakable hardness in her blue eyes. He recognized it because he saw the same look in the mirror every time he viewed his reflection.

"You might want to sit back down." Jessica motioned for the chair, but her eyes were on the man Luke didn't trust right now. And trust was everything to him.

"I'll stand. Thanks," Luke responded.

"I told you he wouldn't fall for it." A kick of sarcasm bit through her words as she stood before the man, her hands settling on her hips.

"He passed the first test, but we'll need to run more," the guy said as if pained by the idea.

"Tests?" Luke pinched the skin at his throat as he faced his sister, a rush of unease gathering up his spine.

Jessica brushed a loose strand of blonde hair off her face. "Can I take point on this?" She directed her question to the man, clearly a superior, which didn't make a lick of sense since she worked for a civilian cyber company.

"It was your idea to bring him in, so yeah, I suppose." He extended his palm. "Will Hobbs."

Luke's eyes widened as he gripped his hand. "The Ghost?"

Will Hobbs had been a legend in the SEALs back around the time of 9/11. The man had basically reinvented what it meant to be a Teamguy. He and Luke belonged to the same exclusive fraternity, which must have been why Luke had sensed a familiarity about him.

It was the job of a SEAL to stay in the shadows, and Will had been a master at that. But the last Luke had heard, Will worked for the Department of Defense.

So, why was he standing before Luke right now, and what was Jessica doing with him?

"I need answers, Jessica."

"I'll be outside when you're ready." Will tipped his head in Luke's direction, but the icy edge in his eyes remained.

Jessica waited for Will to leave and inhaled a deep breath as if she were about to go diving without the proper gear. "So."

"So." He stood before her with his hands tucked beneath his armpits.

"I'm not who you think I am," she said softly.

"Yeah, I'm getting that." He cleared his throat and kept quiet after that, waiting for her to drop something seriously heavy on him.

"I was recruited from MIT my last year of school. I went to the Farm when I was twenty-two, and my job at Henly Computers has been a cover ever since."

"You're CIA?" He couldn't believe it. How the hell could his baby sister be government and he not know it?

Her eyes cruised the room before finding his again. "No one knows. Not Mom or Dad. *No one.* I'm sorry I had to keep this from you."

He turned his back and shoved his hands into his pockets, his mind racing faster than the bullet from his 50-caliber sniper rifle.

"Why are you telling me now?"

"Because I need you." Her voice dropped an octave, and

she walked around him and toward the laptop on the table. "Your country needs you."

"My country has me." He stood next to her and looked at the screen. "What the hell are you talking about?"

She began clicking through various case files of operations, including some ops he'd led as master chief. "I know about your missions. I know your kill count. Hell, I've provided the DOD with some of the intel needed to greenlight a few ops."

His sister's government-talk blew his mind. "And?" He pressed a closed fist onto the table and glimpsed a woman he didn't recognize anymore.

Seven years in the CIA. Seven years of lies.

But he was familiar with lies, wasn't he? Only his closest friends knew he was a SEAL, and they only knew because they were military, too. He didn't have friends who weren't in the service, or at least former Teamguys. He'd even lost touch with his college buddies.

It was hard to carry on a conversation with most people when work was your life and your job was classified.

"These are either the missions that were screwed up because intel got leaked to the press," she said while pointing to new data onscreen, "or the ops that never got the *go* from Congress or the DOD because they were in friendly nations."

He straightened, his spine going stiff. "What's your point?"

She looked away from the screen and rested a hand on her collarbone. "Ever since bin Laden was taken down our Tier One operatives have been increasingly in the public eye. It's become more difficult to stay out of the spotlight." She found his eyes, and an almost grim look reflected off her irises and slammed into him. "And even though you guys pretty much operate under different rules, there's still too much red tape."

This wasn't new to him, but he waited for her to get to the point.

"Will got approval from President Rydell . . ."

"For what?"

"We want to form a team to run more covert special ops. We want you to lead ten men—all active duty SEALs."

"Why poach from the SEALs? Why not recruit retired Teamguys?"

"Will thinks we should recruit men who are still at the top of their game."

"This is crazy."

"Crazy or not, it's going to happen. The team will be on call for the powers that be."

He almost laughed as he stepped back from his sister. "Which powers exactly?"

"Secretary of Defense Tom Handlin and CIA Director Paul Rutherford. And, of course, POTUS. If they need something done that can't be on the books, they'll come to us. Only a handful of people will know about this."

He continued to eye her like she was, in fact, nuts.

She took a breath before continuing, "You'd be handling the sensitive jobs we can't get Congress to approve, or other matters that may involve dipping our toes in friendly nations. Hell, some ops may take place on American soil. The funding won't be great because we need to stay under the radar, but the jobs will be impactful."

"Sounds illegal to me." He shifted his gaze to the ceiling. "Besides, I don't want to step on the Feds' toes and get into hot water by operating in the U.S." He turned and closed his eyes when she remained quiet. "Why'd you lie about being kidnapped?"

"To prove to Will you're the man for the job. He's worried because we're family you and I can't work together, which is ridiculous since I put you in harm's way in the past. Of course, my intel was always spot on." She touched his back.

"I can't believe you're a spy. Mom and Dad should never have let you watch that *Alias* show growing up. You always wanted to be like that CIA character." He made a *tsk* noise and faced her.

"Luke . . . this is serious."

"You think I'm kidding?" He shook his head.

"I guess it runs in the family then." She gave him a shy smile.

"So, you're asking me to lead some black ops group—and what else, exactly?"

"Co-lead, actually. I'll run it with you." Her lips tightened for a second. "We'll recruit SEALs with limited family obligations. We'll need a good cover though."

He half-grinned. "An alias?"

"How does Scott & Scott Securities sound?"

He laughed. "Like we're going to be lawyers."

"No, not even I could fake that. But I figure the best way to hide is behind the truth. Well, a version of the truth."

He rocked back on his heels, trying to wrap his head around everything.

"We'll run a security company." She crossed her arms. "It'll look as if our people retired and work in the private sector. Government contractors or whatnot."

"Then you might consider actually hiring some retired SEALs, too."

She opened her mouth to object, but he raised his hand.

"Hear me out." He quirked a brow and smiled when she nodded. "Hire some younger vets to run the day-to-day operations of this tactical security company. They won't be privy to what we're doing on the side, but it'll look more legit if we have more people. Plus, they can run things when we're not around."

"It might be hard to keep it a secret from a bunch of SEALs, but I get what you're saying. I'll talk to Will."

"And where does Will Hobbs fit in with all of this?"

"He'll be our only point of contact, the one to alert us to a mission."

Luke thought about everything carefully, but didn't know what to say. He didn't want to leave his platoon, but the idea of his sister getting hurt had his stomach wrenching.

"There's an important caveat . . . if an op goes south—"

"The government doesn't know us," he finished. "We're on our own."

She gave a hesitant nod. "So, what do you think?"

Instead of answering, he asked, "How'd you move up so quickly in the agency? You must be damn good if Will came to you with this idea."

A smile lit her face as she pointed a finger at her chest. "Came to me?" She playfully rolled her eyes, her blues softening. "I'm the brains behind this."

"And you really want to give up your cushy CIA gig to do this deep-cover stuff?"

She chuckled and swatted at his arm. "'Cushy' my ass. I've been holed up in barracks not much different than yours these past several years."

His eyes narrowed even though a slight smile tugged at his lips. "How the hell did you pull the wool over my eyes all these years?"

"My boss thought it'd be dangerous for you to know the truth in case I ever needed an extract. He was worried you'd, literally or figuratively, jump ship to save me."

"And Will seems to have a similar idea about me."

"What would you have really done if you thought I'd been kidnapped?" she asked.

"I guess you'll never know because I won't let anything happen to you."

"Does that mean you're in?"

"You think I'm going to let someone else take point on this, with you at the helm? No damn way. I've got your back, sis. As always."

She threw her arms around his neck. "Thank you. You need to jump through a few more hoops for Will, but I promise you won't regret this."

CHAPTER ONE

ISTANBUL

Five Years Later

"I'M BEGINNING TO REGRET THIS GIG. MAYBE I OUGHT TO start a normal life." Luke kept his voice low as he walked through the bazaar. The place was like a maze, and despite having his people on comms to help him make the right turns, today he felt like Alice after she went down the rabbit hole. He was in a tourist Wonderland with signs pointing every which way, making him dizzy.

"Give me a break," Jessica sputtered through the earpiece. "I know you don't like malls, but come on; you don't even know the word *normal*."

The Grand Bazaar may have been one of the first malls in the world, but damn, it was just too much. Most of it was enclosed and gave off the vibe of a cave. The bazaar covered over sixty streets and had more than four thousand stores. Heaven for shoppers, and hell for a SEAL.

The place made him itchy: the buzzing of voices, the

people jamming up near him from left and right as they bargained with shopkeepers as he passed. Too many people meant he could be taken out easily by a sniper, or lose his target.

"American, yes? Can I interest you in this gorgeous handmade carpet?" a Turk asked as he slowed near one of the storefronts.

Luke was dressed in jeans, a long-sleeved shirt with BIG APPLE printed on it, and cowboy boots. Between his wardrobe, blue eyes, and a complexion lighter than most Turks', he may as well have been wearing a *MADE IN THE USA* stamp on his forehead.

It was one of the few times in his life he wanted to be identified as an American in a foreign country.

"No, thanks," he said, checking his impulse to answer in the native language.

In the SEALs, if you didn't know something you had to learn it. Preparation was vital to survival. And the black ops group he now co-led, which was so secretive it didn't even have an official name, was no different. He required more knowledge because he didn't have the entire government working behind the scenes.

"There's a military-aged male about a half klick away from you." His crew member Owen's voice came through the line. "I'm going to move in closer to confirm the target," he said. "Keep past the rugs and swing a right once you see the belly dance skirts."

"Copy that," Luke said.

"The target has stopped moving, and he's talking to another military-aged male. I'm uploading the images to my program for facial recognition, but by sight, it appears to be Ender Yilmaz," Jessica said a few minutes later.

"He's a hundred yards up on your right. You got him in your sights?" Owen asked.

Luke spotted the target up ahead. "I've got him."

"Make sure he sees you," Jessica directed.

"Roger that, boss lady."

Ender was about five feet ten, with dark hair, brown eyes, and a trimmed beard. His face had been a permanent imprint in Luke's mind ever since the prick shot him in the arm three weeks ago.

Luke slowed as he neared Ender, trying to ensure eye contact.

Look at me, motherfucker. A second later, the target lifted his head and locked onto Luke, recognition dawning on him.

Luke walked past him, his eyes remaining connected with Ender's, and then he purposely increased his pace, breaking into a fast walk, appearing as if he wanted to escape. "Is he following me yet?"

"Yup. He's hanging back, but you've been marked," Owen answered.

Luke exited the bazaar, following the signs to find his way to the street. "Heading for the car."

A few minutes later, Luke arrived at his rental. Once inside the little blue sedan, he shifted his rearview mirror and watched Ender hop inside a taxi behind him. "He's tracking me."

"Perfect," Jessica said into his ear.

CHAPTER TWO

WHY ISN'T HE RESPONDING? SHIT. EVA REFRESHED HER EMAIL a few more times, but no new messages appeared.

She put her phone in her back jeans pocket right as the director yelled, "That's a wrap!"

They never finished shooting four days ahead of schedule; they were always a week behind, which currently left her with a dilemma.

After filming, she'd planned on leaving Manhattan and heading to her place in the Adirondacks to get some writing done. With this unexpected extra time, she wanted to head there now.

But she couldn't, could she? Well, not unless Travis Davenport replied to her email that begged him to change the terms of their agreement.

She'd rented out one of her cabins in the mountains to make some side money, but that wasn't the actual issue. No, it was the fact that the guy had demanded that her *other* cabin on the 100 acres of land she owned remain unoccupied.

And had he not offered to pay five times her booking fee, she'd have told him *hell, no.*

Given her profession as a screenplay writer, her overactive imagination had her creating about a hundred different scenarios as to why this man would want the land to himself.

She'd run a thorough background check on him, and Travis appeared fairly boring: a businessman from North Carolina.

Normal-looking guy. Normal job. Normal everything.

Almost too normal.

She should've said *no*, and then she could be heading up to her place now.

Damn it.

She'd spent the last month dreaming about her vacation; she was itching to move her fingers over a keyboard and finish her screenplay.

And now, she even had four extra days.

Four days of solitude to write.

As much as she craved a break to work on her script, she still loved her current job.

Being a screenplay writer and a co-producer for a hot drama that had already secured two more seasons on one of the primetime networks—it was a dream position, and she'd worked her ass off to land her current role.

"You guys killed it." Eva waved a hand in the air to fan away the smoke still settling from the last scene, then directed her attention to her best friend, heading her way.

"Are you thinking about your script?" Jayme asked.

"How'd you know?" Eva snatched a pink frosted donut off the table near the director's chair as more of the crew streamed past them and toward the exit.

"You always have that constipated look on your face when you're stressing about it."

Eva cracked up. "Oh my God, I do not."

Jayme grinned. "So, I take it you haven't finished."

"No, I keep rewriting it. It'll never be good enough to pitch at this rate." She bit into her donut. *Maybe if I have those extra days.*

Jayme eyed the dessert like it was a hot guy with a six-pack, standing, sweaty and naked, in her living room. God, Eva would give anything for that vision to actually be waiting in her loft when she got home later.

Who am I kidding? I'd run out screaming and calling 911.

"Well, we have three weeks off before we start shooting again. Why don't you use that time to work?"

"I have plans to write when I go to my place at Lake Placid, but I—"

"Just pitch it to your dad," Jayme interrupted. "Stop being so crazy, and give him the script."

Eva shook her head and polished off the rest of her donut, relishing the sweet taste that kicked in the back of her throat.

One of the perks of being behind the scenes and unknown, unlike Jayme, meant she didn't have to live on salad. Carbs were her best friend, and how could one survive without her BFF?

"I'm not putting my real name on it. Dad doesn't even know I'm trying to make a play for Hollywood, and I'd like to keep it that way."

Jayme's eyes tightened, determination competing with the Botox injections in her forehead. She'd been on Eva for months about this issue, ever since Jayme discovered her true identity.

It'd been hard keeping the truth from her, but once Eva's brother showed up at her door to surprise her for her thirtieth birthday—it'd been game over. Everyone in the film industry knew Harrison Reed, and Jayme had practically fainted in her dangerously tall heels, nearly collapsing right into his arms that night.

"Only you would do this, you know. Anyone else would kill to be the daughter of an iconic director. And don't get me started on the rest of your family, especially"—she looked around—"Harrison."

"I don't want anyone to know who I am, or that I'm working in the industry." Aside from making money from renting the cabins her parents had sold to her as "Eva Sharp," she didn't take a dime from her wealthy family. The Reeds were to Hollywood what the Kennedys were to D.C., minus the tragedies.

"No one earns anything anymore. It's all about who you know. And you know *everyone*."

Eva's lips pinched together as her eyes journeyed the room, taking in the remaining crew. "So, what will you do with your time off?" she asked, hoping to deflect.

"Nope, you're not getting off so easy." Jayme smoothed a hand through the air with dramatic flair. "Picture this: Everly Reed, Oscar-winning—"

Eva puckered her face like she'd eaten something sour. "Shhh."

"You're so damn stubborn. If I didn't love you like a sister I'd probably rat you out."

"You just want to stay in my good graces so you can get cozy with Harrison. The way you swooned over him that night . . . please, woman. You think I don't know you have the hots for him."

"And who doesn't?" She laughed.

"True." They grabbed their coats and purses and left the studio, following the last few people out. "So, where are you spending your time off?"

"Probably on a beach. I don't know. I might throw a dart at the map and see where life takes me."

"I wish I could be like you." Eva smiled.

"So, come with me." Jayme stopped walking once out on the street and faced her. "We'll have a girls' trip. I'll get a few of us together, and we can get out of this cold weather and have hot guys serve us mojitos."

"As tempting as that sounds—"

"You have a script to finish. A script that'll end up in the junk pile unless you put your real name on it."

"I shouldn't have such an unfair advantage."

Jayme looked up at the cloudy sky, rolling her tongue over her white teeth. "Don't the rumors bother you? I'd lose my shit about some of the things people have said about you. I mean, about the former you."

Eva stepped out of the way of the foot traffic and leaned against the exterior of their usual coffee shop. "I don't care about that, but what I do care about is going to my cabin."

"Uh, okay—and that means, what exactly?"

"It means I've made up my mind. I'm going to the mountains tonight, whether Travis wants me there or not. There's enough room for the both of us." *And maybe he won't even know I'm there. I can be invisible.*

"Who the hell is Travis?"

* * *

TRAVIS'S TEXT CAME TOO LATE. EVA WAS A FEW MINUTES from the cabin and had no intention of turning back.

As the taxi driver made the last sharp turn before entering the final road, his message popped up on her phone: *You can't come. That's not the deal we made. This is non-negotiable.*

She reminded herself he was a businessman, and so maybe that's how business people talked.

"Too late," she whispered under her breath and stowed her phone back into her purse.

"What?" the cab driver asked.

She smiled and adjusted her black-rimmed glasses. "Talking to myself. Sorry." She clutched her purse against her puffy winter jacket, her pulse quickening when they neared the home.

Maybe the renter wouldn't notice her, anyway. The cabins were several acres apart, and the snow would be falling soon, reducing visibility.

"It's going to storm pretty bad. You sure you're going to be okay at this place all alone?"

His eyes caught hers in the rearview mirror and a sudden barrage of Tweets played out in her mind: *Taxi driver attacks woman staying alone in the woods during a freak blizzard. Woman turns out to be part of the Hollywood Reed family. She's lied for years about her true identity. Why? What horrible secrets is she hiding?*

People would be disappointed to discover that her life was uneventful, plain, and super boring—well, compared to her siblings' at least.

"I won't be alone," Eva lied and nearly choked on the words as they rushed from her mouth.

He nodded and returned his attention to the drive. "You have food and everything if you get snowed in?"

A couple of days ago, she'd had her cabin stocked by the manager who looked after her place. "Uh, yeah," she answered as they rolled up the driveway.

She eyed the two-story red cedar home. Memories from her youth raced to mind—the few peaceful moments in life when her family escaped to the cabins for a little R&R with no cameras in sight. They hadn't come as a family since her parents split over two decades ago, but the memories hadn't faded with time, even though the vacations had been rare blips in her normally chaotic Hollywood childhood.

Her younger brother playing guitar on the porch swing.

Her sisters swimming in the lake and dancing on the dock with her.

And, of course, Harrison, sneaking off with every pretty girl with a pulse this side of the mountain.

A soft sigh left her lips as she swallowed the past and let it simmer once again in the corner pocket of her mind.

Once inside the place, the smell of roasted hazelnuts flooded her nostrils as she dropped her bags inside. *Nice touch on the manager's part.*

A lick of worry darted down her back as she thought about her current tenant and neighbor. What if Travis, aka Normal Guy, had a scope or binoculars and spotted her?

She hurriedly closed all of the blinds before plopping down on the brown suede couch in front of the massive stone fireplace.

The flight out of the city had been short, but the drive from the airport to Lake Placid had taken her longer than expected. The night sky would be dropping down like a movie curtain within a few hours.

The land Eva owned had a view of the lake, but her love for the place had more to do with her memories and the breadth of solitude it could give her.

But was she crazy to be alone in the mountains, especially with some guy so close by, demanding "alone time"? Just because his background check cleared didn't mean he wasn't some crazy killer. Everyone was normal until they suddenly weren't . . .

"I've got to shut off my brain," she said as a cold bluster of air moved down her spine.

Maybe drinks on the beach with Jayme would've been a better idea. Before she could close her eyes, a sudden banging had her startling upright to her feet.

"We need to talk," a voice sounded from outside, followed by another hard tap that shook the door.

"Shit." *Normal Guy?*

"I know you're in there. Open the door."

Yeah, sure. Is he insane? Her heartbeat took a panicky climb. "Who is it?"

"Travis Davenport."

"I just got your text. Sorry." She approached the door, trying not to trip over furniture on her way through the dimly lit room.

I'm going to die in the woods because I'm a moron.

"You need to go before the storm hits," he said, his voice a little calmer now. But damn, it was still deep and laced with something else—a gruff sexiness she hadn't expected from Normal Guy.

Sexy could still be dangerous. Probably even more so.

"Can you open up?"

Both palms went to the door as her heart ticked up to the speeds of an Indy racecar driver. "Can you slide your ID under?"

"I don't have it on me."

Of course, you don't. "Yeah, and how do I know it's really you then?" She stole a quick look behind her, wondering if her father's gun was still in the safe upstairs. He came to the place once or twice a year when he wanted to escape the public eye. Since the land was no longer registered under the Reed name, it was the perfect destination for someone in need of hiding.

"It is me, and I won't hurt you."

A sense of alarm buzzed through her arms and she staggered back, assessing potential outcomes if she opened the door. "I-I promise I'll be quiet, and you won't even know I'm here. Okay?" A tremble poked through her voice, even though she desperately tried to steel her nerves and remember the combination to the safe upstairs.

Whose birthday did her dad use for it?

Probably Harrison's.

"You need to leave. This isn't up for negotiation."

"I'll return your money, but I can't go. Besides, I got dropped off, and I'm alone." *Just great. Perfect. Nothing like giving him permission to bust the door down and hack me into little pieces.* She pressed the heel of her hand to her forehead and took shallow breaths.

"Can you please let me in? I won't hurt you. I promise. You ran a background check on me, right?"

"That doesn't mean anything." She placed her hand on the wall, searching for the light switch.

"If I wanted to hurt you, I would've done it already."

What the hell is that supposed to mean? Her spine bowed with unease as she flicked on the light and adjusted her gaze in the now lit room. "I'm sorry again about the mix-up, but this is my home, and my plans changed, so here I am . . ."

"You need to *go.*" A grittiness bit through his words, loud enough to penetrate the thick door.

"I already explained I—"

"I'll drive you to the airport, but we need to leave now before the snow gets worse."

She moved to the closest window and shifted the curtains a touch to steal a glimpse outside.

"Can we please talk face-to-face?" he asked.

She slowly edged back to the front door and rested a hand on the knob. "I'd like you to leave."

"I can't do that." His voice had changed. It was more intense. More *everything.*

"It's almost dark, and the storm's going to be bad. It won't be safe here."

"But for you, it will be?"

"Don't worry about me." He was quiet for a moment. "I need you to trust me. I'm trying to keep you safe."

The word *safe* hummed in her ears like a soft echo on repeat. There was something in the sound of his words that made her want to believe him.

Am I overreacting? "One minute." She went into the kitchen, spinning around in circles like a dog chasing her tail. She needed a weapon, but she was too frazzled to think straight.

She grabbed the largest knife she could find and walked back to the door. "You promise not to hurt me?"

"Of course."

Her eyes fell shut for a brief moment as she tried to steady her heart rate. With her free hand, she cracked open the door.

But, holy shit, the man standing before her wasn't Normal Guy.

No, there was nothing normal about this tall, well-built man with the bluest eyes she'd ever seen.

Not only was he gorgeous—he wasn't Travis at all.

CHAPTER THREE

HE HELD BOTH GLOVED HANDS PALMS UP, NOTING THE
woman's knife.

When Jessica had informed him the email account for
Travis Davenport had received a message from the owner of
the cabins, he'd phoned Eva immediately but his calls went
straight to voicemail.

His last-ditch effort of a text to keep her away had clearly
failed, but scrubbing the mission wasn't an option.

His men rarely operated on U.S. soil. They tried to avoid
it if possible, especially since they had significantly less to
work with: no air support, drones, or missiles. Minimalistic
ops so his crew wouldn't draw the eye of either the public or
law enforcement.

But in this case, their target was supposedly hiding within
U.S. borders with no desire to leave, and they needed to lure
the bastard out into the open.

"The photo of me online is a little out of date," he said
since the woman's hazel eyes narrowed beneath her glasses.

People say eyes are the window to the soul, but Luke also
saw them as the gatekeepers to wisdom—he knew the depth

of one's intelligence. He could tell from one long look into her irises that she was brilliant, which could prove troubling for him.

Her gaze dropped from his face and traveled down the length of his body. "You're lying. You're not Normal Guy." She cleared her throat. "Travis."

How could this woman see he was a fraud even though TSA at JFK couldn't? "I'm not going to hurt you."

"Go, please." She started to slam the door, but he wedged his booted foot in the jamb.

"I'll cut you," she threatened, but fear flowed so strong through her voice he knew she wouldn't actually go through with it.

Well, he hoped not. He needed his hand. He wanted to shove the door inward, but what if she fell back and cut herself? He couldn't let an innocent woman get hurt, but if she stayed at the cabin she might as well paint a bull's-eye on her forehead.

Jessica had done her homework and chosen the best location in New York: 100 acres of unoccupied land. And yet, here this woman was . . . occupying it.

"Just back up before she accidentally stabs you or herself," Jessica said into his earpiece.

He followed her advice, knowing his sister was right.

A second later, the door closed in his face.

"Reason with her, but if she doesn't listen, you'll need to subdue her. I don't think we have much time," Jessica said.

"I'm not gonna hit her, and I don't have any drugs on me," he answered in a low voice.

He took a couple of steps back to assess the entry points of the cabin. He didn't want to breach the place if he didn't have to, but could he talk this scared woman into leaving her home with a stranger? Probably not.

"Figure it out and fast."

"Roger that." He knocked on the door again. "Listen, lady, if I really have to, I'll come inside on my own, but I'd rather have an invitation." He pressed his ear to the door, listening, but all he heard was the cool whisper of the wind as it brushed his cheek.

A few minutes passed, and she asked, "What do you want?"

His palm pressed to the frame of the door, and he bowed his head as he thought about what to do. He knew how to deal with criminals and terrorists—but a frightened woman in the woods? She had no intention of leaving because of the storm, so he'd have to be more creative.

"Listen, my ex-wife's a little crazy, and so I needed a place to go where she wouldn't find me. But she tracked my receipts, and if she comes up here and discovers a woman—"

"I could make up a better lie than that. Try again," she snapped back.

"She's right, you know," Jessica said, and Luke rolled his eyes.

"All I can say is that you're in danger, and if you stay here, you'll get hurt. That's the truth."

The woman remained quiet for a moment, and then he heard the click of the lock. But this time when the door opened he found himself staring at the muzzle of a rifle instead of a knife.

Luke cocked his head and eyed the weapon. If it were any other day, he'd almost find the sight amusing. He'd bet the petite brunette had never loaded a gun before, let alone shot one.

He eased back a step and relaxed his stance, hoping to come across as less threatening. "I'm not the enemy," he said calmly.

"How can I trust you when you clearly lied to me about who you are?"

"I'm safe." He lifted his gloved hands and placed a palm over his jacket, on top of his heart. "I swear."

Her gaze drifted to his Tahoe parked in the driveway. "Please pack up your stuff and go," she requested.

Luke covered his ear to better hear Jessica as she said, "Drop her off at the rest stop three klicks east of our location. We'll have Owen there, waiting."

Owen added, "I'll hold on to her until the op is over. We can't risk her running to the police."

Although he didn't want to hold her captive it was better than having her wind up as collateral damage.

Luke couldn't confirm aloud, so instead he took a hesitant step her way, noticing the tremble of her trigger finger. The safety was on, though, whether she realized it or not. "Eva, right?"

She swallowed, and a soft pink flush crept over her skin. "Yeah."

"I'm going to take that from you, okay?" He kept moving in her direction, scanning the surroundings behind her, ensuring she wouldn't trip and get hurt when he disarmed her.

Before she had a chance to react, he swiftly wrapped a hand around the stock of the gun, tipped it up, and yanked the weapon from her hands.

"I don't want to die." She held her palms facing him, terror filling her eyes.

He removed the ammo from the chamber and unclipped the magazine, and then tossed the weapon onto a nearby couch. He didn't need to wipe it down since he still had on gloves. "And I'd like to keep you alive." He pointed to her jacket. "Put that on. I'll grab your bags, and let's get you out of here."

"I don't understand," she said, but was finally listening to him, thank God. She slid her arms into the sleeves of the coat and took a tentative step his way.

"The less you know the better." He lifted her bags and motioned to the front door.

Once her luggage was stowed in his trunk she strapped in next to him in the Tahoe, and he removed his gloves and started up the engine.

"Who are you really?" she asked as they reversed out of the driveway.

"I told you."

"You're not some normal businessman from Charlotte, are you?" She removed her semi-foggy glasses and rubbed them against the material of her shirt beneath her jacket.

"You still want normal?" Jessica, the ballbuster, asked.

He almost laughed at his sister's words, but Eva would officially think he was nuts. "I'm no one important" was all he could say.

"I don't believe you."

His spine stiffened as he glanced at her again out of the corner of his eye. She placed her glasses back on and dug her fingertips into her denim-clad thighs. Her nails were short and pink, and he suddenly envisioned what they'd feel like biting into his shoulders.

She had the hot librarian look going for her: wavy dark hair stopped just past her shoulders, no makeup, a straight nose, high cheekbones, pouty lips, and gorgeous eyes beneath the glasses. She was probably shy and completely unaware of her beauty.

Her lip wedged between her teeth, and she cast him a quick look before he redirected his focus to the road.

Jesus. There was something about her, and it had the muscles in his legs tensing as he drove. He needed to focus, but it was hard with the sweet smell of her perfume drifting to his nose, reminding him of how long it'd been since he'd had sex.

He'd been on op after op for months, and he hadn't had time to take a moment to breathe, to inhale the scent of a woman.

Maybe after this mission, he could take time off and have sex with some gorgeous woman on a beach somewhere. That's all it'd be, though—sex. He wasn't allowed to have a meaningful relationship. His life was one giant secret, and there was no room for a woman, especially not someone who'd need more than the web of lies he'd have to spin.

"Where are we going?" Her soft voice broke through his clouded thoughts. "The city is the other way."

Lies bubbled to the surface of his mind, but for some crazy reason, he didn't feel like voicing them. What was it about this woman that had him wanting to speak the truth—a woman he'd known for all of fifteen minutes?

Before he could say anything, Owen's voice was in his ear. "Two unmarked black Suburbans and an eight-foot rental truck are heading in your direction. They're less than four klicks out. I have eight heat signatures inside."

"Get back to the cabin," Jessica said.

Luke let off the gas, careful not to slide on the snowy roads, and made a U-turn.

"What's going on?" Eva's voice strained with concern and her hands clenched into fists on her lap.

He heaved out a deep breath. "There's been a change in plans."

* * *

"You're going to have to run that by me again." Eva's eyes widened.

"Run into the woods as far as you can get and wait until someone comes for you."

"I-I can't. You're not making any sense." She started gasping for air.

"Listen, some really bad men are going to be here any second. They'll search both cabins, and if they find you inside they'll kill you." He stepped back, snatched a phone from inside his jacket, and pressed it between her palms. "Turn this on in an hour. Someone will track your location and rescue you."

She shook her head and stumbled back, almost falling onto the bank of snow behind her.

"We don't have time. Do you hear me? You're going to die if you don't do exactly as I tell you."

"I'll freeze to death in the woods. Or animals will—"

"You won't die out there, but if you stay here you will. The men who are coming probably won't burn the house because they won't want the attention, but they'll murder any witnesses."

"What men?" She zipped the phone into the pocket of her jacket.

"You're right about me. I'm not who I said, but I'm also telling the truth about wanting to keep you alive."

Jessica's voice filled his ear again. "They're coming right at you. The snowfall is slowing them down, but I'd say you have less than two minutes."

"The snow is falling fast enough, so if you hurry, it'll hopefully cover your tracks," Luke told Eva.

It was getting darker out, and without Luke's night-vision goggles he wouldn't be able to see well for much longer. He assumed the men coming would have NVGs with them, though.

"I can't do this," she cried, as he grabbed her two bags from the Tahoe.

"Wait! What are you doing?" She came up behind him and grabbed his arm.

"I need to get rid of these." He didn't have time for explanations. They were down to the wire.

"My computer. No, that's my life!" she screamed, but it was too late.

He tossed the bags over the thirty-foot drop on the left side of the driveway.

"No!" She bent forward, pressing her hands to her knees.

"Go," he roared a moment later, frustration burning the blood in his veins as worry began to warp his sense of control.

"Who's coming? What about you? Where will you go?" she asked, even though she continued to stare over the cliff as if he'd just tossed a body instead of bags.

"I'm staying here." He unclipped his pistol from its holster, which had been tucked out of sight beneath his jacket —not that he planned on using it when the men came.

Eva turned in his direction and almost stumbled over the cliff upon noticing his drawn weapon. "Who the hell are you?"

"Don't worry about me."

He pressed a hand to his ear so he could hear Jessica. "We've lost visual now. They'll be there any second."

"Fuck. I'm gonna go dark now. You copy?"

"Copy," Jessica said. "And we'll rescue her; don't worry. Owen's already on his way."

Luke tossed his earpiece over the cliff and then grabbed

Eva's arm, forcefully yanking her in the direction of the woods behind the cabin. "We're out of time."

"I don't want to die."

"You weren't supposed to be here," he said gruffly, having reached the edge of a thick brush of leafless trees.

She faced him, anger and fear tangled like a fierce and dangerous dance within her gaze. "Why is this happening?"

"It doesn't matter."

"If I'm going to die, I want to know why."

"You're not going to die" was all he said, and then he turned his back to assess their tracks. "Now, go into the woods."

"Come with me," she cried.

He looked back at her. "I can't."

"Why not?"

"Because I'm the bait."

CHAPTER FOUR

THIS CAN'T BE HAPPENING. SHE CROUCHED IN THE WOODS, peering down at the half dozen men in the driveway alongside the cabin Travis had rented.

She had been right all along. She'd die in the woods.

Afraid running would make too much noise, she opted to stay in place and be as still as humanly possible.

Her fists had remained locked tight in front of her lips, and she'd stifled a scream upon witnessing Travis surrender his gun and sink to his knees on the snowy driveway.

He hadn't put up much of a fight, and for some reason, that surprised her. From the moment she'd laid eyes on him, she'd taken him for a man who wouldn't give in so easily.

Bait? Did he want to be taken? It didn't make sense. But what the hell did she know?

Three sets of headlights illuminated the driveway: two SUVs and what looked like a rental truck people used for short distance moves.

One of the masked men forced Travis's hands behind his back and began nudging him in the direction of his cabin.

Other men were already inside, and every light had been

turned on. She assumed they were tossing the place, but what were they looking for?

Her shoulders jerked at the sudden sound coming from . . . *shit*, from her. Her cell phone was still on and inside her purse. She'd almost forgotten she had it.

Curses came from the driveway and gunfire sprayed the woods.

She wasn't on set.

These weren't fake bullets.

No! She snatched her phone from her purse, turning off the call from her brother Harrison, and kept low as she ran, trying to dodge the bullets.

She tripped and fell, hitting her head on something hard as a loud voice boomed, "STOP!"

Eva had to get back upright so she could move again even though the gunfire now ceased.

Her breaths were shallow and tears streaked her cheeks, but her legs felt weighted down by lead as she rose.

She gasped when someone grabbed her from behind. "No. Let me go." She struggled, trying to break free, but two more people swooped before her.

"Stop resisting, or I'll kill you now." An accented voice found her ears and her knees buckled.

"Please, let me go," she cried, even though her plea would be in vain. She was up against three figures in the dark, and they were probably armed.

Within ten minutes, she found herself back at the cabin, being pushed indoors.

Her palms landed on the floor, her knees banging against the hardwood. She slowly lifted her head to find Travis's blue eyes pinned to her face.

He was on his knees, his hands behind his back, and he was shaking his head ever so slightly as if disappointed.

"Don't hurt her." His gaze veered to an armed, masked man off to his right.

"Why shouldn't we?" the man asked, his accent unrecognizable to her.

"She's important to me." Travis looked at Eva again, as if he were trying to send her a message with his eyes.

But she wasn't receiving it. "No, I—" One of the men pressed something hard into her back, forcing her flat against the floor now. She turned her cheek to try and prevent her glasses from breaking. They pressed hard against her face, digging into her skin.

"If she's special to you, all the more reason to put a bullet in her head."

Oh, God. She squeezed her eyes closed, preparing for death. But how does one do that, exactly?

"She works with me. She knows everything," Travis rushed out.

Peering out of one eye, she caught sight of the man's dark shoes as they inched back a couple of steps from her body.

"Malik will want her brought in with me," Travis added, making things worse in her eyes.

"She doesn't matter. Kill her," the man said so casually she couldn't comprehend his words.

"Ender, wait!" Travis yelled. "The USB's been destroyed!"

The sentence held no meaning to her, but she prayed to God it'd somehow keep her alive.

"Who has the code?" He pointed the gun at her and then switched it to Travis.

"She knows five digits of the code, and I know the other five. It keeps us both alive," Travis said.

Code? A foggy haze secured itself in her mind like a self-defense mechanism that would protect her from pain if a bullet pierced her flesh.

"And how do I know you're telling the truth?"

"You don't. The question is *can you take the risk?*" Travis's self-assured tone with not the slightest waver in it, almost comforted her.

Murmured voices in another language continued as she thought about all of the things she still wanted in life and might never get a chance to experience.

"Get her up," the man growled, and her stomach muscles banded tight.

She struggled, floundering like a wet fish on the dock as they lifted her. "Get your hands off me!" she begged once standing.

The man referred to as Ender removed his mask, and she shut her eyes.

Wasn't seeing someone's face the kiss of death—or was that only true in Hollywood?

"Strip," he demanded in a low, guttural voice that had her skin crawling. His black brows dropped as his dark lashes lifted, his eyes traveling the length of her body.

"No." She looked at Travis, hoping for a savior, not sure what the hell kind of mess she'd gotten herself into.

"You didn't make me strip. You can pat her down with her clothes on." Travis's voice was rough and intimidating, but the man cocked a gun her way and angled his head, ignoring him.

"Fine. Tell me the code, and she can stay clothed." The man edged closer to him.

"Sure, so you can kill us both, here and now?" Travis's face tightened, and a slow creep of redness spread up his throat and then deepened as if anger had burst through and he could no longer hold himself back.

The man redirected his attention to Eva after a breathy huff fell from his lips. "Strip."

"Don't make her do this." Travis started to move in her direction, but two masked men roped their hands around his arms in an attempt to hold him back. He simply dragged them along with him. "Don't disgrace a woman like this."

"Make her do it, or she'll die. We'll roll the dice as to whether you lied about the code or not." Ender's lips twisted into a grim sneer.

"They're making sure you're not wired," Travis said a moment later in a softer voice.

"You can leave your undergarments on," Ender said.

She swallowed the rise of bile in her throat. The pain in her stomach traveled north and into her chest, and her entire body began to hurt. "Okay," she surrendered.

Eva slowly removed her jacket and bent forward to unzip her knee-length brown boots. Her fast pulse pricked her neck as she went through the motions of stripping down in front of complete strangers.

The men forced Travis back to his knees. It took four guys to get him there. While he'd dropped easily in the driveway earlier, for some reason, he'd become more of a lion inside the cabin—ferocity filled his eyes.

Her cold fingers reached for the hem of her long-sleeved sweater, and she nervously lifted it over her head. She immediately clutched it in front of her chest, but the man—Ender—stepped in and grabbed it from her. "You hiding something?"

"No." She could feel Travis's eyes on her, but when she looked at him, he wasn't staring at her body like she was sure the men in the room were—no, his eyes were burning with hate, with something dark and primitive. It was as if he were ready to charge at the men in the room and tear them to shreds.

"Pants, too." Ender motioned for her to hurry.

As she unzipped her jeans, another masked man at her side began speaking in a different language. He held two phones in his hand, the one Travis had given her, plus her personal cell.

Shit. "See, I'm okay." She opened her arms wide as Ender circled her.

She flinched when he snatched her glasses from her face and stomped on them with his booted foot—and then snapped a photo of her with his phone a moment later.

"Get dressed. We're going." The burn of Ender's gaze was like a hot iron on her skin.

She scrambled for her clothes as the men forced Travis back to his feet.

He whispered, "Sorry," as he brushed past her on the way out.

Sorry was reserved for spilling coffee on your blouse or for deleting your favorite show from the DVR.

Sorry was not for getting you kidnapped and probably killed.

Ender escorted her to the rental truck once dressed, and Travis was already sitting inside. His ankles were tied and his hands were behind his back, attached to something that appeared bolted to the floor.

Before she knew it, she was positioned in the same way, but directly across from him.

The door fell shut a moment later, and they were left alone in the dark.

With her chin tucked against her chest, she closed her eyes and tried to come up with a plan. But she had a feeling she couldn't write herself out of this mess. This was a serious plot twist in her life, and she was damn sure there'd happy ending.

* * *

"ARE YOU OKAY?" TRAVIS ASKED ONCE THE ENGINE PURRED and they were on the move.

"Of course I'm not," she hissed.

"I'm sorry," he said a minute later. "You were never supposed to get dragged into this."

"Four days early. Why did we have to finish filming four days early?" she whispered under her breath.

She tilted her head back and squeezed the emotions down her throat, trying to find some sense of calm, but it was damn next to impossible.

"Why'd you lie to them about me?" Tremors shot through her arms.

"To keep you alive," he said softly. "Otherwise they'd have put a bullet in your head and burned your body."

"Burned my . . ." She couldn't even finish the sentence.

She wasn't on a TV show, she reminded herself. This was reality. But how could this possibly be *her* reality?

She was boring.

Flannel pajamas–History Channel–and–black coffee boring.

Everly Reed was glamour, not Eva. And she hadn't been Everly in three years.

But God, after tonight, she'd give anything to have her old life back if it meant she'd live to see another day.

"What's your real name? I keep calling you *Travis* in my head, and I know that's not who you are." She narrowed her eyes, trying to see better. She could finally make out his shape, at least. His broad frame was hard to miss.

39

"Luke. I'd offer to shake your hand . . ."

Luke. It fit better. If he was telling the truth, of course. How could she ever believe anything he said? "What the hell happened back there? You owe me that much after I've been shot at, forced to get nearly naked, and—"

"I'm so fucking sorry," he rushed out. "You weren't supposed to be there."

"You keep saying that, but this is insane."

"You're going to be okay."

His steady voice should've reassured her, but how could they possibly be fine after all of this? "I think we're outnumbered."

"Once my team realizes you've been taken, too, they'll come get us." Disappointment wrapped tightly around his words.

"You don't want them to come for us, though, do you?" Her body grew stiff.

"I don't want you getting hurt, which trumps whatever was supposed to happen."

"And what exactly was supposed to happen? Who is Malik? And what USB—or code—do they want?"

A minute of silence swept the cool interior of the truck before he answered. "I can't tell you anything. I'm sorry."

"Since these guys think I know half of this code, I ought to be clued in." She was close to snapping like one of her younger brother's worn-out guitar strings.

"The less you know, the better, but I promise you'll be safe soon. Why don't you try distracting yourself while we wait for an extract?"

"Distract myself?" Tears crept into her eyes. "And what do you suggest for a distraction? You have a harmonica on you? You want to sing folk songs?" She faked a laugh. "Right, you're cuffed to the inside of a truck, and so am I.

I'm thinking there's nothing that will take my mind off our imminent death."

"You're not gonna die."

She wished she could see his eyes; she was always good at reading people. "I'm thinking we are. Your so-called team won't be able to find us because that man took my phone, and, I'm assuming, yours, too."

"My people are tracking me, don't worry. They'll need to wait for the right moment to rescue us. We're driving in the mountains during a snowstorm, which makes things trickier."

"How can you be so calm right now?" She shut her eyes. "Are you government? Police? FBI? DEA?"

"Something like that."

His words had her lifting her chin and opening her eyes. "Okay, so that's good. Why didn't you just tell me that?" She arched her back and shifted on her bottom, trying to keep her limbs from going numb. "Your people can outnumber these guys then, right?" She took a sobering breath.

"It's more about quality than quantity," he said, his vagueness testing her nerves.

Being in the dark with a stranger and some serious bad guys behind the wheel should've broken her; but somehow, she found herself clinging to hope. Without hope, she'd have nothing left, and so . . .

"Why'd you rent my cabin? Why were you bait? Bait for what?" Her questions pinged off the metal walls, and she impatiently waited for his response.

After a minute, he said, "None of that matters. Focus on staying calm. Okay?"

She bit her lip, wishing she could click her heels like Dorothy and be back home right now. "If you really want to provide me with a distraction, at least talk to me. Tell me something. Anything."

But, of course, he remained quiet.

"I'm screwing something big up, aren't I?" Sudden guilt tugged at her heart. "Your people are only going to come for us because of me; you wanted to be taken, and so now . . . shit."

"This isn't on you. Try not to think about it."

She shot him a humorless smile, forgetting he wouldn't be able to see her. "Sure. You told me not to come. You told me to run in the woods . . . so this *is* my fault."

"No," he said firmly, but he didn't offer more than that.

"If I didn't ruin your plans, what would've happened?" She hung her head, knowing she was wasting her breath. The man probably couldn't tell her anything if he was part of some three-letter agency.

"Why'd you show up to the cabin?" he asked instead.

"My job finished earlier than expected, so I wanted to come up here. I like the quiet. Being at the cabin always helps cure my writer's block."

"You're a writer?"

"Yeah. I'm a showrunner for a TV series, but I'm also working on a screenplay. I'm stuck on the ending. Of course, you chucked my life's work over a cliff, and so—"

"You don't have a backup?"

"Yes, but it's not going to be the same."

"Well, what's your script about?"

"You won't talk, but you want me to?"

"It's that or silence. Take your pick."

"I'm not a fan of talking about myself," she said softly a few minutes later.

"Neither am I."

"No surprise there." Her hands were officially numb, damn it.

"But I wasn't asking you to talk about yourself. I asked about your script."

"True." Movies and TV had always been her entire world. Films were her comfort zone; even after she'd tried to escape the life, she'd found herself right back in it by working on *SEAL Security*. Destined to be, she supposed. "Well, it's an action movie. Maybe you'd like it. It involves the FBI hunting down a serial killer."

"Not what I expected."

"Really?" A dark brow arched. "And why is that?" God, she was nearly forgetting where she was right now, her heartbeat even beginning to settle to its normal rhythm. "Do I have to be a guy to write an action movie?"

"Didn't say that."

"Well, what were you expecting?"

"Something lighter. Happier."

"I guess looks can be deceiving."

"You have no idea," he said in a low voice. "So, uh, what TV show do you work for? And what is a *showrunner*?"

"A showrunner's basically a writer and producer. I help come up with storylines, and then I'm on set during filming." She'd give anything for tonight to have been a scene from the show instead of real life. "Maybe you've heard of it. *SEAL Security.*"

"As in Navy SEALs?" There was a hint of humor in his voice, and it bothered the hell out of her.

"Is that funny to you?" A slip of anger dug into her tone.

"Not funny at all," he said, but she could hear his smile, even if she couldn't see it.

"Well, I assure you, the show is very realistic."

"I've never seen it, and I wouldn't know how true to life it is since I'm a businessman from Charlotte."

"I, uh—" The truck hit a bump in the road, cutting her off.

They fishtailed, giving her a serious case of whiplash. Had she not been tied down, she probably would've flown across the truck and landed on his lap.

"That's them," Luke said a moment later, his words stealing her breath and catching her off guard. "Tuck your chin to your chest."

"What? I don't hear anything." The truck flipped on its side a second later and her head banged against the wall. She looked up to see Luke hanging above her; his hands must've been still anchored to the truck behind his back. That had to hurt . . .

There was no way the cuffs would hold his weight for much longer, though. She jerked her head to the side and closed her eyes when Luke crashed down on top of her.

He looped his arms over her neck, the chain of his cuffs probably broken, and he pulled her in, shielding her with his body.

Her teeth chattered and her limbs vibrated as the truck slid on the road, bouncing from side to side, most likely off the guardrails.

Luke held her tight, her head beneath his chin, as gunfire rippled through the air like the popping of fireworks.

Machine guns or rifles, she wasn't sure, had her cringing with each blast, worried she'd get hit. The noise intensified, much louder than the props used on set earlier that morning.

Everything happened lightning-fast once the truck finally stopped skidding along the road.

"Don't move," Luke said into her ear, as bullets continued to ping the exterior of the vehicle like a tap dancer on speed.

"Not like I can." Her shoulders flinched with every shot.

The gunfire finally ceased, and a moment later, the sound of the truck door sliding open had her craning her neck to the side and away from Luke's chest.

Who was there?

Friend or foe? At this point, could she distinguish between the two?

A beam of light shone on her face, causing her to blink and avert her gaze. Luke lifted his hands above her head and shifted into a seated position before her.

"Luke?" It was a male voice, and she had to assume he was a member of the good-guy team.

"Is it over? Are we okay?" The desperation to live, to survive this hell of a night pierced through her words.

"Yeah, it's over," the voice answered. "Anyone get hit?" the man asked once before them.

"I'm okay," she answered, surprised by the fact that no bullet had penetrated the walls of the truck to shred her flesh.

"I'm good," Luke said.

"I won't hurt you." The man began to work at her hands, holding a small flashlight between his teeth.

"Took you long enough," Luke scoffed as the guy untied her ankles.

"Yeah, well, this was one situation we didn't account for." After freeing Eva's hands and feet, he tossed Luke the flashlight and keys.

Luke worked at the rope binding his legs, then removed the metal bracelets still circling his wrists, the broken chain attached dangling from one of the loops.

Eva shook her arms at her sides, trying to revive the feeling within them, and then Luke took her by the elbow and guided her out of the truck.

Harsh lights met her eyes from the SUV's high beams positioned opposite of her.

A shriek ripped from her throat when she noticed a dead body in the snow bank off to the side of the road, and she cringed and turned toward Luke, burying her face in his chest.

His hand rubbed up and down the center of her back, the stroke of his fingers, even atop her jacket, somehow soothing her.

"Are they all dead?" she asked, her words probably getting lost against his hard chest.

But he answered, "Not sure. Can you give me a minute? Will you be okay?"

He stepped back, and she peered up at him, the car lights from behind casting a glow around him as if he were some sort of savior. A hero, maybe. "I guess."

"Stay here and don't move. Try not to look at anything, either, okay?"

She swallowed the terror that stuck in her throat and managed a nod, then scanned the group of men walking around, dressed in tactical gear. Military-style fatigues and bulletproof vests. They had guns strapped to their legs, and some still had rifles in hand as they scoped out the scene.

Eva spotted one woman amidst the group. She had a ball cap on, but her long hair was in a ponytail, and her eyes were focused on Eva, even though she was speaking to Luke. She spoke what sounded like German, and Luke answered her in the same tongue.

"You good?" The man who had untied her was at her side now.

"I'm alive, so I guess I'm okay." She watched as more men appeared. They knelt alongside the dead body closest to the truck and lifted it.

Her stomach twisted, and her skin started to sweat, despite the freezing temperature and snowfall, so she rushed to the edge of the road and bent over the guardrail to throw up.

A moment later, a hand was on her back. "Shit, you okay?" Luke asked.

"No, nothing about this is okay," she said, her voice trembling. She wiped her mouth and slowly turned to face him. "They're putting bodies in the trunk of that SUV." She swirled a finger around in the air. "That doesn't seem like something the police would do."

"Police?" The blonde woman approached. She didn't appear to have an accent despite the German she'd spoken moments ago.

"Who are you people? You're not the good guys, are you? You lied." *But he protected me in the truck.* She attempted to brush past Luke as if she could actually make a run for it, despite her heart telling her he was safe.

Luke captured her arm in one swift movement and tugged her back to his side.

"We *are* the good guys. Those men"—he jerked his chin toward the bodies that were now being carried—"are the dangerous ones."

She tried to pull free from his grasp, but his hold was too tight. "Yeah, well, they're dead. So, let me call the police and tell them what happened since I'm thinking you're not a cop."

"I'm afraid we can't let you do that," the woman said and then looked to Luke. "She's going to be a problem."

A heavy sigh fell from his parted lips. "Get Knox over here. Find out if he has anything on him that'll help."

Shifting, Eva pressed her palms to his chest and looked up at him. "Please let me go. I-I won't tell anyone what happened tonight."

He grasped both her arms, the exact opposite of what she wanted to happen. "Unfortunately, I can't let you leave. You got yourself involved in something, and until we know how to fix it, you'll be staying with us."

"I don't *want* to be involved." What she wanted was to be back in her New York loft. She did not want to be on the side of a mountain with a bunch of dead bodies and strangers with guns.

Luke leaned forward, his mouth close to her ear, and a strange sensation washed over her. "I wish you didn't have to be, either," he whispered, and then a darkness dropped over her mind, and everything went black.

CHAPTER FIVE

LUKE ASSESSED THE SCENE.

Twelve assault rifles with optical and thermal scopes attached, eight pistols, and three shotguns. Not to mention the unused flashbang grenades and shit-ton of body armor.

Eight dead bodies. Three vehicles they needed to dispose of.

A female civilian caught in the crossfire.

And one failed operation.

Luke watched as the rest of his team worked to cover up the area as fast as possible. Thankfully, it was late, and with the storm few people would be traveling the roads. His people had set up a detour sign a half-mile back in each direction to prevent any potential witnesses just in case, though.

"Ender's still alive! We've got a pulse," one of his team members shouted.

Luke circled the truck on its side and eyed Ender's body sprawled on the road outside the passenger side door. "Get him out of here fast. Don't let him die," he ordered and looked at one of his other buddies, Liam. "Make sure you get samples from the dead and cross-check their DNA in the database. I want IDs on all the vics."

"Got it." Liam helped lift Ender's body, and then Luke turned around to see Knox on approach, his teammate who helped him and Eva out of the truck.

"This is why I really hate operating on U.S. soil," Knox said. "Eva's resting like Sleeping Beauty in the back seat. Too bad she'll remember everything when she wakes from her nap."

It'd make it a hell of a lot easier if the drugs Knox had given her could erase the last few hours of her memory. He'd spoken to his sister in German regarding the op, hoping the woman wasn't fluent, but he was afraid Eva already knew too much. If she were to go to the police with her story, Luke would have a hell of a lot of explaining to do, and he wouldn't be able to use the guise of Scott & Scott Securities as a cover this time.

"This is a disaster." Luke swiped at the snow hitting his face and curled his hand into a fist. "If only this woman had shown up tomorrow."

"Yeah, talk about shit timing," Knox said when Jessica came before them with her phone in hand.

"I got the GPS location to where Ender was headed, but I'm assuming when these assholes don't check in, Malik won't show at the rendezvous."

"You're still certain Ender and Malik are working together?" Luke asked.

"Why? Something happen back there that's given you doubts?" Jessica asked.

Luke thought back to what went down at the cabin. "If Malik really had his brother killed, why would Ender work with him? Why would Ender work with the man who murdered his dad?" Luke scratched at his chin, wet from the falling snow.

"We've been through this before: that's the intel we were given," she said, but he sensed the echo of suspicion in her voice as well. The intelligence passed on to them wasn't always accurate.

He pinched his shoulder blades together for a moment and relaxed them. "I don't want to make assumptions at this point. We need to keep Ender alive so we can find out what's actually going on."

"You know he won't roll over. There's a reason Ender wasn't at the meet four weeks ago with his father. He didn't approve of the deal his dad made with the CIA, which is probably why his dad didn't give him his code," Jessica replied.

Speculation, he thought, but kept it to himself this time. Jessica had more faith in the CIA than he did since she used to be an agent.

"Ender had to have been there watching the meet, or he wouldn't have known to follow the CIA operative after the mission went to hell," Knox chimed in.

"I doubt he'll give up the second code. Hell, he may not even know it himself. Malik may not have told him." Jessica tapped at the screen on her phone. "Our men are now en-route to the location where Ender was planning to take you."

"Which was where?" Luke asked.

"North of Poughkeepsie, about eighty miles outside Brooklyn."

"No one will be there." Luke cracked his neck and leaned against one of the SUVs, his mind running through all the different scenarios they had planned for, none of which had actually happened.

"Nothing like a five-foot-five brunette to fuck shit up.

Who would've thought? Guess we ought to update our contingency plans," Knox said sarcastically, his Southern drawl dragging through his words. "You think we can turn these goddamn lemons into some lemonade?"

A tight smile met Jessica's lips. "If you're suggesting we make a trade with Malik—first, we've got to find where he's hiding . . . and second, I doubt Ender's life is valuable enough for him to make that deal."

"Shit, we gotta try something," Knox responded.

"We'll figure it out, but Sleeping Beauty's caught up in the middle of this all now, too." Luke's teeth clamped tight.

"We can't let her talk to the press or police," Jessica responded while staring at the ground, a scowl on her face. She hated failing as much as he did.

"I'm not just talking about that. Before Ender and his men brought Eva into the cabin, they took my picture, but—"

"We accounted for that. They'll get the match we planted for you," Jessica interrupted.

Luke shook his head. "Yeah, well, we didn't account for them taking a picture of her."

"Christ. Do you think Ender already texted or uploaded her image?" she asked.

"Get Ender's phone unlocked and decrypted as soon as possible, but let's assume the worst. We'll need to protect her," Luke said.

Her hands rested on her fatigue-covered hips. "President Rydell's waiting for news. Will can't leave him hanging. We'll have to let him know the mission's been compromised."

Failure wasn't an option, though. The SEALs liked to say *the only easy day was yesterday*, and God, was that true, especially right now.

"Don't tell him anything yet."

"You want me to lie to the president?" She took a tentative step his way.

"Have Will tell him there's been a change in plans. Tell him we have Ender in custody now, and we'll update with new details soon."

"And if Ender remains comatose, then what? We can't keep this from POTUS. We have seven dead bodies on our hands."

"You could've kept some of them alive—and maybe left Ender in better condition." A crease formed in Luke's brow.

"Ha! You're no one to talk after what you did three weeks ago," she exclaimed.

"That wasn't my fault," Luke grumbled.

"Whether Ender survives the night or not . . . we need to figure out another way to find Malik," she said.

"Well, Malik needs the code as much as I need his, so he'll be looking for me." Luke spotted his teammate Owen walking up the road in their direction.

"Sorry I'm late," Owen said. "When I went in to get your girl and discovered she'd been taken, too—"

"My girl?" Luke rolled his eyes. She was about the last woman he ever wanted to see again right about now.

How the hell had a writer screwed up one of the most important missions his team had been on since starting five years ago?

"Guess we chose the wrong place to lure Malik's men to," Owen said. "What do we know about this Eva Sharp woman?"

"I only did a quick background check on her before we signed the rental agreement. She didn't matter then," Jessica answered.

"Looks like she matters now." Owen jerked his thumb

toward the SUV. "Can't exactly ditch her along with these terrorist motherfuckers."

Failure.

Fuck failure.

"Hell, we blew the op to save her, so we're going to have to ensure she stays alive and kicking." Luke tensed. "Especially if Ender got the chance to tell Malik what I told him."

"Which was?"

"She knows half the ten-digit code, and I know the other half," he added dryly.

"You did what?" Jessica came before him, ignoring the snowflakes catching in her long eyelashes.

"What choice did I have? They'd have put a bullet in her head."

"So, not only do they have a picture of Eva, they'll want her brought in as much as you." Jessica blew out a breath. "Just great."

Owen secured his pistol and looked up at them, placing his hand as a visor to shield himself from the high beams from the nearby SUV headlights.

"You guys handle the bodies and let me know as soon as our men reach Poughkeepsie," Luke instructed and then went over to the other SUV with Sleeping Beauty in it. "And give me hourly updates on Ender's status. Keep the prick alive."

"And what will you do?" Jessica asked as he got behind the wheel of the Range Rover.

"Get Eva somewhere safe," he answered. "Let me know if you find anything of use off the phones."

Jessica nodded. "Malik's going to be pissed when Ender doesn't report. He'll assume all his people are dead."

"Malik *allegedly* killed his own brother, so tomato

fucking *toe-mah-to*. He'll only be upset that he doesn't have me." Luke slammed the door shut and started up the car.

Jessica knocked on the window. "You forgot your go-bag," she said as it scrolled down. "Your new ID, credit cards, and cash are inside. Plus, your favorite firearm, of course."

"Thanks." He nodded and set it on the passenger seat. "Be safe."

"You, too."

He shifted the rearview mirror to catch sight of Eva lying in the back, asleep. "Now what the hell am I going to do with you?"

* * *

HE CHECKED HIS BURNER PHONE WHEN IT BEGAN TO RING AND went into the hotel bathroom and closed the door, hoping not to wake up Eva. "Tell me you have news," he said straight away.

"The address brought our people to an abandoned factory. And unfortunately, no one was there. We have two men in position, but I'm betting Malik and his men won't show," Jessica said.

"If Malik ever planned on showing." Luke stared at his tired eyes in the mirror, wishing this had all ended as planned. "What's Ender's status?"

"Still breathing, and our very expensive doctor is trying to keep him that way. Ender's under the knife now."

"Okay. Good." He swiped his hand down his face, allowing it to fall back to the countertop. "If the same people who were after Malik's brother are now after him . . . he'll be getting desperate, especially with Ender off the grid."

"Malik may have already cut a deal with the terrorists.

His brother's death and the safe in exchange for his own safety."

"These are all guesses. But if you're right, and Malik doesn't hand these people over both access codes for the safe, someone will be out for his blood. And although it'd be nice to have someone else take him out for us—"

"POTUS still needs Malik's code and the location of the safe," Jessica finished for him.

"We'll get it," he said as confidently as possible. "But I don't want to stay at this hotel for another night. Can you find me some place to bring her?"

"You planning on babysitting this woman?"

It wasn't his idea of a good time, but what choice did he have? It was his responsibility now, since he had gotten an innocent woman involved in this mess. "For now."

"Never thought I'd see the day when my big brother played house."

His lips pressed into a tight line as he fought the urge to offer a snarky retort.

"And, Luke, we've already screwed this woman's life up enough . . . so don't complicate shit with her."

"What the hell is that supposed to mean?" He stood erect and backed away from the counter, eying the door, wondering when Eva would wake. He didn't know how potent a dose Knox had given her.

"I know you." She cleared her throat. "You and a gorgeous woman alone for however long sounds like a shit combo to me. Maybe there's a reason why you've never been assigned to babysitting."

"Because I'm too fucking valuable."

Jessica went quiet, and he knew he'd probably pissed her off.

"You get their phones unlocked?" he asked.

"Yeah, I was about to bring that up before I got distracted."

He mumbled under his breath. "And?"

"The photos were sent, but the receiving phone line's been killed. We can't ping a location."

"Great." He dropped a mouthful of curses. "Just get me a place that's owned by a spook and not being used." He paused for a moment as he thought about Eva. "And when you have the name of whoever will be stocking the place, get it to me. I have a few special requests."

CHAPTER SIX

"WHAT'D YOU DO TO ME?" SHE SAT UPRIGHT AND BLINKED A few times, trying to focus on her surroundings.

She was on a bed and in what appeared to be a hotel room. Her jacket and boots were off, but she was still clothed, thank God.

"We gave you something to help you relax." Luke tucked his hands in his khaki fatigue pockets. "Can you see without your glasses?"

She was still too tired to even feel angry. "Those are a Clark Kent thing," she said softly, in a bit of a daze.

"A what?"

"I, uh, don't need them."

Luke stood alongside the bed now, and she eyed the veins on his forearms like they were a decadent showcase of male power. When he shifted a step back, she also spotted ink peeking out from beneath his black short sleeve shirt.

"You didn't need to drug me. I would've come willingly."

"Sorry, but we couldn't take any chances." His blue eyes darkened for a moment as his gaze swept up the length of her body before seizing hold of her eyes.

Even in a semi-foggy state, there was something about this man that both calmed her and made her shaky. "Where am I?"

"Somewhere safe." He cocked his head. "Why don't you go back to sleep? We'll be leaving in a few hours."

"Leaving to where? People are going to worry when I don't check in. I-I need to make a call."

"I can't let you do that."

"Why not?"

"Because you're in danger."

"What are you talking about?" She thought back to the whirlwind of a night that had happened . . . well, she wasn't sure when it had happened. Had it been hours ago or days? How long had she been asleep? Her stomach tightened, hunger stirring inside. "You told those men I had a code." Her eyes closed with the memory. "You did it to keep me alive. I remember now. So, you think they'll come after me?"

"Most likely."

"Are you going to use me as bait?"

"The thought has crossed my mind."

His words had her eyes opening, her chin lifting to look at him. A hint of a smile brushed across his face so fast she almost missed it. "Didn't you kill everyone?"

"Most, but the important ones are alive." He pressed his back to a closed window and continued to study her.

"Who do you work for?"

"We've been through this before. It's still classified," he said, his voice all cloak-and-dagger-like. "Boyfriend? Husband? Who might wonder where you are?"

Her lips pursed in thought. "My brother's very protective. He's the one who called. I didn't think to turn off my phone in the haste to try and get to safety."

He went over to the desk for a minute. "Who's your brother?"

She didn't want to tell him his name, but she had a feeling he'd find out anyway. "Harrison Reed," she said softly. "Can you let him know I'm okay?"

"Give me his number, and we'll send a message. We'll have it appear to be coming from you and out of New York."

She breathed a sigh of relief. Harrison's name hadn't triggered any change in Luke's eyes. Maybe he didn't know of her family.

She dropped her feet to the side of the bed and prepared to stand.

"I wouldn't do that yet," he said, without even looking at her.

Did he have eyes in the back of his head? "I need to pee if you don't mind."

He tucked his phone in his pants pocket; his pants had a ridiculous number of pockets, she realized. And then he faced her and reached for her hand.

"I can walk by myself, thanks." She tugged her hand free of his. "You've done enough." She slowly brushed past him, trying to ignore the size of his muscular arms in the process.

She shut the door and splashed some water on her face, contemplating how far she could get if she tried to make a run for it. Even though she wanted to trust Luke, a man who had shielded her body with his own, she also didn't like the idea of being a prisoner. And what if he did end up using her as bait?

No, his people had rescued her to keep her safe, blowing whatever operation they had planned in doing so.

Operation: a word she was familiar with because of her TV show. But this shouldn't be happening in real life, not in her life, at least.

She eyed herself in the mirror and wiped the faint bit of mascara from beneath her eyes. It was the only makeup she ever wore on a daily basis. Now, she looked about as tired and plain as possible. But looks didn't matter, because she'd almost died tonight. Still, there was a hot badass guy out there right now, and for the first time in years, she had a sudden desire to be seen.

A tap at the door startled her. "You okay in there?"

"Yeah. Give me a second." After finishing up, she went into the room. She positioned herself at the edge of the bed, and he sat across from her at the desk and leaned back.

Over six feet tall atop strong and powerful legs—she could just tell, at least. His blond hair was short, but not too closely cropped, and his strong chin and hard cheekbones were covered in stubble. He had such a commanding presence about him that maybe should've intimidated, and yet, she found comfort in his rugged sexiness and obvious strength.

"I don't have a choice in any of this, do I?"

"For starters, your life is probably at risk," he replied.

"And if my life weren't on the line?"

"What my team and I do is—"

Irritation bunched tight in her stomach and she snapped, "Classified. Got it."

He looked past her and at the wall, as if eye contact was suddenly awkward. It gave her a chance to eye the tattoo on his bicep peeking out from his shirt sleeve; her eyes widened at the familiar tatt. "You're a Navy SEAL, aren't you? Or you were, at some point, right?"

He jerked his attention to her lightning-fast, his eyes catching hers, and she noticed how blue they actually were. Nordic or Northern European descent, she had to assume by his Viking-like perfect structure and features.

"What?" He stood and grabbed a dark long-sleeved shirt draped over the office chair, and pulled it over his head. "Just because you write for a SEAL show doesn't make you an expert."

His eyes shifted to the floor, and she focused on the black military boots he wore.

Yup, *military* might as well have been carved into every inch of his body. Why did the man who'd wreaked havoc in her life, while also being a savior, have to be so damn good-looking?

The last thing in the world she needed to be thinking about was what he looked like naked.

She couldn't believe a SEAL heartthrob stood before her, whether he'd admitted to it or not. Teamguys, as they seemed to call each other, tended to be cagey and secretive, but what had blown her mind was his ability to make her legs tighten with some foreign need when she should've been scared shitless.

She refused to be a cliché and fall for the hero, especially a hero who'd gotten her into this hot mess.

Even in her own screenplays, she'd never willingly let the woman get wet with desire within sixty seconds of meeting the guy who'd saved her. She had standards for her characters, and so, damn it, she wouldn't—*no*, she *couldn't* think about this man before her as anything other than that. *A man.* A man who'd better get her out of this storm.

"Actually, I am a bit of an expert on the military," she finally said as confidently as possible. She'd spent the last two years researching anything and everything about the military, with particular regard to SEALs. Her friends at work joked she was a walking *Wikipedia.*

"Mm-hm. Sure you are." He found her eyes again, and the

sizzle she didn't want snapped straight down her spine and into her toes.

It's the drugs. It has to be.

"So, what about you?"

"What about me, sweetheart?" He cocked a brow, the amused twist of his lips disappearing fast.

"Do you have someone at home who might be worried about you?"

His mouth parted, but he didn't say anything. He kept staring into her eyes as if she held all of the answers in the world. He looked speechless, and she wasn't sure how she'd rendered him that way.

"You okay?"

His jaw beneath that sexy stubble clenched briefly. Even in a semi-lucid state, she realized this man tried damn hard to hide his emotions.

"Shouldn't I be the one asking you that?" He heaved out a deep sigh. "You're handling this pretty well. I have to say I'm surprised."

She was a little shocked, too. "I'm alive and no longer shackled inside a truck." She shrugged. "Could be worse, I suppose."

Her boring little life had shattered and fallen into pieces the moment this man had knocked on her door. Why hadn't she listened to him? Why hadn't she stayed away like he'd asked?

No normal person paid five times the rental fee because of privacy. "I'm an idiot. I should never have rented my place to you." She stared down at her nails, the paint beginning to chip as a result of the insane night she'd survived.

"It's hard to find property at the last minute. Your place was a lifesaver."

"Until I ruined everything for you. I just wish I knew

what you were trying to do." She nervously glanced up, regret filling her. "But I know you can't tell me."

"You already know too much, I'm afraid." He turned his back, walked over to the wall, and braced against it with both palms.

She stared at his ass in the fatigues, even though she fought like hell to look away. "I won't tell anyone anything. You can trust me," she whispered. "If you're really who you say you are . . . *a good guy* . . . then I'd never want to do anything to jeopardize your work." She cleared her throat. "Maybe you shouldn't have let your people save me. You were okay with being taken; maybe I'd have been okay, too."

He glanced over at her but didn't drop his hands. "The potential loss of civilian life is not a risk we're willing to take."

Civilian. God, you're so military.

"Were those men terrorists? Will you tell me that much?"

He faced her and crossed his arms, casually leaning against the wall now. The room was too small for a man with such an unassailable presence. He clearly wasn't military anymore, or he wouldn't be operating on U.S. soil, so she had to assume he worked with the FBI or Homeland Security.

She was safe, then. But, she'd like to be home within three weeks, before work started up. And, at the very least, before her family started asking questions about her whereabouts, and the world discovered Everly Reed had been living as Eva Sharp.

She hung her head at the realization that her identity might be exposed, anyway. "They took a picture of me without my glasses," she said under her breath.

"Yeah, which is why you're in danger. And then they'll figure out your name is on the property deed of the cabins."

"Right, but they might also figure out that my life is a lie."

* * *

"I'VE GOT YOU ON SPEAKER. EVA SAYS THERE'S SOMETHING we should know." Luke held the phone between them.

"I'm pretty sure she's about to tell me her name is actually Everly Reed." Jessica cursed through the phone, and Luke's eyes narrowed in distrust as he stared at Eva.

What right did he have to be angry, though, when he'd said he was Travis Davenport?

"Everly? Who is—"

"She's famous. Well, her family is," Jessica cut him off. "I just found out when I did some more digging."

"Sorry, I never heard of you or your family," Luke rasped, clearly upset.

"Well, get familiar," Jessica said, and Eva shrank back onto the bed. "They're always in the spotlight, and her brother Harrison also owns a media outlet and newspaper."

"Great." Luke's free hand balled at his side, and it had Eva tensing. "We really picked the perfect cabin to rent, didn't we?"

"I-I'm sorry." Some sense of responsibility clung to her like wet clothes after getting caught in a rainstorm. What if people died because she'd been rescued?

"This is my fault. I should've done a better job picking the cabins, but we were on a time crunch," Jessica said. "Plus, whoever created her new identity did one hell of a job. It took me awhile to discover it."

"I promise I won't tell my family or anyone about you guys," Eva said, trying to come across as even-toned as possible, despite the fear hollowing out her stomach.

"Why'd you change your name?" Luke asked.

"I don't want the world to know who I am, probably as much as you don't want them to know about you." She bit the inside of her cheek. "So, you can trust your secret is safe with me."

Luke stepped away and shielded his eyes from her by turning his back. "See if there's any chatter about her. Look into both names."

"If anyone is looking for her, I'll find out and hopefully track down a location," Jessica vowed.

"Do you think these people you're after will find out who I really am?"

"They'll probably assume Eva Sharp's an alias, so they'll dig," Luke answered.

An alias? Jesus. "What about my family, then?" The realization that her parents and siblings might get caught up in all of this suddenly hit her. "They have a lot of security, but . . ."

"Send a credible tip to the FBI. Lead them to believe her family is in serious danger, so the Feds will keep a watch out, and ensure her family ups their security," Luke suggested.

Eva had to assume Luke and this woman weren't FBI. Otherwise, why would they need to send a "tip"? Why wouldn't they just tell the Feds what was going on? Well, unless they were super deep under? Her thoughts would run nonstop until she sank her teeth into the truth.

"We leave in a few hours. Did you secure a location?" Luke edged closer to the hotel door and put the phone back to his ear. "You're off speaker." He peeked at her, but she guiltily looked away.

After a minute, he ended the call.

"Try not to worry about your family, okay? I know it might be hard, but we'll ensure they're safe."

She nodded. "Okay. But there is one thing you could do that might help."

"Yeah?"

"I'm starving." Her fingers splayed across her abdomen. "I probably shouldn't be thinking about food at a time like this."

"We can get room service before we go."

"Thanks. Uh, is it pancake or burger time?"

"I think rich people call it brunch."

She couldn't stop her eyes from rolling. "I'm not rich."

"Sure, honey. And a frog's ass isn't watertight."

"Now, that's just gross." She puckered her lips. "And you really are a SEAL, aren't you?"

He dragged a large hand down his face, his eyes damn near twinkling. "What?"

"Knowing you were once one of the most elite operatives on the planet will make me feel safer." She swallowed the hard knot that formed in her throat.

"What makes you think that wouldn't make me more dangerous?" he asked in all seriousness.

CHAPTER SEVEN

"Do you have a hollow leg? I've never seen a woman eat so much."

"I eat when I'm nervous." She moved the plate of food away and caught a smile lingering on his lips before he got rid of it.

"What else do you do when you're nervous?" He hid his hands in his pockets as his gaze fell to her lips, which induced a strange twitch of emotions in her chest.

Think about you naked, apparently.

"I dance."

"You what?"

She rolled her shoulders back and wiped her mouth with the linen napkin. "When I'm waiting on an important call from the studio, or nervous to open a letter of . . . normally, rejection from a director about a script . . . I dance."

"Like, at a club?"

"No, like in my apartment while wearing fuzzy socks and jamming out to Led Zeppelin or something high energy."

"Huh." He faked a cough and turned his back. "Are fuzzy socks mandatory?"

"Oh, for sure." She rose, feeling much better after having eaten. She'd hopefully killed any residual effects of the drugs by shoving a ton of food into her mouth. "Do we have a long drive ahead of us? I'd love a shower, but I won't have anything clean to put on, so I guess I'll wait." She nervously patted her thighs as she waited for him to face her.

"Going just south of the Poconos. Not too bad of a drive."

Her heart pitter-pattered in her chest. "And will you be staying with me at this location while you and your people decide what to do with me?"

"I'm on babysitting duty. We both need to stay out of the spotlight until we have a plan." He finally turned and looked at her.

"Why you? I mean, if you were bait before, why wouldn't you want to be found again?"

"We need to cover all of our bases before I offer myself up," he said dryly.

"Oh. Well, I hope you believe me when I say I promise your secrets are safe with me."

"Promises don't go a long way with me, I'm afraid."

"Did someone burn you before?" She closed her eyes, wishing she hadn't voiced her thoughts.

"Trust has to be earned, sweetheart."

The huskiness of his voice had the hairs on her arms pricking to attention. "That goes both ways." She opened her eyes and asked, "How long will we be holed up together?"

"Hopefully, only a few days. I'm not looking forward to this."

"Yeah, me either, Captain Commando."

"If you did your research, you'd know SEALs don't like that term."

She lifted a brow. "What makes you think I don't know that?"

He grunted and turned away, whispering under his breath, "Why couldn't you work for a medical show?"

* * *

"Big enough for you?" Luke leaned inside the doorframe of the kitchen that connected to the living room in the so-called "safe house" they'd arrived at ten minutes prior. The home sat on several acres of land and had a six-foot fence surrounding the property.

"Could be bigger," she said.

"Forgive me, Miss Beverly Hills. Forgot who I was talking to." He flipped his gaze to the ceiling.

"It was a joke." She sighed. "I live in a tiny studio in New York. Basically, anything with two levels is massive to me. I told you I'm not rich."

"I still don't get it." He strode across the room to where she stood, her back against the large kitchen island. "Why change your name?"

"I'll tell you if you tell me who you are," she said without dropping his gaze.

His eyes were like a pair of blue magnets, pulling her to him and straight out of her comfort zone. He continued to stare at her for a gut-agonizing minute, the tension building between them so much it had her palms going to the counter on each side of her. And then he sidestepped her and went straight to the fridge, and she expelled a breath.

"I had the place stocked with food, and I got you some stuff." He grabbed two bottles of water and surprised her by tossing one her way. He sucked down nearly the entire bottle then said, "Come with me."

She put her unopened water down and followed him out of the kitchen, down the hall, and up the set of stairs that split at the middle, branching both left and right. The house was decorated like it was stuck in the '90s, with pastel wall colors and brass everywhere.

"Why didn't your people use this place to lure those men to?"

He stopped walking midway down the hall, and she nearly collided with his frame. Muscles strained atop muscles —but not in the bulky kind of way . . . in the annoyingly good-looking way.

She flipped on the nearby light switch so she could better see his eyes and try to get a read on him when he faced her.

"You're not going to stop trying to get information out of me, are you?"

"I'm a curious person."

"Which makes it hard for me to believe you'll keep what happened to yourself." Frustration passed over his face. He started to turn, but she caught his arm.

"Just give me something to go on, okay? I have so many stories spinning in my head, and it's making me a little crazy."

His gaze shifted to the floor, and she wondered if he were actually contemplating opening up. Her heart raced, but she wasn't sure if that was due to the feel of his arm beneath her palm or her desire for answers.

"We couldn't use a government-owned property, which this is. And hotels and such run the risk of casualties."

"And you didn't want witnesses," she added, but he didn't confirm.

He shifted out of her grasp and continued down the hall.

When she followed him into the room, her heart leaped into her throat.

"You got me a computer?" There were shopping bags on

the bed, but it was the MacBook sitting next to them that held her eye like a flashing beacon.

His hands disappeared into his pockets as his gaze cruised the room and then found her eyes. "Sorry about tossing yours. I figured you could write while we're here, so you don't lose your mind from boredom."

She almost hugged him.

Almost.

"Thank you." She stood in front of the bed and smoothed her hand over the top of the silver laptop. "Why am I guessing what's on your bed is a lot different? Probably heavy artillery."

"You do want to be kept safe, don't you?"

"Yes, but do you really think anyone can find us here?"

His eyes tightened a little. "No, or I wouldn't have brought you to this place."

Good. "Are these bags full of clothes?"

"I didn't know your size, so it looks like they bought out the store."

She peered into the closest bag and smiled as she reached for one of the items and held it. "Fuzzy socks?"

"That was a last-minute addition. In case you get nervous at all and feel like dancing."

"Hm." She shifted the bags out of the way so she could sit, then began nervously fiddling with the pair of pink socks. "This is surprising."

"Well, I owed you a computer, didn't I?"

"No, the computer's not surprising." A grin teased her lips. "That, you should've done." She lifted her attention upward, her lip catching between her teeth at the sight of him. "But the socks . . ." She let her words drift for a moment. "The socks make me think you have more going on"—she waved her free hand in a small circle in the air—"beneath that hard exterior of yours."

He cracked a smile. "Do you always judge a book by its cover?"

"When it comes in a package like yours." Her gaze dipped below his belt and a warmth crept up her pale skin, and she knew she'd be red.

"Do you want to grab a shower, and then we can eat?" he asked.

"Uh, sure."

"Did you happen to get my purse and phone back from those men?" Although she was sure he wouldn't let her call anyone.

"My people must have them. Sorry."

Just great.

"I'm three doors down on the right if you need me."

Her focus slowly skirted up, landing on his arms, but she couldn't get herself to meet his eyes.

"Do you think there's any makeup in these bags?"

"Why would you need makeup?"

"Right. I guess I don't." Considering she only wore mascara, it was insane that she suddenly wanted to add a little color while she was hidden away.

"I'll cook after I shower."

"You can cook?" she asked, finally forcing her eyes to his.

"As long as it's microwavable or comes in a box." He winked and left.

CHAPTER EIGHT

Luke allowed the ice-cold water to pelt his skin before he changed the setting to the rainfall mode in the shower.

His head dropped forward, and his fisted hands pressed against the tiled wall. He had to get this woman off his mind.

He was on an op, and not just any op—one that could lead to the takedown of half a dozen terrorist groups all over the globe. He couldn't allow his dick to compromise the mission.

But damn, ever since this woman had come blazing into his life yesterday he'd had the burning desire to shove his tongue into her mouth and grab that beautiful dark hair of hers at the same time.

He tried to fight back thoughts of her, but it wasn't working.

After getting out of the shower and toweling off, he swiped the beads of water from his short blond hair, spiking it up a little, then wrapped the towel around his waist and went into the bedroom.

He opened the military-grade laptop he'd had delivered and popped onto a secure feed. His curiosity was piqued, and if he was going to spend the next few days—or hell, weeks—protecting this woman, he wanted to know more about her.

Midway through his search about Everly Reed and her ridiculously wealthy and famous family, an incoming call from his sister had him taking a deep breath.

"Hey," he answered.

"President Rydell's not happy," she said straight away. "But, he's trying to be optimistic about our capture of Ender, even though it wasn't part of the plan."

He exited the secure internet search and closed his computer. "And did you tell Will about Eva?"

"Yeah, and you know how he took it."

He grumbled. "Well, I still doubt Ender will give us anything." He stood and kneaded the muscles at the base of his spine, the tension building. "I assume he's still alive?"

"Surgery went well, but we're waiting to see if he'll wake up."

"'Kay. Anything on the GPS location?"

"I'm not going to hold my breath anyone will show."

"And I have to assume Malik's men won't go to the address for my fake identity," he noted.

"No, but we have someone watching, in case. We're stretched thin right now."

"Shit, I know. Too bad we couldn't pull some of our men from the company to help out."

"Yeah, I wish." Luke released a sigh. "Anything new from the CIA about why the hell their man went rogue and killed Malik's brother?"

"Aside from the same BS—that Malik must've paid Reggie Deeks a shit-ton of money to stab our country in the back . . . *nope*. Nothing new."

"They confirm payment between Malik and Reggie to back up this theory?"

"Will couldn't give me an answer, and if he pokes around too much it could tip someone off to the fact that we're doing damage control for the CIA's mess."

"I'd like to know how Malik managed to find out which CIA operative was going to the meet with his brother. Hard to believe Malik could access that intel and then get lucky enough to pay Reggie off to kill Odem Yilmaz and steal the USB."

"Yeah, so what are you suggesting? A mole in the agency?"

"There's a reason why only four people in the world outside our team know of our existence. Hard to know who to trust these days," he said dryly. "And I'm sure as far as the CIA's concerned their guy never existed."

"Yeah, well, the traitorous son of a bitch really doesn't exist anymore since you killed him."

Luke stood in front of the mirror over the dresser, eying the new scar on his arm from the bullet that grazed his skin three weeks ago. "I didn't mean to kill him."

"I don't blame you. I just wish we could've taken Reggie in alive to get some answers. Hopefully, Ender can help us now."

Had Ender Yilmaz not shown up and shot Luke at the precise time he'd been about to fire a round at Reggie's arm —he never would've missed and pegged the CIA operative in the heart.

Luke dragged out a frustrated breath. "Nothing like feeling like we're in a pressure cooker."

"We'll figure this out. We always do. Just try and get some rest."

He nodded as if his sister could see him. "Anything new on Eva? Everly, I mean?" Her face scrolled through his mind like a hot flash.

"I'm sure Malik's people will find out who she really is." She cleared her throat.

"Yeah, okay, keep me posted." He ended the call and dumped a bag of clothes onto the bed, but a knock at the door had his body tensing.

"Hey, it's me." A pause. "Well, obviously . . . if it weren't me, we'd have some unwelcome house guests, huh?"

"You need something?" he called out and swallowed a lump in his throat, his body tightening up again, as if he were Pavlov's dog and his bell had been rung—and, damn, he was salivating over the idea of losing himself inside of her after the frustrating hell of the past three weeks.

He needed a break. A moment to breathe and not worry about terrorists.

But this was the life he had chosen.

He wouldn't change it, not for a minute.

But he also wouldn't mind at least one damn night off.

"I, uh, there wasn't any shampoo in the bathroom or the bags you gave me. Do you have any I can use?" she hollered through the door, and he felt like an idiot for making her yell the request—but his mind had . . . wandered.

"Yeah, of course." He grabbed it from the bathroom and opened the door a few seconds later.

She staggered back a step, her eyes widening.

"What's wrong?"

"You're naked."

His gaze dropped to his lower half, noting his towel still secured in place. "No, I'm not."

Her palm covered her eyes. "Close enough." Her chin tipped up to the ceiling, and a beautiful shyness swept over her features.

He couldn't see her eyes, but her nose crinkled, her lips

disappeared inward, and her neck and ears were in the process of tinting pink.

"Here."

She reached out, swatting the air in search of the bottle without dropping her other hand from her eyes.

He pressed it against her palm, too damn amused to say anything else.

"Thanks," she whispered and fled, running away as if he'd been covered in explosives.

He crossed his arms, leaning inside the doorframe until she was out of sight, his body below the waist rock-hard now.

Back to the shower it was . . . because there was no way he'd endure an evening with her without first relieving some of the pressure. He was already wound up from the failed op; he couldn't let this woman be his undoing.

* * *

"MACARONI AND WINE. INTERESTING DINNER COMBINATION."

He lowered the glass from his lips and eyed her as she strode to the table in a pair of black leggings and an oversized white tee that hung loose off her shoulder.

"You're wearing the socks. Are you planning on dancing tonight?" A smirk met his lips.

She sat at the table and pushed her semi-damp hair to her back. The woman was naturally beautiful. Makeup? God, she didn't need any. Her hazel eyes had captured his attention the moment they'd locked on to his yesterday.

"No dancing, but they're too comfortable not to wear." She looked at the bowl of macaroni and smiled. "Looks perfect." She lifted the glass of wine he'd poured right before she'd come into the kitchen. "But I'm not sure how I feel about my bodyguard drinking while on duty."

He took a long and purposeful swig of his wine. "No one will show up here. Besides, I can shoot better drunk than most men can shoot sober."

Her long lashes lifted, and her eyes journeyed across the room as if she were looking everywhere possible to avoid him. "And have you ever shot drunk?"

"I've had to shoot on morphine while taking enemy fire, which is a close enough comparison." He sat down, and his body tensed at the realization of what he'd said.

Her lips twisted in a knowing smile. "Military team?" She circled her index finger in the air. "Or while on this team now, the super secretive one?"

Christ. He cleared his throat and dug into his pasta instead of answering.

"Why morphine?" she asked when he remained quiet. He shoveled food into his mouth to keep himself from leaking any more info to this woman like she was some Greek siren and he was under her spell. "Were you hurt? I mean, I assume that's what happened."

He contemplated what to say, but the mission where his helo had crashed into Pakistan was classified. "Leg injury." He wondered if attempting to keep this woman in the dark would be worse than giving her some piece of the truth. So far, she'd managed to get more out of him than almost any other woman, and he'd only met her twenty-four hours ago.

He'd never had issues with the military assumptions from women over the years, but he'd always remained tight-lipped about being part of DEVGRU.

Sometimes the lies burned his throat and tore up his insides, especially when talking to people he actually cared about. But those lies also kept people safe.

"I was Navy, but now I run a tactical security company

with former military guys. That's all I can say, and so, if you could stop prodding, that'd be great."

"Fair enough." She closed her eyes and then licked the drop of wine from her lips.

He rolled his neck around. The second shower had done nothing to help relieve the desire that was flooding through his veins at hyper speed. He'd done his best not to think about Eva while jerking off, it felt creepy somehow since they barely knew each other; but she'd kept popping into his mind anyway.

"This is my favorite. German Riesling?"

"Yeah."

"I didn't take you for a wine guy." Her lashes lifted, and she drank more.

"You seem to be making a lot of assumptions about me. I thought we addressed this issue already—about book covers and all."

"Bad habit, I guess."

He leaned back and gripped the sides of his seat, hooking his feet around the legs of the chair.

"Speaking of German wine, was that German you were speaking last night?"

He nodded, not sure why he'd even answered.

"And the woman you were talking to, who is she?"

"You're still asking questions."

"I can't help myself. So, are you two dating?"

He dropped his head forward, and his lips curved at the edges. She just didn't stop, did she? "No, we're not."

"Hm. Well, if I were writing a story about all of this, I'd have the male lead fall for someone like her."

He looked up. "Oh, yeah? You wouldn't have the guy fall for the woman he'd rescued?"

"No, that's been done too many times before, and I pride myself in being more unique than that."

"Really . . ." Based on the color of her cheeks, his words had impacted her. He shouldn't have said it, but he couldn't help himself.

"Well, um, do you speak any other languages?" She nervously fiddled with the fork, stabbing at the food without bringing it to her mouth.

"A few," he answered.

"By-product of your job, huh?" It was more of a statement than a question, though.

"I'm half German," he said with a shake of his head, pissed at himself for relinquishing any additional details.

"Oh, yeah? How'd that happen?"

"My German mom and American father cohabitated."

She let out a soft laugh.

"What?" He raised a brow. "I'm not going to say *sex*. They're my parents, for Christ's sake."

Another laugh brushed across his skin. "True, but I was thinking more along the lines of how your parents met, I suppose."

"You always need a backstory, don't you?"

"If I don't know one, I tend to make it up. It's my job." Her hands fell into her lap as she rolled her tongue over her teeth. "Tell me more."

Why wasn't he surprised she'd want to dig deeper? But his family origins weren't exactly classified. "Pops was military. He met my mom while stationed in Germany. I was born over there, and then we moved to Naples before heading to the U.S."

"Military brat. You moved a lot, huh?"

He nodded and swirled the golden liquid around in the glass.

"And I assume you lived in the south, based on the slight bit of Southern in your speech. Mid-Atlantic?"

Damn, she was good. She almost got him to answer *Tennessee.* "How about you? Did you move a lot?" He needed to get off the topic of his life and fast. Pretty much the rest of his life story was off-limits. Answering every question she might ask with *classified* would get boring real fast. He was sure she was much more interesting.

"More times than I can count."

"I guess we have that in common."

"Yeah, but it looks like you were okay with the constant change of scenery since you joined the Navy. But me, I hated it. Well, as a kid I did, at least."

"So you decided you needed a change?"

"Look who's prodding now." She smiled.

"Well, I did look into you before you showed up at my door, trying to get a glimpse of me in my birthday suit." His eyes narrowed as he waited and hoped for that gorgeous shyness to take up residence on her face.

"I was *not* trying to see you naked. And you shouldn't have answered in a towel anyway."

"My naked chest has never offended anyone before," he quipped.

"Well, it, you know . . ." Her cheeks flushed, and she swallowed and looked away.

This time, it was his own bottom lip tucking between his teeth as he quietly observed the mysterious woman before him.

"We'll make a deal to never wear towels in front of each other. Okay? We can shake on it if you'd like." He extended a palm.

"You're a smart-ass, huh?" She brushed away his hand,

knocking over his wine glass in the process. "Shit." She stood and went around to his side of the table.

He looked up, ignoring the wine now on his sweatpants, and found her attention focused on his crotch. Her mouth rounded, and he cleared his throat and pushed away from the table to grab a paper towel.

"Sorry."

"It's fine. Let's get back to you." He pulled the material away from his body to pat the pants dry. "Why do people think you're either searching for God in the mountains of Tibet or sobering up in rehab in Europe?" He tossed the towel, refilled his glass, and perched a hip against the kitchen island.

"Oh. Well, no one knew where I'd disappeared to, and so people just made assumptions."

"And it doesn't bother you they think you might be a drug addict?" He scratched at the base of his throat. "Unless, you, uh, have that problem." Shit, for all he knew, she did.

"If it means I have my privacy, they can think I'm dead for all I care." Her shoulders arched back. "And no, aside from trying pot once in high school, it's safe to say I'm a good girl."

Good girl—he'd gotten that impression, for sure.

And now his cock was hardening as he thought about tossing this "good girl" onto his bed and making her come until she saw fucking stars.

He advanced closer to her, thankful Eva's tee was long enough to cover her ass in the leggings that clung to her curves like Saran Wrap. Maybe he'd bend her over and—

"I don't have any kind of sad story, by the way."

He had figured she might be hiding some ugly truth of her past, but when she faced him, he didn't see any hint of sadness in her eyes, which was good. "So, what's your story, then?"

Her fingertips tucked into her palms at her sides, and she shifted her weight to her right leg. Her nerves were getting to her. Was he making her uncomfortable?

"I was sick of being in the public eye all of the time. I wanted to eat a piece of pizza or go for a swim without cameras in my face."

"I guess that's got to be annoying." In his line of work, he could understand the desire for privacy. Hell, his life depended on it.

"All of my family is in the public eye in one way or another. My older brother hates to have his privacy invaded, too, but he's so rich he can hire a wall of professional wrestlers to protect him from the paparazzi everywhere he goes."

"Are we talking Oprah-rich or . . ."

She nodded. "He's got connections and helped me get the new identity. He didn't even question me when I asked for help."

"There have to be some perks to being part of a famous family." Her dad had directed some of his favorite action flicks, and his own father had had a massive crush on Eva's mom when Luke had been growing up. It was a bit surreal.

"Getting to know Sly, Keanu, Bruce, Denzel . . . Those were some of the highlights of my life, I guess."

"Wow."

"If we make it out of this alive, I can get you an introduction to anyone you'd like."

He set his glass down on the counter. "You'll make it out alive," he said in a steady voice, needing her to believe him. "But, do you think these movie stars will remember who you are since you've been on the DL?"

Her mouth opened, but she didn't say anything.

"I guess even in hiding, you ended up back in the media business, though."

"You can't escape blood, and the industry is in mine like the military's in yours. It's just before, the expectations on my shoulders were heavy—like Atlas-holding-the-globe-on-his-shoulders heavy. If Everly Reed fails, it'll be a disaster, but if I plummet my career to its death as Eva Sharp, no one will care." She cupped her mouth, her eyes widening a hair as if she hadn't meant to slip out that admission.

Her eyelashes fluttered, and she lowered her hand and sucked in a panicky breath before releasing it.

He stayed relaxed, simply watching her—waiting for her to spill more.

"That, um, wasn't my original reason for leaving that life, but maybe it's the reason why I maintain this new identity now. Well, aside from trying to make it because of merit and not name." A plump bottom lip tucked between her teeth for a moment, and it had his heart slowing as his body grew ready for something—*someone*—he couldn't possibly have.

"Glasses, minimal makeup, plain clothes. I learned if I slouched and didn't make a lot of eye contact, people wouldn't see me anymore. I became Plain Eva. And as far as the actors at the studio are concerned, I'm a struggling writer pinching her pennies, hoping for a big break." She sidestepped him, brushing against his body in the process.

He turned to see her heading to the table to clean up, even though they'd barely touched their dinner. "I'm not quite sure how you can look in the mirror and see yourself as plain. Or how you could ever think you could possibly be invisible."

She lowered the bowl she'd been holding back to the table and both her palms landed alongside it. "It's true."

He came up behind her. A hint of coconut and flowers

caught his nostrils. He wasn't sure what type of perfume his buddy had bought at the store for her, but he'd done a damn good job. She smelled like a sweet summer day on an island somewhere.

His fingers ran through her silky strands as he whispered close to her ear, "I see you."

Her head dropped slightly forward as if his words had weighed her down.

He didn't know what the hell he was thinking being so close to her, but he couldn't seem to get himself to back away. Always in control of his actions, but he was inexplicably drawn to this woman.

"I should get some rest." She turned, but he'd been so close she bumped into him, and he caught her arms and staggered back a step to find her eyes.

He didn't want to let go. He wanted to take her out of this hell he'd dragged her in to and find a way to erase all of her problems.

"Not hungry, huh?" he asked, his body tightening with a continued and unexpected need to be near her—to continue to hold on to her.

"Just tired." Her tongue rolled over her teeth as she held his gaze. "Th-thanks for the food."

He released her, took another step back to give her space, and looped his thumbs in his front pockets. "I'm here twenty-four seven if you need me to whip you up another fine meal."

"Thank you." She moved out of his reach, but as she started to exit the kitchen, she paused mid-step and peered back at him. "Luke?"

"Yeah?"

"Thank you."

"For what?" His brows furrowed.

"For whatever it is you're doing. I assume you're trying

to keep people safe. And also for, you know, shielding my body from bullets in that truck."

He didn't know what to say, and so he did what he always did when someone thanked him—he forced a stiff nod and kept quiet.

CHAPTER NINE

Luke tapped at the screen on his armband, checking
the cameras positioned a mile away from the home. He'd get
alerted if anything larger than a squirrel passed the one-mile
line. In the middle of the night, a deer had woken his ass up,
and he hadn't been able to fall back to sleep.

Now, it was quarter past six, and he decided he'd do a
couple laps around the property before Eva woke.

"Where are you going?" Eva asked from behind, taking
him by surprise. No one ever got the drop on him. He was off
his game.

He turned to see her mid-yawn. Her hair was messy in a
sexy kind of way, and she was in silky pink pajama bottoms
with a matching top.

She'd forgotten a bra, and so he forced his focus back to
her eyes.

"For a run. Do you want to join me?"

"Uh, you know that expression, *if you see me running, it's
because someone's chasing me*? Well, that'd be me. I
don't run."

He grinned. "What do you do to stay fit?"

"I think our definition of staying fit is drastically different. You probably spend three hours a day in the gym to look like that."

"Hardly. All genetics."

"Funny." She peered at the front door, her brows drawing together. "Is it safe to go out there?"

He pointed to his wrist. "This place is off the grid, but I also have cameras, so don't worry."

"What about the fact that it's twenty degrees out?"

"Honey, when you've swum in waters below zero, this is like a walk in the park."

"SEAL," she mouthed, which induced an eye roll from him.

Persistent. "I'll be back soon."

"I can make us coffee and breakfast while you're out."

He nodded. "That'd be great. Thanks."

As his hand wrapped over the doorknob, she added, "Be safe."

"Will do."

Once outside, he sucked in a breath of the crisp Pennsylvania air. It was the second week in January, and they were in the mountains, which reduced the temperature even more. But the weather never bothered him. He'd been conditioned to handle all kinds of environments.

On his fifth lap around the edge of the property line, Jessica phoned him. He hoped to hell she had good news.

"What's up?" he asked, his breath catching visibly in the air. "Ender awake?"

"Not yet, but I have an idea."

"Yeah?" He glanced back at the two-story house a hundred feet or so behind him, ensuring Eva wasn't in sight.

"I think you should show your face at the Turkish consulate in New York on Monday."

"We ruled that out as a possibility a few weeks ago."

"Yeah, and a few weeks ago, only Ender Yilmaz knew what you looked like. Malik didn't have any photos of you. We had no choice but to find Ender to try and draw out Malik. It's a different game now. If there's anyone dirty at the consulate, then Malik will have sent a photo of you so they could be on the lookout."

"That's a big *if.* He's not going to show his face in Manhattan, even if I show mine."

"Malik will have eyes on the consulate. All you need to do is walk in the building."

"We can't operate in the city. Too many people. Too many possible problems."

"So you get in and out quick," she replied.

"And then what?"

"We're working on a plan. I know you have your hands full babysitting, so let us handle this." His sister sounded confident, and he knew she was brilliant, but he hated not being actively part of the strategizing. He'd always helped make the plans, and this was killing him. "We have three days until you need to be in New York. We'll think of something by then. And maybe Ender will wake up in the meantime."

"What about Eva?" he asked. "Am I bringing her with me? Will I pass her off to one of our guys in New York once we're there?"

"No," Eva shrieked from behind.

Had this woman really snuck up on him twice in one morning? "I gotta go." He ended the call and faced her. "What are you doing out here?"

"You were gone longer than I expected, so I got worried. I came to find you." She had ski pants and a matching pink jacket on. His guy had packed everything for her, so it seemed.

"And if something had happened to me, what would you have done?" He arched a brow, genuinely curious.

"I'm resourceful."

"Sure, you are." He strode closer to her. "Let's go inside." He could hear the clicking of her teeth. How long had she been outside, if she were still cold in that getup? This woman was becoming even more trouble than he'd anticipated.

"I don't want to stay here alone, nor do I want to be passed off to someone else." Once inside, her hands landed on her hips.

"Well, I'd obviously never leave you alone." He closed the gap between them, her cheeks losing the tinge of rosiness from the cold air. "But, I can't exactly keep you with me forever." Even if he did wonder what she'd be like in bed, or maybe on a desk, with her glasses back on.

"As amazing as *forever* sounds"—she actually rolled her eyes, which had him fighting back a smile—"I barely trust you, which means I certainly won't trust some new guy."

"Why're you being sexist? What if it's a woman I have protect you?"

And the pink on her cheeks was alive again. "Why would you go to the Turkish consulate? Were those men who took us Turkish?"

He progressed closer to her, and she inched back, bumping into the staircase banister. "How much did you hear?"

"Enough," she bit out, but confidence didn't carry with the word. A crease in her brow formed as she studied him from his running shoes to his fleece jacket. "You're going back out as bait, huh?"

He removed his jacket and draped it over the banister. "Did you make coffee?"

She tilted her chin up. He'd take that as *yes*.

He left the foyer and made his way into the kitchen. Mid-pour, he heard her soft steps from behind. Why hadn't he heard her outside? He really did need a vacation if this five-foot-five woman could get the drop on him. He made a mental note to tell Will he'd be taking a few weeks off once this operation was tied up.

"I won't go anywhere or stay here with someone new . . . not unless you tell me the truth. Fuck classified."

He almost dropped the coffee mug at the sound of her curse. She had appeared too delicate for such a word, but maybe he'd misjudged her, as she had him.

"Well, I can tie you down if I have to. Staying here right now isn't an open invitation; it's a requirement." His voice deepened, and he slowly turned to face her. "If you've misunderstood the arrangement, perhaps I need to re-explain."

There was a quick glimmer of something in her eyes, something that said she wanted to be tied down by him, and not in the way he'd meant. Not that he'd ever tied up a woman—after cuffing and binding people in war, the last thing he wanted was to simulate any scenes in the bedroom that took him to any place dark.

He cocked his head and smoothed a hand from the base of his throat down his chest as he considered what to do with the stubborn woman before him.

"Let me be clear." She edged closer, leaving less than a foot between them. She was invading his personal space, and for some reason, it didn't bother him.

"Yeah, Hollywood? What do you want to tell me?" He dropped his gaze to her mouth, unable to miss what he knew he'd catch—an angry but sexy twist of her lips.

She stabbed a finger at his chest. "I'm here because you got me into something dangerous, and I'd prefer to keep my limbs intact. I'm not your prisoner, and last time I checked, kidnapping was illegal."

He brought his mug to his lips while casually capturing her wrist. He took a sip of his coffee, and she wrapped a hand over his, trying to break free. "Princess, I can do whatever the hell I please."

Her eyes flicked up to his face. "Princess. Hollywood. If you're going to choose a nickname to try and offend me, at least stick with one."

He released her, and she stumbled back, her nostrils flaring. From her neck to the tips of her ears, she was flushed. And he had the desire to trail his lips over the reddened flesh, to distract her from the nightmare he had, in fact, dragged her into.

"You may be trying to come across as rough and tough——some badass commando," she said, emphasizing the last word, "but there's more to you than that. You ruined your operation to save my life, and so whatever this thing is you're doing right now . . . well, it doesn't fool me." She whirled around and strode with her head held high out of the kitchen.

At the sound of her shoes running up the steps, his heart settled back to its normal beat, and he dropped down onto a bar stool at the kitchen island. The woman had balls to talk to him like that.

Why the hell did that have to turn him on so damn much?

CHAPTER TEN

"I DON'T WANT TO SEE YOU," EVA CALLED OUT WHEN LUKE knocked on her bedroom door. "I need more than the hour you've given me to cool off."

"You know I can get in, whether you choose to let me in or not."

She shoved the MacBook off her lap. "If you come in, you'll see me naked." That lie would stop him from breaking down the door, right? She hoped so, at least.

"Great. I could use something to cheer me up after a Hollywood star all but stuck her sharpened claws in me earlier."

Eva dropped her feet to the ground and stood, fired up. "Wow. Are you that big of a wuss that you can't take a couple of cat scratches?" She pressed her palms to the door. "And don't even think about referring to me as a pussy as a retort."

"The thought never crossed my mind, Hollywood." There was a definite amused chuckle that swiftly breezed through his words.

"I was never a star, by the way. I did my best to avoid

being on screen. I just got dragged into the limelight by being surrounded by stars."

He was quiet for a moment. "Are we gonna keep having this conversation through the door?"

"Kind of how everything started with us." She lifted her head. "Better than you seeing me naked, anyway."

"Hm. I don't know about that."

"You wish, Commando." This man could melt her insides like butter with one look, but she'd never let him know the power he wielded. She had to stay resolute; she had to get him to give her some sliver of an idea as to what she was really up against. What if something did happen to him? What if she were left in the dark and had no way of protecting herself from an enemy unknown to her?

She hoped nothing would happen, but he was clearly in a dangerous line of work, the kind of work where any day could be your last.

How does one live knowing that tomorrow isn't promised? Of course, the same held true for everyone with a pulse, didn't it? There were no guarantees, but in his case, he was literally putting himself in front of men with bullets, and so the risks were amplified.

She wondered what life would be like if she lived each day to its fullest. She'd been hiding so long, too afraid to step out of the shadows that clung to her now, she had no idea what it'd be like to be carefree. She'd been so by-the-book and "good" as Everly Reed to prevent the media from ever writing a salacious story on her, she really hadn't gotten a chance to live all that much.

"Are you going to open it, or what?"

"Well, do you have anything new to say? Or did you come here to show me your tail between your legs in hopes I'll be a good girl and forgive you?"

He didn't respond, but she had a feeling he was merely biting back some one-liner in reference to her *good girl* comment. She almost wanted him to piss her off so she wouldn't open the door and have to look into his too-damn-blue-to-be-true eyes.

"I'll let you in if you tell me something. I'll even sign some nondisclosure agreement."

"Yeah, sure . . ."

"Wives of SEALs have to sign one," she noted, remembering her research.

"Are you my wife?"

"A man like you won't ever get one, will you? Not while you're chasing bad guys."

"Can you please open the door?" he requested, a throatier sound to his voice this time. His patience was clearly wearing thin.

"Do we have a deal?" She eyed the door and tightened her grip on the knob as she waited.

"One question only."

"Three," she sputtered back.

"One."

"Three."

"Two," he bit out.

She flung the door open with a triumphant smile, getting exactly what she'd wanted. What she hadn't expected to see was the SEAL standing before her in navy workout shorts that stopped just above his knees, and no shirt again. A sheen of sweat rolled over his muscles, and the slight chest hair across his pecs made him even hotter.

"So, looks like you're the only naked one."

"We need to work on your definition of *naked* again." He brushed his hand through the air in her direction as he studied her clothed body.

"Were you working out?" She hadn't meant to stare at his abs or the hard planes of his body . . . or the shoulders that were perfect for grabbing onto while making love.

God, this man didn't make love, did he? No, his body was made for much naughtier things. No, he probably screwed women all the way to Oz and back.

"And this is why I shouldn't have opened the door."

"Say what?" He sat on the edge of her bed.

Did I say that aloud? Shit. "Nothing." Her eyes widened when he lifted her laptop and held it before him. "Put that down!" She rushed toward him, snatching it from his grasp.

One dimple she hadn't noticed before popped in his right cheek as his eyes caught hers. He'd never smiled big enough to expose his teeth before. "Are you writing a sex scene in that script?"

"You wish." She closed the laptop and placed it on top of the dresser. "I didn't mean—"

"Relax, Hollywood."

"Maybe I would if you stopped calling me that."

"Maybe you'd relax? Or maybe you'd write about sex?" He smiled again, and her heart danced.

He stood and tucked his hands in the pockets of his shorts. The material was that breathable kind of fabric, but it was also thin. She could make out the line of his very impressive package. She had a feeling if they exchanged any more banter he might just show off even more.

At this rate, her lip would become a permanent fixture between her teeth. "I never write sex scenes, by the way. My scripts always fade to black. If the director wants to be more creative, so be it, but I can't write the vulgar details of such scenes."

"Vulgar, huh?" His shoulders rounded back, which had his chest lifting. "You have a thing against sex?" He angled his head to the side, his blues traveling the length of her body, upward from her toes.

"I don't like writing about it. Too many moving parts." She flipped her wrists as if dismissing the idea.

"Maybe you haven't had the best experience to draw from."

One step.

He edged only *one* step closer to her, but that one step was so powerful, it had her bumping up against the dresser.

Predator. Prey.

Check. Check.

The look in his eyes made one thing perfectly clear: he wanted her. And maybe she'd only be a casual lay. Maybe that's all the man was capable of—and *maybe* she should be offended by a man wanting her sexually while he's supposed to protect her, but her body didn't seem to give a shit. Her body craved the rough hands of this stranger running over every inch of her.

There'd only been one time in her life when white-hot lust had crept up on her, making her weak with the insatiable need to have sex.

Craig Louis. He'd been a childhood TV star who'd lured her into his trap of charm and sexiness, and she'd given him her virginity at seventeen. And Craig had dumped her as soon as he'd realized dating her wouldn't land him a role in any of her father's movies.

"My two questions," she rushed out, deciding to protect her heart, even if her body didn't want to listen. She wasn't quite ready to live freely yet, especially with a man like this, a man who could clearly pulverize her heart with one crushing flick of his wrist when he dismissed her later. Not that he'd probably have a choice in the matter given his top-secret life. "I want my two questions."

He heaved out a deep sigh and looked at the ground briefly. When his eyes found hers again, the smoldering look faded, and fast.

And why was that disappointing to her? She'd been the one to flip the switch.

"What do you want to know?"

She walked past him to the en-suite bathroom and grabbed a towel. "First, wipe that sweat from your body. It's distracting."

His lips curved when he caught the towel. He loved making her uncomfortable, didn't he? Surely he could tell by looking at her she was fighting the impulse to squeeze her thighs together. She couldn't stop herself from imagining how it'd feel to have him part her legs with his knee and press his mouth to her center.

"Hurry," she cried, as he continued to slowly torture her by rubbing the towel across his tan body. *Who the hell is still naturally tan in January—other than actors?* And his tan was definitely a result of the sunshine. No way in hell this man cooked beneath fake rays.

"Sorry, ma'am."

She'd prefer Hollywood to *ma'am*. "*Ma'am* is for teachers, mothers, and anyone over forty."

"Really?" He clenched the towel tight between his palms. "Want me to grab a shirt, too, before I break government protocol and answer your two questions?"

"Like you'll tell me anything too classified," she snapped.

"'Fuck classified,' right?"

She spun in the other direction because it was the only way to steal her gaze away from the ripple of his flesh. "Sure," she whispered, a chill snaking up her spine when she felt his breath meet the nape of her neck like it had last night at dinner.

He shifted the hair over her shoulder. His lips brushed against her earlobe, and the honest-to-God, only-happens-in-the-movies tingles swept from her neck down the curve of her back and to her ass.

"What are you doing?" she meekly asked and her eyes fell shut.

"Making you as uncomfortable as I am," he whispered.

Didn't he know she'd crossed that line basically the moment he told her she needed to hide in the woods or die?

Sexual tension was a blip on the radar compared to her life being threatened, wasn't it?

But she couldn't stop herself from asking, "I make you uncomfortable?"

Another warm breath kissed her skin, and this one had her breasts puckering to new life, getting overly optimistic that a touch after a long dry spell was imminent.

"You want me to talk about my job, and *that* makes me uneasy."

"Oh," she said, a whisper of disappointment softly echoing inside of her.

His hand curved over her shoulder. "Sure you don't want to back down?"

She almost groaned, wishing they were merely in the midst of verbal foreplay and sexual innuendos. Life would be much easier if this moment was about a wild hookup, and she wasn't in the woods with a SEAL who'd covered her body with his not even forty-eight hours ago to protect her from a barrage of bullets.

Bullets—it should've been bullshit. But, nope. This was reality. She'd crashed the biggest party of her life, and now she was paying the price.

"Should I go, or do you want to get this discussion over with?"

A coolness crept across her neck, and she realized he'd stepped back. "I thought about Googling the name *Malik* in relation to a consulate in New York," she softly began while facing him, "but I didn't know if I'd set off some sort of crazy bad-guy alarm in doing so."

He visibly swallowed and let go of the towel. "I should shower."

She reached for his wrist without thinking, her eyes widening. "Luke!"

He smirked, but glanced at her hand atop his arm. "Kidding."

"Not really the best time for humor."

He squinted and gave a half shrug. "I can't seem to help myself around you."

"Oh, yeah?" She let go of him. "And why is that?"

"You're cute when you're angry."

"You already know so much about me, huh?" Her brow creased.

"I do have an entire dossier on your every movement since birth." He stepped back and lowered himself to a seated position on the bed. "Thirty. Parents divorced at age seven, and you bounced back and forth between your mom's place in New York and your dad's in Malibu. You have two brothers and two sisters. Don't get me started on the number of stepsiblings you have from your parents' multiple marriages afterward." He took a brief pause. "Perfect grades throughout school, except your junior year, when you dated that actor Craig . . . talk about a bad influence."

Her mouth dropped open, but she couldn't find the words.

"Graduated cum laude from USC in L.A., and did a double master's after at Boston University. Went off the grid three years ago and reappeared as Eva Sharp." He scratched at his short beard. "A natural brunette, but I'm guessing

you're rocking darker highlights right now for your disguise."
He paused for a moment, and his Adam's apple moved in his
throat. "And you have the most beautiful hazel eyes I've
ever seen."

Her heart took up residence in her throat. "That's not fair.
You can browse *Wikipedia* about me, and as for you—I don't
even know your last name."

"Life isn't fair. If it was, you wouldn't be here with me
right now. You'd be at your cabin writing your movie, living
your lie of a life."

"Don't make it sound like that. Besides, who the hell are
you to judge?"

He slowly rose, and she did her best to remain grounded
as his eyes drilled into hers as if he were on the brink of
stealing her every thought.

She couldn't back down now. "Does anyone know the
real you?" She poked his chest—his very naked chest. "It
must make for a lonely life."

"Clearly you know me, so . . ." He started to turn, but she
flattened her hand against his flesh, and he remained
before her.

"Don't walk away from me. I want answers." Confidence
rushed through her raised voice.

The stubborn set of his jaw tightened; he eyed her hand as
if it were a grenade. "It is lonely," he rasped as if he hadn't
meant to admit that.

Guilt curled into a tight fist in her abdomen at the
realization of how she'd talked to him—to a man who clearly
put his life on the line for the country.

"You drive me nuts," he said. "You've been making me
crazy since I first saw you."

"I—"

He gently gripped her chin and slanted his mouth over

hers. He parted her lips with such an intense need it had her almost falling. But, of course, his hand swooped to the small of her back to keep her upright.

Her hands slipped between their bodies, and she guided them up his hard chest, groaning against his full mouth as he tugged at the strands of her hair, tipping her head farther back so he could deepen the kiss.

She wasn't sure who would break first, but in her gut, she knew it'd happen. One of them would blink, one of them would bow to desire, and the other would hold to the sense of responsibility.

And in three, two, one . . . Luke, the dedicated and *responsible* SEAL, tore his mouth from hers and released his grip as if she were a butterfly in his palms and he had to set her free.

Her hand swept to her mouth to cover her nearly swollen lips.

His eyes darkened to a different shade of blue, a color meant for midnight and stolen kisses in some secret garden. "Goodnight," he said in his signature husky voice.

She was grateful he hadn't apologized for the kiss. Brief as it was, it'd been exhilarating.

A rush of energy had exploded through her body the second his tongue had swept into her mouth, and everything inside her came to life: pop, sizzle, and spark.

She sure as hell knew it'd be a moment she'd never forget, and so, she went to her bed, opened her laptop, and decided to change her fade-to-black sex scene to one with a little more color.

CHAPTER ELEVEN

"Wow. You're good." She didn't wait for an invite and brushed past him into his bedroom.

"You keep showing up after I take a shower." He tightened the towel around his hips.

She whirled around and stabbed a finger in the air, a scowl marring her lips. "You tricked me. You distracted me with the kiss, so I'd forget about my questions."

"That wasn't my . . ." He allowed his voice to trail off as amusement pinned him still. With a lift of the chin, she edged closer as if she could intimidate. *Good try, Hollywood.*

"Is that a SEAL tactic?"

"Yeah, we go around making out with terrorists to get them to—" *Did I just admit I was a SEAL?* He cleared his throat and sidestepped her to go to the bathroom and get dressed. This wasn't a conversation he planned on having wearing only a towel.

"You're frustrating." Her voice dangled along the fine line between exasperated and defeated.

He stopped outside the bathroom, and his arms swooped up. His palms landed on the exterior frame of the door. "I'm the frustrating one, huh?" Her eye contact was on point when he faced her again, but he could tell she wanted to lower her gaze, and it made his cock twitch. "You're the one who has been a thorn in my ass ever since you broke the deal and showed up at the cabin."

"They're my cabins!"

He stabbed a finger at his chest. "And I paid for them."

"That's semantics." She waved a dismissive hand.

"Not really," he grumbled before retreating to the bathroom.

"You're not walking away from this conversation. I want my questions answered."

"You can join me in here, but I plan on dropping this towel in a second to get dressed." With his back to the vanity, he folded his arms.

"Go ahead," she said, but heat stained her cheeks.

Oh, he would. Did she not realize that? But he also knew he'd have to give her mouth-to-mouth and resuscitate her after. Maybe that'd be a hardship he was willing to endure.

"No more deception. I want answers."

He scoffed and crossed an ankle over his foot, and he could tell his casual stance further pissed her off. "I'm not deceiving you."

"I need to know what I'm up against." She dropped her eyes to the checkered tiles. "What partial code will these assholes try and torture out of me?"

"I won't let them get to you."

"You can't know that for sure."

"Listen." He took a breath, trying to steady his emotions. "It's my job to keep civilians from knowing about all of the evil in the world. You'd never be able to sleep at night if you knew the news barely scratches the surface of the kind of shit I've seen . . . and *stopped*."

"I'm not just anyone," she said softly. "I'm in this with you now, whether I want to be or not."

He stepped forward and placed a fist beneath her chin so his gaze could meet her eyes. "And this isn't a story. You can't write yourself out of it. This is real life, and real life is messy."

"That's not fair. Don't try and make me out to be some naïve girl," she whispered, her bottom lip trembling.

His jaw locked tight at her slip of emotion. "It's hard for me to figure out whether you're scared, and your walls are on the verge of crumbling, or if you really are strong enough to get through this."

She kept her eyes on him, her lips tightening. Maybe she didn't know either.

"What good will come from you knowing?" he asked when she kept quiet.

Her eyes became damp, and his arm dropped heavy at his side.

"If I have to die, I want to know why. I want to know what I'm dying for."

He lightly gripped her shoulders. He'd never made this promise before, but he couldn't get himself to say anything else. To believe anything else to be true. "You're *not* going to die. How many times do I have to tell you that?"

"Please," she murmured, the sound like the first prick of a tattoo needle—it pierced his flesh.

His stomach dropped knowing he was about to break protocol. He was the king of rules and regulations, a stickler for policy. His men fell in line behind him, so why was he going to be the first to let a civilian in on a mission? But she already knew so much at this point. Did it even matter? "Can I at least get clothes on first?"

She softly nodded and wiped at the tear on her cheek.

He took his time getting dressed in the bathroom once she'd left.

A million thoughts and objections raced through his mind like a derailed freight train—everything becoming jumbled in a sudden crash.

When he entered the room, he found her sitting on the bed, denim-clad legs stretched out in front of her. Her gaze slowly drifted his way.

"Where do you want me to start?"

"How about from the beginning," she said, not skipping a beat.

"I'll tell you what I can without too many specifics, but I can't give you details about me. Okay?"

She nodded.

He tucked his hands beneath his armpits. "Five weeks ago, a man called the U.S. government and asked for protection."

"He was in danger?"

"Yeah. He worked with criminals around the world if it paid well. He didn't care about a cause, only financial gain." His words were like a slap of betrayal toward his superiors for sharing the information and unease continued to fill him. "His name had been on Interpol's list for years, but he never stayed in one place long, and because he was more of an intermediary between terror groups, it proved harder to catch him."

"So, who'd he need protection from?"

"The guy had stockpiled intel on all of the groups he'd ever made deals with—his own insurance policy if shit ever got hairy."

"But it backfired?"

"Someone," he said while waving a hand in the air,

"maybe even more than one organization discovered he'd been holding intel that could be damaging."

"Why not just blackmail them like he planned?"

"You're quick." He shifted his weight to one leg and pressed a palm to one of the four bedposts. "He never got a chance to. He was shot but managed to escape, and that's when he called the U.S. for help."

She looked up in thought. "In exchange for protection he'd provide the U.S. with the intel he had on every terrorist organization he'd ever worked for?"

"Yup."

"That could be really useful. What happened?"

He thought about the failed exchange four weeks ago between the CIA operative Reggie Deeks and Odem Yilmaz, but he couldn't share that much with her, even if the info was on the tip of his tongue. "One access code to the safe was provided, but he mentioned he also had a silent partner in all of this, and that partner had a code as well. To access the safe, both codes must be entered at the same time or else all the data will be lost."

"Really? Sounds like a script I wrote last year and pitched to Hollywood. They turned it down, saying it wasn't realistic enough." Her lips twitched into a smile but quickly faded. "What happened next?" She sat up taller.

"That silent partner was his brother—Malik."

He allowed the name to sit with her for a moment, so she could connect the dots. "That's why Malik's after you?"

"Yeah. Malik's brother—Ender's father—was killed before he could provide that information. The assumption is that Malik had him murdered to get the code."

"The man who had me strip, it was his dad who'd made the deal and died?" She arched a brow.

"Yeah."

"Why would he work with his uncle then? That seems strange to me."

You and me both.

"How'd you get a hold of this guy's code if he died?"

He heaved out a deep breath. "I managed to obtain it three weeks ago from the guy who killed him."

"I assume our government still wants the contents of the safe. So, you need Malik, and he needs you."

"Precisely." He nodded, slightly baffled by the conversation he was having—with a civilian, of all people. A gorgeous woman from Hollywood.

"You used yourself as bait to try and get Malik to come for you so you could get his code." She pressed her fingertips to her forehead. "Why would Malik have his brother killed? Wouldn't he need protection, too, for the same reason his brother did?"

"The story we're working with is that Malik and Ender saw him as a traitor for making a deal with the U.S. even if his reasons were to stay alive—which is why he probably never gave his son the code."

She dropped her hand and stood. "Sounds like you don't believe that."

He gave a half-hearted shrug.

"Hm. Well, was this Malik also on Interpol's radar before all of this?"

His stomach tightened with regret. "No one knew about him."

"That's hard to believe." She took a few tentative steps his way, focusing on his eyes as if searching for answers.

"Yeah, well, he's a diplomat and has been living under our goddamn noses in Manhattan."

"Oh, God."

The reality was sinking in for her, and he scratched at his jaw, not sure what else to say.

"I can see why you're so angry with me."

"I'm just angry. Period," he said in a low voice.

"I guess I really did screw everything up." She dropped back onto the bed, and her palms covered her face.

He sat next to her. "We'll make it work out. Don't worry." He'd get his target, but he wasn't sure what the hell would happen to Eva once the dust settled. "Do you regret knowing all of this?"

"No, I don't think so." She rose and hooked her thumbs into her back pockets.

"Are you sure you're okay?" He clasped his hands together, resting his elbows on his thighs as he observed her, worried about the terror that clung to her face, wishing he could take back his words and keep her safe from the ugly world once more.

"I'll fake it until I make it. That's what I used to do when I was Everly."

He stood. "And how'd that work out for you?"

Her lip briefly caught between her teeth. "Not so great, I suppose."

"I'll get you through this."

She nodded and headed for the door, her normal confident stride off.

"Don't go," he found himself sputtering unexpectedly, and a pair of hazel eyes met his.

After a deep breath, he shook loose the swirl of desire that became hard and greedy in the pit of his stomach. Bad timing to want a woman after dropping such a bomb, but in his line of work, when was it a good time? "Let me help take your mind off everything."

She pivoted all the way around. "You can wipe that cocky smile off your face."

He laughed. "I was thinking maybe we could play a game."

A chill must've swept down her spine because he noticed the slightest tremble in her shoulders at his words. "I'm talking chess, not strip poker." Although he wouldn't mind so much putting all of his cards on the table and making a couple of loose wagers that could end with his tongue in her sweet mouth again.

"Of course you'd want to play a game that involves strategy."

"What's wrong with that?" He smiled again, probably the "cocky smile" she'd called him out on moments ago.

Another step had his hand landing on his chest, the feel of his own heart pounding against his palm like the moment before he'd fast-rope out of a helo. "You want to play something a little friendlier? We can check out the office and see what they have."

God, was he really offering to play a board game when all he wanted was to spend the next couple of hours making out like bad guys didn't exist?

How'd he go from talking about terrorists to imagining himself deep inside of her? Being away from his team and out of the driver's seat on an op—it was throwing him off.

"I guess I could use a distraction. I doubt I'm up for writing, anyway."

"A distraction it is, then." He just had to remind himself that sex could *not* be the distraction, even if it'd be the best possible one.

CHAPTER TWELVE

"ARE YOU FRUSTRATINGLY GOOD AT EVERYTHING?" SHE restacked the playing cards and shuffled them as he smiled, his Pacific blues landing on hers, which had her breath catching, inducing a small cough.

"Pretty much." He stretched one leg out and pulled his other knee closer to his chest. "Had to keep busy when deployed in between ops."

"I'll bet you were the master of *Call of Duty*." A smirk stretched her lips at the image of him playing video games with a bunch of guys overseas.

He held one of the green tassels from the throw blanket they were sitting on in his hand, closing a fist around it. "More of a *HALO* fan. Word is I still have the best score of the game."

"Why am I not surprised?" She started to deal the cards but paused before sliding him the last one. "What was your nickname? You had one, right?"

He dropped the tassel, and his body grew stiff.

Before she knew it, he'd stood and turned his back.

Shit. They'd been having a lighthearted conversation

despite what she'd learned earlier, and now she'd probably spooked him by bringing up his so-called "classified" life.

Wine, a roaring fire, and packed bookshelves . . . she'd almost forgotten why they were secluded in the woods. Well, until now—until the moment a quietness seized hold of the room, leaving only the crackling sounds of the flames.

Luke's fingers brushed across some of the thicker spines on one of the bookshelves, and he tipped one back and held it. "Skywalker."

"Huh?" She released the cards, forgetting the game of Spades they'd been about to play, only able to focus on the way his muscles stretched the soft fabric of his long-sleeved tee.

"The guys liked to call me Skywalker."

"You're a *Star Wars* fan?"

"No, I'm not a sci-fi kind of guy, but during new-guy hazing, they duct-taped me to a chair and forced me to watch a few of the movies."

A light laugh escaped her lips. "Must've been torture," she teased and stood.

His shoulder blades pinched back as he reached for another book. "It was a nightmare, but the damn name stuck, whether I wanted it or not."

"I'm sure you got payback at some point."

"Of course," he said, glancing back at her.

She folded her arms and tried to steal a glimpse at the new book he held. "Tolstoy?"

"What? I can't appreciate Russian literature?" He placed *War and Peace* back in its place and faced her. Only a few inches of space separated them, and it wasn't enough, especially when his eyes dipped down to her parted lips. "You're not judging me again, are you?"

"I'm finally learning not to do that, Skywalker." A tiny

hint of a smile crept up her face as she envisioned him lounging in a chair with a glass of German wine in one hand and the pages of Tolstoy beneath his fingertips. This man made of steel had more sides to him than she could count, and each time she discovered a new one, her sense of desire to know even more heightened.

When his eyes breezed to hers she staggered back a step.

"I was a history major in college."

"Meaning you had to read a lot?" She smiled. "My bachelor's degree was in history, too."

"I know." He grinned.

"Right. I forgot." Nerves tangled thick and hard in her chest before dropping into her stomach like the large ball at midnight on New Year's Eve. A slow countdown and then— bam!—an explosion of energy lighting everything up. Yup, that was her right now. On fire with a sudden burst of desire to jump the man before her and unleash her stress onto him.

So, they'd only known each other for a couple of days— didn't a near-death experience afford an unusual bond? Or was that only in the movies? Sometimes the line between reality and fiction became blurred.

"We have that in common, too, I suppose." She turned, but at the feel of his hand on her forearm she stilled, and her eyes dropped closed.

"Tell me how else we're alike," he said.

The sexy gruffness in his voice had her inching into dangerous territory with flashing warning signs all over the place . . . but she didn't want to take the detoured route or heed caution. She wanted to throw herself right into danger if it meant getting a second chance to feel his lips blazing a trail of heat over her skin again.

It was insane to be thinking about sex after she'd learned a terrorist wanted her, wasn't it?

One thing was abundantly clear: no more boring Eva. No, the moment she'd received Luke's request to rent her cabin, her life had taken a drastically new course.

"Well, neither of us can be in relationships," she surmised.

"Why can't you?" He didn't lose his hold of her, even when she shifted to better view him.

Her eyes flicked skyward. "Busy with work."

"You're sure that's the only reason?"

"Why would you ask that?" A queasy unease had her stomach tucking in. Could he see through her rickety walls so easily?

He angled his head when she nervously focused on him again. "You tell me."

She wanted to pull away, to protect herself from the naked truth. But at the same time, she had a burning desire to release everything she'd held pent up inside for years, the weight of her name that pulled her under like the rough ocean currents.

"Eva, tell me what the dossier couldn't."

She swallowed the hard knot in her throat, noting the heavy rise and fall of his chest, and the strength of him, even though his touch on her forearm was featherlight.

"I'm scared," she admitted.

He continued to assess her with no change on his face, so she couldn't really get a read on him. "Scared of what?"

She closed her eyes. "I'm afraid of divorce. Afraid of having multiple failed relationships, like my parents. Afraid of being used for my name and living a lie with someone because of it."

At the feel of his touch on her face, her lids lifted, and his thumb made a small sweeping circle on her cheek.

"I want someone to love me for me, you know? Not for

my family's name and money. Not to land a role in one of my dad's films." She wet her lips, a touch of saltiness there. "But I didn't think it through, did I?"

He palmed her entire cheek before his hand slid through her hair, holding the side of her head. "How so?"

"Because how can I ever start a relationship based on a lie?"

His eyes narrowed and dropped to her mouth for a brief moment, but he didn't say anything.

"We're both pretending to be other people, so we have that in common, too, I guess," she said while trying to dodge the heavier emotions before they turned from a slow drip to a downpour.

His face hardened, and the slack in his jaw disappeared when he captured her eyes once again. "I'm not pretending with you."

She sucked in a sharp breath. "Me, either," she said, almost breathlessly.

His forehead touched hers. "This thing between us doesn't make sense, does it?"

She pressed her lips together, but before she could respond, he leaned back to gather her face in his hands and kiss the ever-loving hell out of her.

Hard and almost punishing at first.

His mouth left hers for a brief moment, his lips hovering before hers as he stared deep into her eyes as if seeking reassurance from her.

She gave a quick nod.

He moved closer to her, kissing her again, which had her walking backward as his tongue roved the inside of her mouth.

With closed eyes, she continued to move until a piece of furniture blocked her backward path.

Luke's hands found her hips, and he lifted her up and onto the desk. She wrapped her legs tight around him as he leaned into her, never breaking the kiss.

Hungry and fierce. Ravenous.

His hard length pressed against her, and she desperately wanted to free him.

Both hands braced against the desk on each side of her once he stepped back, his eyes raking her body. He cupped his mouth, and she wasn't sure if he was trying to prevent himself from coming back to her or strategizing his next move.

She bit her lip and arched her shoulders with anticipation, hoping for the second option.

He peeled off his shirt and unbuttoned the top of his dark denim jeans, exposing the gorgeous cut of his muscles.

"What do you want me to do?" she whispered.

"Besides get naked while I go down on you?"

Her thighs instantly tightened. "Ohh."

A flicker of excitement crossed his face as he motioned for her to rise. He took her lip between his teeth, gently biting, as he shoved off her pants and underwear and slid a thick finger across her soaking wet center.

He released her lip but didn't stop pleasuring her with his touch between her legs. "Take off your shirt. I'd do it for you, but my fingers are a little busy right now." His other hand wrapped around her hip bone and bit into the flesh of her ass cheek.

Her pulse slammed hard at the side of her throat, and she fought the urge to rock against his palm as he took his sweet time touching her. "You're not coming yet, honey. My mouth will be taking care of that." A slow roll of Southern came from his voice as a wave of pleasure tore through her and shot up into her chest, making her nipples harden with the need to be sucked by his perfect mouth.

"It's hard for me to take my shirt off with you doing that." She closed her eyes and held onto him, fighting back the desire to orgasm. He was barely touching her, and yet, she was on the brink of losing her mind.

"If you want something bad enough," he brushed his mouth over hers, "you find a way."

Her fingertips dug into the hard planes of his chest, and her hands skated slowly down his abs.

He gripped her ass even harder, and she gasped. "Shirt. Now," he all but grunted.

Gathering the hem in her hands, even though his body was practically melded to hers now, she wrestled with the material, trying to lift it without banging him with her elbows —she didn't want to kill the mood by hitting him.

"Bra," he rasped as his finger plunged deeper inside, which had her tightening her muscles and arching forward even more.

"Breathtaking," he whispered against her lips without even looking at her breasts once they'd been freed from the confines of her bra. "Lie back."

He let go of her, and she shuddered from the loss of his touch, but the promise of what his mouth would soon bring gave her hope.

"On the desk?" The massive oak structure could easily take her weight.

"I have every intention of pleasuring you to the point where you forget both of your names." A quick wink had her heart elevating as she positioned herself onto the desk once again.

He dropped his pants and boxers, his impressive length, roped in thick veins, drawing her eyes. He wrapped a hand around his shaft and pumped a few times as his blue eyes darkened. His gaze swept up from her toes to her heated cheeks in one fiery hot moment.

"I've wanted you like this ever since I saw you in those glasses."

Her fingertips curled into her palms at her sides, and she leaned back onto her elbows but kept her gaze focused on his. "You have some sort of secretary fantasy? Or librarian?"

"As long as you're the star of the show . . . I don't care what you call it." He closed the gap between them and pressed a hand to her stomach. His index finger made a circle around her belly button before tracing a line up the center of her body.

Her tongue peeked between her lips to wet them, and desire pooled between her legs as he palmed her breast. Her spine hit the desk as he gripped her outer thighs and scooted her butt almost off the edge. He lowered himself to his knees and parted her legs.

The moment his tongue darted up and down her sensitive flesh, her hands pounded the desk at her sides and she bucked up off the wood. *Holy shit.*

"Hang on, I'm only just starting."

Little dots appeared from the bliss that glided through her. She didn't want to orgasm in less than a minute, but when he added more pressure with his fast tongue, coupled with his fingers . . . she came undone. She broke into a million pieces, not sure how she'd ever get put back together.

And maybe she didn't want to, either.

"Don't stop." She kept her hands knotted as she rode the wave of ecstasy for as long as possible.

And once her heart slowed to its normal rhythm, he was on his feet, brushing his lips across hers as his fingers skirted the side of her body. "Are you ready for me?"

"God, yes."

He stood and grabbed a foil packet from his pants pocket.

"Stay on the desk." He stroked himself a few times before rolling it on.

"You came prepared, huh?" Amusement lit her insides, as well as gratefulness for the protection.

"I'm always prepared for every situation." His fists met the desk, and he nuzzled his face against her neck before biting her earlobe. "I just didn't prepare myself for meeting you."

His words had her spine bowing, her body growing ready again.

She wanted to blast out of the shell of a life she'd been hiding in and be with this man.

Tomorrow wasn't promised, but if the sun gave birth to a new day like always, and she was alive and kicking to see it —she'd worry about her emotions then.

Luke kissed her softly, his tongue nudging her lips open. He pulled himself tight against her by wrapping her legs around him, and he positioned himself at her center, never losing touch of her mouth.

While standing, his powerful thighs up against the desk, he filled her in one move.

His body was a gift from God. And right now, he was all hers.

Her lips left his as she started to fall back from his hard thrusts, thrusts that pretty much woke up every nerve cell in her body, sending her into orgasmic shock.

His hand swooped to her spine, holding on to her even if she were like dead weight against his palm as he rocked in and out of her.

She gathered her strength and roped her arms around his neck to help them stay connected, certain she'd never be the same again after tonight . . . but she'd never regret this moment, even if the moment chipped away a piece of her heart.

"Eva." He said her name like a broken moan into her ear when he pulled her tight against him.

"This is—" She cut herself off as her breathing competed with her words, and she felt him tensing and jerking inside of her.

He held her in his arms after he'd orgasmed, as if he never wanted to let her go, as if the world had wanted them to meet and this was all part of destiny's plans.

His chest lifted and fell with slow breaths as he stared into her eyes. She didn't know what to say or how to act. She'd never felt like this before, and it wasn't just about the sex. No, it was about the moment—right now. The moment when the curtain lifts to expose what happened between two people, and everything is raw and exposed.

This moment—this moment was theirs. It was the moment Hollywood chased after, attempting to capture on screen.

She was feeling it—whatever *it* was.

"You okay?" His pupils constricted, and his mouth set into a hard line as if worry had taken hold of him.

She nodded and attempted to corral her thoughts. "I'm great, actually."

His dimple popped, but he kept quiet and eased out of her.

"So, what do you suggest we do now?" She covered her chest with her arm, a sudden shyness fighting her previously brazen nakedness.

"Well, we could try the bed next, with you on top." He arched a brow. "If you're up for it? I mean, we do have time to kill."

"It'd be the logical thing to do, I suppose," she said softly, allowing her arms to drop to her sides to expose her breasts.

"I'm a sucker for doing what's logical," he said and pulled her back into a crushing embrace.

* * *

HE PEPPERED HER WITH KISSES. HIS TONGUE DARTED OVER her belly button, and she stifled a laugh. "You were right," she said before releasing a lazy sigh—the kind you reward yourself with after having mind-blowing sex.

He propped his head up with a couple of pillows, and she ran a short fingernail over his pec and across the slight dusting of chest hair.

"Of course, I am." He cleared his throat and brought her palm to his mouth. "About what, though?"

"You told me I needed a better experience to draw upon for the sex scenes in my script." She chuckled. "And you just gave me an entire night of memories to utilize in the future."

He laughed. "So if you ever make a movie, I'll know the hot scenes were based on our time together?"

"Not that you need another ego boost."

He laced their fingers together, resting their hands atop his strong heart.

"I can't believe we did this, though. I mean, given the situation we're in—are we nuts?"

He rolled his head to the side to look at her. "I know I am, but I accepted that long ago." He winked and looked skyward. "I do things that scare the shit out of me all of the time, which has to be one of *Webster's* definitions for the word *nuts.*"

"I don't know about *Webster,* but . . ." Her breath hitched at the realization of his words. "Are you saying what we did tonight scared you?" It was hard for her to imagine Luke being scared of anything, especially of her.

He pinched the bridge of his nose and closed his eyes, but he kept hold of her hand.

A blanket of thoughts dropped over her mind, like her yammering aunt who told the same stories over and over again at Thanksgiving. Her brain wouldn't stop creating stories, trying to interpret the words followed by the painstaking silence.

He squeezed her hand tighter. "There's a fear that creeps up the back of my neck and dips into my mind right before I jump out of a plane or scale whatever need be on God's green earth." His tone was dark, his admission shocking, and when she looked back at him, his eyes were open but glued to the ceiling. "And when I go down a fatal funnel—aka, an alleyway—I fear death. When a bullet barks out of my rifle and pink mist sprays from the impact of the round in my target—my heart dies a little at the fear of whether or not the kill was justified, even if the guy was an asshole."

This time, she added pressure to their held hands, to signal to him she was listening—that she cared. She had no words, though. How does one respond to what he'd said? For the first time, even in her head, she was speechless.

"Hollywood," he said, catching her eyes, "has it wrong. We're afraid. We have fears. But fear isn't the enemy. Fear is what drives us to survive, to live to see another day. Fear keeps our brothers alive during enemy fire. It motivates us to do our absolute best in any given situation."

Her mouth rounded in understanding, and a rush of anger whipped through her when she realized she'd judged him, yet again. Assuming that a man like him couldn't possibly be afraid of anything.

"But this," he sucked in a sharp breath and let it out

through his nose, while raising their palms a few inches off his chest, "scares the shit out of me. And it's the kind of fear I don't know how to face. How to handle." He closed his eyes once more, as if the contact between the two of them was too hard. "I can navigate the depths of almost any challenge, but there's one thing I've always run from."

"What?" she whispered, but she knew the answer in her heart.

"Allowing myself to ever feel anything for someone. It's a line I've never crossed."

Her heart worked harder as he let go of her hand and shifted to his side. She sat up on her elbows, and the pad of his thumb pulled at her lower lip. "Are you saying you want to cross it?"

"We barely know each other." His brows pulled together as he held her cheek. "It doesn't make sense, right?"

"I don't know anything anymore ever since you showed up in my life." The taste of something more, the promise of something to come, cut into her mouth, and she swallowed her fears and tried to stay in the moment. "I wouldn't take tonight back, though. As insane as it sounds, I don't know if I could ever rewind the last few days and let the memories of our time together slip from my mind." Tears crept into her eyes. "Does that make me a bad person?" Her voice rocked from emotion. "I screwed up your mission, and we're both in danger, but all I can seem to focus on is the way you make me feel when you look at me."

"And how do I make you feel?" He leaned in closer, his mouth hovering near hers.

A teardrop hit her parted lips. "Seen," she whispered.

CHAPTER THIRTEEN

HIS VIBRATING CELL ROUSTED HIM FROM SLEEP, AND HE groaned and slapped his hand on the table in search for it.

He knocked it to the ground and lifted his head to look over at Eva, sound asleep next to him.

Her hair covered most of her face, and when he sat up, he shifted the mass of dark locks off her cheek so he could better see her.

So damn beautiful. And smart. And witty. Also stubborn, in a breathtaking way.

The moment he'd taken her into his arms, he'd known he was in trouble.

He had one rule for not only himself, but his team, and he was terrified this woman had the potential to blow it to pieces.

Four days. Had it only been four days since they'd met?

Today was the day she was actually supposed to show up at her cabin. But today was also the day he realized he was capable of something he thought he'd buried deep inside of him for the sake of the job.

Country first.

Country always.

But . . .

He let out a soft but frustrated sigh and dragged his palms down his face before grabbing his phone off the floor.

A text popped up from Jessica a moment later.

Emergency. Call me.

He walked naked over to the window.

Waiting for the line to connect, he opened the blinds and looked out at the mountain in the distance as the sun roared to life like a giant ball of fire from behind the top peak.

"I need you on a plane within three hours. You think you can make it to Philly in time?" Jessica cut straight to the point.

"What about the consulate and New York?"

"Malik Yilmaz just showed his face outside the French Embassy in Monaco. He looked right at the camera as if saying, *Come get me, motherfuckers.*"

"What the hell is he doing there, and how did he get out of the States without us knowing about it?"

"No damn idea, but believe me, I'm looking into it. I'm also checking to see if he or his brother ever traveled to Monaco. Will alerted POTUS to the change in plans. I'm enroute to the airport. I'm taking a flight to Nice in two hours, then the team and I will drive to Monaco from there."

Luke glanced back at Eva, stirring in her sleep. "Do we have any assets in Monaco that can try and get a location on him in the meantime? Anyone we can trust, I should say."

"Yeah. Remember Harper Brooks? She's a CIA field agent, and she's stationed outside Nice. Will didn't want to bring anyone outside our team into this, but we can't risk losing Malik, so he's sending her in now. I've got my facial recognition program running—if he's still there, I'll find him."

"Good." Luke's shoulders relaxed at the idea of this all hopefully ending soon. "Do you think Malik's taking a page from our playbook and trying to bait us to him?"

"Looks that way. Why else would he risk leaving hiding?"

He grabbed his strewn clothes off the floor, catching Eva's eyes when he stood upright. "I take it Harper can't grab Malik for us, so we can call it a day?"

"Sure, wiseass."

"Everything okay?" Eva whispered, sitting now.

"Yeah," he mouthed and added, "Give me a sec."

She nodded and fisted the sheet close to her skin.

"Why are we flying commercial? Do you want him to know we're coming?"

"We don't have time to coordinate a military flight, especially without raising any alarms as to who the hell we are—and I can't get a private jet on such short notice. Besides, Malik's expecting us."

He held the phone to his ear with his shoulder while pulling on his boxers and jeans, and then a thought hit him like a bullet, and he slowly turned toward the stunning woman in bed. "What about Eva?"

"She comes with us," Jessica said after a few seconds of silence passed.

"I don't like this." Taking Eva to Europe with him? How could he put her in even more danger?

"We don't have a choice. There's no time to arrange a bodyguard for her, and aside from two of our guys staying back to babysit Ender's comatose body, everyone needs to be in Monaco."

"I'm not a huge fan of walking directly into a trap," Luke muttered.

"Since when do we do that?" A long breath came through

the line. "Just call me when you get to Philly. I'm making arrangements for two new IDs and passports to be delivered to a locker at the bus terminal outside the airport. Once I have confirmation, I'll get you the passcode to the locker."

"Okay. Be safe." He ended the call, tucked the phone in his pocket, and then settled his hands on his hips as he studied Eva standing nervously before him with her lip between her teeth. "You ever been to Monaco?" It was home to the rich and famous—so, maybe . . .

"Yeah, actually." She smiled.

* * *

ON THE PLANE, EVA PEERED AT HIM AND A HINT OF A SHY grin touched her glossy lips.

She'd stopped in one of the stores at the airport and bought mascara and gloss. She was a natural beauty, but the gloss did have him wanting to suck the cherry flavor right off her lips.

"How are you feeling, Mrs. Cross?" He reached for her hand beneath the tray table.

She rolled her tongue over her lips, and he knew she was purposefully teasing him, which had him hardening already. This woman was something else. "Okay, *Mister* Cross, given the circumstances."

Thrown into danger, and yet, she could still roll on the fly with him. Who the hell was she? He wanted to know more and more about her; he couldn't seem to get enough. He'd found himself pumping her with questions on their drive to the airport.

He shifted the sweater off her right shoulder and pressed his lips to the light dusting of freckles there. "You smell like heaven."

"I smell like I haven't taken a shower." Her shoulders lifted from her soft laugh.

He found her ear. "Actually, you smell like sex."

She looked up to find his eyes again, their noses almost touching. Her hazel irises burned with lust, reciprocating his own desires. He wanted to pin her down and take his sweet time with her, but they were on board a flight with two hundred people, and so . . .

He doubted they'd have time to be together once in Monaco, so he had to relish the time he had with her now, knowing it'd come to an abrupt end once the mission was over.

He'd go back to his life, and she'd go back to—what exactly? Would she ever be safe as Eva *or* Everly? Had Malik or Ender given her name to any terrorist organization?

He sat taller and cupped his mouth as he processed potential outcomes for a woman he barely knew, but desperately didn't want to let go of.

FEAR.

Four letters that packed a bruising punch.

His fear of ever falling for someone, especially someone who could steal his breath, that fear had kept him at arm's length from women. But Eva . . .

"You know what's strange?" she asked softly.

"Yeah?"

"I still can't escape my last name, not even with you." She swallowed. "The Reed name is still a prickle in my side."

"How so?"

She shook her head lightly. "I can't be Everly with you, because that means I'd pull you into the same harsh light I tried escaping from, which would be dangerous for you. For who you are," she said in a low voice, even though her words were masked to others by the high altitude and crying baby two rows behind them.

"Do you want to be Everly again?"

"I don't know." Her palm flattened on the table next to her coffee, and she stared down at her chipped nails. "You may not even want to see me again after all of this is over, but it kills our chances anyway, doesn't it? Even living as Eva— if someone found out who I really am . . ."

He squeezed his eyes closed, fighting the natural recoil inside of him he'd honed so well over the years, which kept him from feeling anything for anyone. "It's not about your last name." A painful blow of disappointment took hold of him, knowing he'd have to let her go, and soon.

"What's it about then?" She looked over at the middle row of people with earphones in, watching movies, then peeked behind her to check for the all-clear to talk. "Because your job is classified?" She mouthed the sentence even though no one could hear.

"It's complicated." He released her hand as the normal, unmistakable coolness attempted to gather inside of him. He lifted his coffee for a chance to gather his thoughts, to fight off the inevitable truth of who he was—needing more time to just be a man, so he could be with someone like her.

"When is anything good in life ever easy?"

The base of his skull met the back of the seat, and he lowered his drink to the table. He shifted uncomfortably, his knees bumping into his tray table, almost spilling his coffee. "Why don't we save this conversation for another day?"

Her eyes drew tight, her lips flattening. "What if we don't have another day?"

"You can't think like that."

She looked away from him and out the small window. "I

thought the fear of tomorrow not being promised helped you survive the day."

"You also have to be optimistic that tomorrow will come."

"It sounds like you constantly have to toe the line. Must make for a hard balancing act."

He stiffened, his fists turning white-knuckled atop the armrests. He had to keep fighting the impulse to spill the truth about why he couldn't open his heart up to anyone, even to a woman like her.

"I can't risk your safety, and I also won't be another widow-maker." His words left his mouth in a rush. "I need some air." He unbuckled, held his coffee, and moved the tray table out of his way to stand.

"We're on a plane."

He set his drink back on the table then pressed his palms to the overhead compartment, and he followed her gaze to the tattoo he'd gotten when he'd first joined the SEALs—a rookie mistake. A mistake that could ID him as a SEAL, but he couldn't bring himself to remove it for some reason.

He dropped his arms. "Bathroom," he said softly and shook his head, hating he was slipping back into his typical, stony façade—a façade she could see right through . . .

CHAPTER FOURTEEN

THE YELLOW LAMBORGHINI WAS LIKE A FLASH OF LIGHTNING, roaring down the road along the French Riviera as they headed to Monte Carlo.

Eva kept her gaze cast out the window and on the Mediterranean Sea, even though it was too dark outside to see anything other than blips of lights from the houses that dotted the landscape built up into the craggy hills.

"We'll be there in ten minutes," he said and tightened his grip on the wheel.

"Quick drive," she responded in a soft voice without looking his way.

A weird fluttering sensation rolled around in the pit of his stomach. Nerves?

His cell was mounted on the dashboard, and his gaze flicked to it when Jessica's number popped on-screen. He decided to put it on speaker, even though he risked Eva hearing something classified. He had to focus on *not* crashing the sports car his sister had arranged for them to rent. Not that he minded driving the beast, but he was more comfortable in a Humvee—something that could handle a battery of enemy fire.

"Do you like my surprise?" Jessica asked when he answered.

"I know this ride isn't courtesy of Uncle Sam, which means it's from our own pocket." He whistled out a breath.

"You're going to Hotel de Paris." She said the name with a French accent. "It's right alongside the Monte Carlo Casino. You'll need to look the part since I checked out a few of the largest suites."

"Are we paying for those, too?"

"We have the cash from the business. Don't get your tighty-whities in such a twist."

His sister's jab induced a small laugh from Eva, and the little sound tapped at his heart. He'd let his sister knock him around any day of the week if it made Eva laugh—even if he shouldn't be concerning himself with such pleasures.

"So, why are you so damn happy?" he asked. "Tell me we have good news."

He could almost hear Jessica's smile through the phone when she said, "I have *great* news, actually."

"Finally." He waited for her to talk, and when she didn't say anything, he added, "You and the suspense-building. Tell me already. We're almost there."

"Our hotel rooms are directly above the two suites Malik checked in to."

"So, we have him."

"Yup. Harper found him. She positioned a camera in the hall light outside his room, so we officially have eyes on his door. We'll know when he comes and goes."

"You know where he is, and you're not grabbing him?" Eva asked, her eyes now sharp on Luke.

He looked back at the road, spotting the lights of the

Monte Carlo Casino off in the distance. "Doesn't work that way."

"Why not?"

"Because this isn't your TV show. We can't go busting down a hotel door in the middle of a foreign country and get into a gun battle," Luke explained, but then wondered if he came across as a dick.

"We'll talk about this more when you get in," Jessica said. "And don't worry, Eva, we have multiple suites. We'll work out the logistics of your sleepover once you've checked in."

He clutched the wheel and shifted gears a little more forcefully than necessary, the car nearly veering off the road. "See you in five." He ended the call, his stomach squeezing.

When Eva didn't say anything else, he realized he probably had been an asshole. And so, when they rolled up to the valet in front of the hotel, Luke turned toward her, his mouth set in a hard line as he thought about what to say.

She cast him a veiled glance before reaching for the handle, even though the hotel staff would open it for her.

"Eva." He let her name sit between them, baking in the silence that captured the small space.

"Let's not keep your team waiting," she said quickly and allowed the valet to help her out before he could apologize— not just for his remark, but for his aloofness on the second half of their flight.

After checking in, he turned to Eva. She was off to the side of the concierge desk, staring up at the ceiling in a daze. "Something wrong? Aside from the obvious, I mean?"

"Remembering my last time in Monte Carlo," she said softly.

"Good or bad?"

"Good or bad what?"

"Your memories from then."

"Oh." A tight smile met her lips. "Still deciding."

"Hm. Well, you ready?"

"Guess so," she said, her voice far too grave sounding.

As they started for the elevators, he wondered if the change in her demeanor meant she was attempting the distance dance, the one where you guard your heart like your life depended on it. Perhaps she realized how dangerous it was to even know a man like Luke.

He had hoped for a little more time with her before they had to carve a harsh line in the sand between them. Maybe she was right to pull away? Everything had happened so fast between them; it might as well end fast.

It's for the better. He'd have to force-feed that line down his throat probably a hundred times before tomorrow, though.

Jessica was in the hall outside the suite when they stepped out of the elevator, the awkward sting of silence still enveloping Eva and Luke.

"Hey." Jessica flicked her wrist and motioned for them to enter the neighboring suite.

Eva walked past Luke and followed Jessica.

"We didn't do formal introductions back in the States," Jessica said once they were in the hotel room. "I'm Jessica." She extended her palm. Eva forced a small smile, and Luke dropped their bags. "I'm the big guy's sister."

He caught sight of Eva's mouth rounding in surprise when she released Jessica's hand. "I didn't see that one coming."

"Most don't." Jessica turned her attention to some of the team crowding the room: Liam, Asher, Owen, and Knox.

Owen was at the desk, and Knox was looking at the screen from over his shoulder.

Asher and Liam were in their civvies, seated on the couch

135

abutting the expansive window. They both wore the same identical amused look on their faces. It was as if they could see plain as day that he and Eva had hooked up last night, and they were rearing to give him a hard time.

Luke lifted his chin in their direction, a silent message to back off and focus on the mission.

"These guys"—Jessica jerked a thumb their way—"work with us. I'm sure you gathered as much before we poked you in the neck a couple nights ago." Jessica shoved her hands in her black jeans pockets. "Sorry about that, by the way."

"Oh, um, yeah—you all saved me, so . . ." Eva shrugged.

"And we also got you into this mess." Knox strode across the room and reached for her palm, his eyes pinned to Eva's mouth. His own lips twitched into a brief smile. "I'm Knox."

"You uncuffed *and* drugged me."

"Mm-hm." He released her hand and scratched at the back of his head as he eyed Luke.

"Owen over there was the one who was supposed to rescue you in the woods, had you not been captured." Jessica pointed to him, but when he didn't look up, Jessica added, "Don't mind him. He tends to zone everyone out when he's in the middle of something."

"I think we can skip the introductions, anyway," Luke said dryly and crossed the fancy room now littered with duffel bags. He shifted the blinds out of the way and glimpsed out the window at the pool down below and the yacht-lined shore. "Where is Harper and everyone else?" He faced the room and folded his arms, trying not to stare at Eva as she stood close to the door, her gaze darting among everyone in the room.

"Once we arrived, Harper took some of the boys back to the safe house in Nice to load up on artillery and other fun tools," Knox said, shoving his hands in his jeans pockets.

"I'm surprised Will's okay with us teaming up with a spook," Asher said from the couch while looking directly at Jessica, the spook-jab meant for her as well.

Jessica stepped over one of the duffel bags and grabbed a computer off the coffee table. "We didn't have an option. Harper was the best choice, and she's worked with Will and me in the past. I trust her."

"Isn't Harper a little curious about what you're doing working this op when you're supposed to be a civilian now?" Luke shook his head at his own question and dropped his eyes to the floor, avoiding the angry look he'd surely be getting from his sister at his choice of words in front of Eva.

Eva was smart enough to figure out Luke wasn't some retired government contract employee, though. But, did it really matter at this point?

Protocol was protocol, but she'd either spill the news about him and the team or not.

"Harper's not going to prod," Jessica said.

Luke came up next to Jessica to view her computer, which showed the camera feed of Malik's room. "Has he left his room since you've been here?"

"Yeah. He's at the hotel bar now." Jessica switched screens. "We hacked into the hotel's feeds. This is live footage. He's been there for the last twenty minutes."

"I still don't get why you don't grab him." Everyone directed their focus to Eva, and it had her signature red creeping up her neck and to her cheeks. "I know you can't make a scene, but isn't getting the safe more important? Isn't it too risky to wait?"

"How much does she know?" Jessica set the computer back on the table, and her hands settled on her hips.

"Enough," Eva answered for him, a pinch of confidence in her tone. And why did it make him proud—the way her shoulders squared back and she eyed his sister as if she belonged on the op, too? "You guys might have saved me, but you did drag me into this whole thing. So, I know what I know, and you'll need to trust that your secrets are safe with me."

Luke noticed Knox fighting a grin, but no one in the room seemed to know what the hell to say. They were probably waiting for guidance on the matter from Luke.

In five years, this had never happened before. A civilian had never been privy to a mission. Civilians had been saved, but they'd never known by whom.

"If a certain someone didn't drop the ball back in the States, we wouldn't even be here right now," Asher said.

Luke noticed Eva staring at Asher's tatted arms, in sort of a trance.

"He sure as hell didn't fly commercial." Jessica's face tightened, and she edged closer to Asher, ready to spar with him. "Not on my watch."

"I just thought you were better than that. I mean, you claim to have created the best tracking program in the world. How could you miss Malik leaving the U.S.—even if he flew private?" Asher rose, casually tucking his hands in his jeans pockets, and stood before Jessica with a mocking grin.

Liam's lips twitched as his gaze snapped back and forth between Asher and Jessica, as if anxious for Luke's sister to sharpen her nails and defend her cyber skills. "Do I need to stand between you two like always?" His Australian accent, still thick, cut even deeper into his tone, and he winked at Eva as if saying *welcome to the club.*

Jessica dragged her gaze up Asher's tall frame. "Blow me."

Asher cocked his head, his teasing smile deepening, his brown eyes dropping to hers.

Before he made a remark that'd push both Luke and Jessica over the edge, Luke stepped up alongside the two and pressed a hand to Asher's chest. "Focus, man." He looked over at his sister. "Keep your head in the game. We don't have time for your usual bickering."

"Um, can I say something?" Eva raised her hand, and the room grew silent as they all faced her once again.

Luke dropped his hand and crossed the room to her, sorrow thickening in his throat as he thought about Eva in this situation.

"Malik wanted you to know he's here, right? Maybe he wants to make a deal?" she asked.

"A deal? Sure, darlin'," Liam said. "His brother tried that and got his face blown off." He stood next to Luke now. "Malik's offered himself as bait, and he's hoping we'll come after him."

"And he'll be prepared," Asher added from behind.

"Let me be bait," Eva announced to the room.

"Hell no," Luke said before anyone had a chance to entertain the idea. "I'm not putting your life on the line like that."

He reached for her forearm, but she retracted it and sidestepped him. "Jessica?"

Oh, she was going to try and go around him? *Not gonna fly.*

"Luke is sufficient bait," Jessica said, and his heart slowed a bit, thankful his sister was on his side.

Eva removed her jacket and held it tight in her arms. She faced Luke again, her eyes pleading. "Malik thinks I know half the code. He'll torture Luke to get the five digits, and then he'll kill him and come after me for the other five."

Luke's arms fell at his sides, surprise cracking through his body like a whip. "What do you think he'd do to you?" he asked, his voice deep as he tried to control the slow boil of anger about to erupt at the thought of something happening to her.

He stepped so close to her she had to lift her chin to find his eyes.

And at that moment, it was as if the rest of the room had faded away, and he and Eva were alone.

Her brows lifted slightly and her eyes widened a fraction as if luxuriating in the warmth of his intense stare.

Or maybe he'd officially lost his damn mind.

"We won't let him take her, but if you two could lure him out of the hotel and somewhere a little less public so we could grab and bag him, that'd be ideal," Owen suggested, interrupting the thick tension between him and Eva.

He shifted his focus to Owen and arched his shoulders back. "She's not part of it. I'll get him to come."

"Can I ask an obvious question?" Eva asked.

"Yeah?" Owen spoke when Luke couldn't do anything other than gape at this fiercely strong woman.

Jessica and the team observed Eva as if she held all of the answers. As if she were this bright, shining light. She drew everyone to her, and he couldn't blame them. He'd been the cliché moth to the flame in her presence the moment she resisted Ender's men to strip, standing her ground against eight armed terrorists. She probably even won him over before that, when she'd pointed a hunting rifle at him.

"What is it?" Jessica asked.

Eva took a sobering breath and offered some distance between her and Luke by stepping back a couple of feet. "If you're able to get both codes, how will you get Malik to tell you where the safe is? Torture?"

"We don't torture people. Not waterboarding, at least. We

have a couple of moral rules we follow," Owen answered and scratched at his throat as he looked to Luke.

"You're okay with murder, but you draw the line at torture?" Eva crossed her arms and scrutinized the room of military personnel as if they were students and she was about to lecture them.

The woman had balls.

And God, did she turn him on.

"There's no guarantee Malik will give us the code or the safe, but we can at least prevent anyone else from getting it," Jessica said when Luke still couldn't get his lips to part and speak, too taken aback by Eva to say anything.

"But it'd be better to get the safe so you can stop more terrorists." Eva edged farther into the room, approaching his teammates. She straightened her shoulders, and any hint of shy red had fled from her skin. She stood in total confidence.

Was she born for this life, and she just didn't know it?

"Of course," Jessica said.

Luke lifted his arm, pressing his palm to the wall. "You think we should give him the code and follow him to the safe," he said, not as a question, more as a statement in line with his own desires.

"We'd love to do that, but orders from above have said *no*." Jessica looked over at Asher who stood behind her, and he narrowed his gaze her way, a hardness to his eyes. He'd been a major proponent of that idea from the get-go and had said, *Fuck what Will wants.*

Asher sent a mock salute to Jessica as if to say *Even a civilian knows what to do . . . so, why aren't we doing it?*

"She's right." Luke let out a pent-up breath and dropped his hand from the wall. "But without the all clear from Will, we can't do it."

Jessica's face was pinched tight in defeat as she eyed Luke now. "Can Luke and I have the room?"

Luke nodded in agreement. "Knox, take Eva to the neighboring suite. Don't let her out of your sight."

"Will do." Knox motioned Eva to the door.

Luke found his sister's eyes and snapped a litany of angry sentences in German—knowing they were about to do battle over this hot-button issue, and he was too anxious to wait until the room had been cleared to start the conversation.

Jessica inched closer and waved her hands in the air, yelling back at him in the same tongue.

"They do this all the time. You'll get used to it," Luke heard Knox say.

Jessica stopped talking and looked at Knox in the open doorway. "Wait, take her to my room, instead." She tucked a hand in her pocket and then tossed Knox a key. "She can stay with me."

Luke shook his head at his sister, but when he looked at Eva, he realized maybe Jessica was right not to have Eva bunk with him.

Owen snatched the laptop with the live camera feeds from the table and followed the rest of the group out a moment later.

"You, of all people, know we can't go against Will's orders," Luke snapped once the door was closed.

The chain of command couldn't be broken, even if he disagreed.

Rules were rules. Breaking an order could end a career.

"How many terrorists can we catch with the intel Malik is sitting on? How many lives can we save if we have access to that safe?" Her teeth clamped together, and her short red nails bit into the biceps of her crossed arms. "Will's playing it safe."

"And POTUS put him in charge. So," he began and edged closer to his sister, his chin dropping almost to his chest as his voice deepened, "are you suggesting we go against the president?"

"No." She spun away and shook her hair loose from her ponytail. "Malik is downstairs." She pointed to the floor as if he'd forgotten the difference between north and south. "I'd love to do what Eva said and just grab him now."

"And you'd be thinking emotionally and not strategically, which isn't like you." He slipped a hand to his sister's shoulder, urging her to face him.

"You're not exactly yourself, either." She paused to take a breath. "We made a deal never to lie to each other five years ago—what happened with Eva, and why does she know so much about us?" She pivoted to catch his eyes, a dark look seizing hold of her blues.

He let go of her shoulder and tapped two closed fists at his forehead, working through his thoughts. "Eva was an unaccounted-for wrench in all of this, but she's a victim—not a tool to be used. We're still on the same page about that, right?" He swallowed, his heart rate kicking up as he waited for his sister to respond.

"You care about her?"

"Like any human life, yeah."

"It's almost like you had that answer already planned." She lifted her brows and gave him a pointed look. "How'd a woman get under your skin in less than a week? Hell, in any time period. If someone is breaking the rules"—she pointed a finger at him—"it's you."

"I'm not falling for her." The muscles in his jaw clenched tight at the lie.

"That's not what I said."

"It's what you meant." He turned, cupping the back of his

head. "I'd feel the same about any woman caught in the crossfires of an operation. I wouldn't want someone innocent getting hurt because of a mission."

"That might be true, but she's different. I can see it all over your face. And on hers."

"And what does any of this have to do with breaking Will's orders and changing the plans?" He stole a look at his sister.

She dropped down onto the couch near the window. "This whole mission is different."

He whirled around. "Damn right it's different. Since when do we let the CIA spoon-feed us intelligence without doing our due diligence first?"

She rested her elbows on her knees and bit into her lip, but kept her eyes on the table.

"How can we do our job when the CIA has only given us half the picture? What if Malik and Ender didn't have Odem killed? What if Ender showed up in Berlin when I took out Reggie, not because he was there to meet with him, but because he'd witnessed his father murdered and followed him, seeking both revenge and the USB? When I showed up and killed Reggie, I changed Ender's plans."

"The CIA must have intel that led them to believe Ender and Malik paid off Reggie and had Odem killed."

"You keep blindly trusting them. I don't get it." He lifted his palms. "Did you see the intel? I sure as hell didn't. What if they lied to Will to cover their own asses?"

"We don't have time to find any of this out."

"Make time," he bit out. "If you want me to even consider breaking protocol and going behind Will's back, I want answers. I want to know what the fuck is really going on and why Malik chose Monaco to bring us to."

Jessica slowly stood. "Just so we're clear, you and I work together. We're a team. I don't take orders from you."

He hated fighting with her, but damn it, they needed to be on the same page, or this shit would only get worse. But he relaxed his stance and said, "We are a team." He blinked a couple of times, clearing his head. "I feel like we're working in the dark, and it makes me edgy. I'm sorry."

She took a small breath and nodded. "I want to do what's right, Luke. And what's right isn't always what's been ordered." A sigh blew from her lips. "I'll learn everything I can about Reggie, okay?"

He nodded. "From his high school girlfriend to who he was last sleeping with, I want to know it. You'll need help from the inside, though."

"Will won't—"

"Harper."

"You're suggesting we bring her in?" She bit her thumbnail in thought.

"Get what you can from her without saying too much. We'll talk to Will later about bringing her on board as needed."

"Okay." She started past him, heading to the door.

"Where are you going?"

"To get the team together so we don't waste any time." Her hand stilled on the knob. "What really happened with Eva in the mountains?" Her eyes swept to his, her question throwing him off. "You're not the same."

"People don't change in four days," he said in a throaty voice, emotion catching in his tone.

"Are you so sure about that?"

CHAPTER FIFTEEN

"This must be a lot for you." Knox flipped through the channels on the TV, his booted foot perched on the coffee table and his hand resting casually on his other thigh as he eyed the screen.

"It's a bit out of the ordinary, but I do work on a TV show about Navy SEALs. I'm guessing you were one before all of this?" She wondered if he'd be as tight-lipped as Luke.

He nodded, which was more than she'd expected, actually.

"How long have you known Luke?" She edged closer to the couch, but her legs were still stiff from the long flight, so she wanted to keep standing.

He scratched at his dark beard, and his light brown eyes lifted to hers. "Since BUD/S. I almost dropped out and rang the damn bell. Can you believe that?" A grin briefly teased his lips. "Luke wouldn't let me do it, though. He told me he'd kick my motherfucking ass if I went anywhere close to the thing. He also promised to buy me a lifetime supply of beer if I didn't give in to the temptation of quitting."

She chuckled lightly. "Why'd you want to quit?" She

rolled her eyes at her question. "I mean, besides how hard it must've been."

"I enlisted to piss off my dad and didn't realize how insane it'd actually be."

"Oh."

"My real name's Charlie." He nodded his head as if making a second introduction as himself and not the SEAL.

She knew a thing or two about double names. "Well, hi, Charlie. I'm actually Everly. So, uh, how'd you get the name Knox?"

He looked back at the screen. "The boys have been calling me Knox since I joined the SEALs because of my father. He's a rich asshole in Washington and has more money than he knows what to do with. He wanted me to be some prissy politician, so I joined the Teams instead."

"I still don't get the name."

"Fort Knox Depository . . . all the gold." He turned off the TV. "I guess I preferred Knox to Rich Boy or some garbage like that."

"Makes sense. So, what does your father think about you now? And are you glad you never quit?"

"Being a SEAL is the best decision I've ever made. I owe Luke for not letting me quit." He dropped his foot to the ground, slid the remote onto the table, and looked over at her. "As for my dad, no idea what he thinks. We don't talk."

Her smile flattened. "Sorry."

He shrugged. "Looks like you know a thing or two about wealthy families, though. Heard you're a celebrity."

"Not even close." She waved a hand in the air and finally sat down. "Most of my family is well-known, though."

"You weren't up for the life?"

"No. Guess you weren't, either." A timid smile fought to capture her lips.

"Luke's a good guy, by the way. I saw how you two were looking at each other back there."

Oh, God. "Oh, um." Her face heated, and she pressed a palm to her cheek.

"I don't blame you for falling for him, even in such a short time. He'd give you the coat off his back and freeze in the cold for you. Hell, we were on an op in Canada three months ago, and he froze his balls off by giving his jacket to this poor guy we encountered."

She drew up the scene in her mind, and her smile broadened. "What happened to the guy?"

"Oh . . . I had to kill him."

"What?"

"Turns out he was undercover."

She arched a suspicious brow. "You're kidding, aren't you?"

"Classified." He winked.

"I am so sick of hearing that word." She sat all the way back and stared at the ceiling, quiet for a moment. "What makes you think Luke likes me? How'd you get that from a few looks?" Her head rolled to the side to glimpse Knox.

"The guy looked like he'd break one of our faces if we let anything happen to you. And he was also looking at you like he wanted to pin you to the wall and have his way with you—to hell if we were in the room." He stood and tucked his hands in his back pockets.

She cupped a hand to her mouth, the intensity of the heat in her face multiplying.

"Luke doesn't get involved with anyone, though. Hell, he even has a no-marriage rule for the team."

She sat up taller. "A rule?"

"None of us has any plans to settle down in the near

future, so it works. But if we ever want to, we'll get booted from the team."

"Wow." Her eyes widened. "Kind of harsh. Does he hate marriage that much? Or is he worried you'll get your covers blown—whoever the hell you people are—if you're married?"

Knox turned and approached the window, keeping his hands in his pockets. "The rule was more of a suggestion up until two years ago. The concern had been that, if anyone found out who we were, they could come after our wives and children."

Keep you safe, Luke had said.

It was one thing to hear the words from Luke, but to receive confirmation on just how off-limits he really was . . . it kicked things up a notch. "And what happened two years ago?"

"Is this how you got to him?" He swiveled around and arched his shoulders back, studying her. "Did you manage to pump Luke with so many questions you disoriented him?" He grinned.

"Am I doing that now?" She bit back a nervous laugh.

"I don't mind talking so much."

"As long as it's not classified?"

He nodded.

"And whatever happened two years ago is classified, right?"

"That'd be a *fuck yes*, to be exact."

A widow-maker . . . She stood, not sure what to make of the conversation. "So, Luke will never settle down?"

"My advice is to wrap up whatever happened between you two in the mountains into a neat little box and store it into your memory bank."

I'm trying. She was going to make a valiant effort, at least. "You're fairly blunt, and a bit presumptuous."

"But I'm always right." A corner of his mouth lifted.

A hard knock at the door interrupted her thoughts. She wondered whether it was Jessica or Luke. She wasn't sure who she wanted to face right now.

"It's me." Luke's deep voice carried clean through the door and right under her skin.

"Be right back." Knox left the room, and she didn't even have a chance to catch sight of Luke in the hall.

She went to the window and looked out at the Mediterranean Sea. It was dark, but the soft glow of hotel lights flickered off the water, and the clear sky allowed the moon to reflect off the surface of the sea.

It should've been a calming sight, and yet, a whirl of air rushed from her lips at the sound of the door opening and then closing behind her. Her eyes fell shut. She didn't have to hear his voice to know she was alone in the room with him.

"Eva."

She pressed both hands to her abdomen, remembering the feel of his body tight against hers as they'd made love. She may not have worked her way sexually through Hollywood, but she knew a thing or two about the difference between sex and making love . . . well, she liked to think she did, since she had to showcase it in screenplays.

"Look at me." The deep timbre of his voice had her unraveling.

Pricks of need poked at her—the need to see him. To face him and look into the pair of eyes that could see beneath her mask and deep inside of her. But she whispered, "No."

"Please."

He was closer. She could feel him behind her, even though she kept her eyes shut. "I'm not mad at you, even if it seems like it." Her voice trembled as sadness skated through her tone. "I understand who you are and what you do."

At the touch of his hands on her shoulders, her arms dropped from her abdomen. His fingertips bit harder into her flesh, then he smoothed his hands down the sides of her body and to her hips. He held her tight against him, and she stifled the moan that wanted to escape from her lips at being so close to him. "What are you doing?"

"Probably fucking up," he said into her ear, and her skin flushed.

She tipped her head back so it touched his chest, and his chin found the top of her head, resting there as if they belonged molded into this position. "You should go. You should go do your job and save the world."

"I will," he said. "But for now, I think . . . I think I want—"

She shook her head and pivoted in his arms to face him before she lost the strength to voice her thoughts and gave in to her desires. "I can't." Her eyes blurred beneath unshed tears. "I can't live in the moment and not worry about the aftermath of it. I thought I could, but that's not who I am."

His forehead dropped to hers, and his hands moved up to her shoulders again. "I know," he whispered.

He held her like that for a few minutes, and she didn't object because she knew it was the last moment she'd get with him.

When he let go, he slowly backed away from her without turning. It was as if he didn't want to lose sight of her.

Her hand pressed to her trembling lips.

How could she feel so much for a man she barely knew? It was the stuff of films and fiction, and not meant for real life.

"You should get some rest. I have to work, so I'll have

someone stay in the living room while you sleep in the bedroom."

"Aren't you tired, too?"

"I'll sleep when I'm dead."

"Not funny."

He finally turned. "Sweet dreams, Hollywood."

CHAPTER SIXTEEN

THE HOTEL ROOM PATIO OFFERED A BEAUTIFUL VIEW OF THE sea. She'd actually stayed at this same hotel five years ago, but it definitely felt different now.

"How's the room service?" One of the SEALs took a seat and slipped on a pair of aviator shades. "No mimosa with breakfast?"

"I'm sorry. There are so many of you. What's your name again?" She'd met six guys in total since her arrival late last night, and aside from Knox—since they'd had their little heart-to-heart—she couldn't keep the ridiculous number of hot men's names straight in her head.

She'd nicknamed this SEAL as the Bad Boy, and it had nothing to do with his longish dark hair and tattoos. No, it was the look in his eyes. He gave off the vibe that he was both a rule-breaker and a heartbreaker.

"I'm Asher." He stole a scone off her plate, leaned back in his seat, and lifted his head in the direction of the sunrays. Monaco was having one of their record high temperatures for January, and she was prepared to soak in every bit of sunlight as a means of avoiding her feelings for Luke or confronting the mess she was embroiled in.

"Is that your real name or your nickname?" She set her fork down, not really all that hungry anymore.

"All mine, sugar."

"And what was your nickname in the SEALs?" she asked, her curiosity piqued. She was already writing his story in her head, almost subconsciously. And in her head, Asher and Jessica had a thing. Or, maybe they would at some point. The tension between them last night had milked the room of oxygen. And usually, there was only one reason why tension ever ran that red-hot. She should know since it'd been like that with her and Luke.

"Fighter Boy."

She chuckled. "Are you pulling my leg? Why not, at least, Fighter Man?"

He swallowed the bites of his scone and washed it down with some OJ. "It sounds weird like that."

"Okay." She flicked her wrist in a come-hither motion. "Details. Why the name?"

"Damn, woman, Knox warned me about you, and I didn't believe him." His dark brow lifted as he peeled the skin off a banana next.

"What?" she asked, a sudden shyness taking hold of her.

"You sure do love questions."

She fiddled with the handle of her coffee mug but didn't lift it. "Well?"

His white teeth flashed in the bright light. "I was a fighter for a couple of years before joining the SEALs."

"Like professionally? In the UFC?"

"Nah, like in underground clubs and alleyways in New York." He chewed his food and added, "I've always been a bit of a rabble-rouser if you can believe that."

"Really? Yup, super hard to believe." She dragged her words through a layer of sarcasm but added a smile. "Do you still like fighting?"

"As long as I have a worthy opponent." He kicked his denim-clad leg up on the table, his black military boot catching her eye.

She couldn't imagine him and Luke working together. They were like fire and ice.

Eva held up a finger. "Be right back."

When she returned, Asher had his hands casually resting behind his neck, and he angled his head her way, the sun reflecting off his glasses and hitting her eyes. "A pen and paper? Is this an interview now?"

"No, but I'd love it if you could help me create a list of names so I can keep everyone straight in my head." She assumed her seat and removed the cap from the pen, poised and ready to jot some notes.

"We don't really want you knowing much about us."

"Too late for that. I just want names, by the way. Not your social security numbers and bank account information."

"Pretty sure your account is a hell of a lot more padded than mine." He looked back up at the sky, far too laid-back for a man on a covert mission. Then again, he did get assigned to her, and not to Malik. He probably drew the short straw.

"I already know Knox," she said while writing his name and *Charlie* next to it.

"And you're fairly familiar with the boss."

She faked a cough, telling him not to go further—hoping he'd get the message. "Aussie accent? That was who again?"

"Ladies' Man Liam."

"What? The accent makes women hot?" She scribbled his name in a rush and reached for her mug.

"Nah, it's his ten-inch cock."

She nearly knocked her coffee off the table as a breath of air whooshed from her mouth.

"Kidding. Relax. I've never confirmed that detail myself."

She was used to working with actors who played the role of rough and tough SEALs on her show, but none of them were actually like *this*. Of course, the keyword was *actor*. These guys were legit.

"Computer guy? Kind of edgy? Or on edge, I should say."

"Owen." Asher released a quick laugh. "Actually, he's a wild man, but when in the middle of an op, he doesn't screw around."

"Okay." *Doesn't screw around*, she thought while jotting down the note. "The pretty woman you like to argue with." Okay, she remembered her name, but now she felt like giving a little feistiness right back to him.

"Jessica—is she pretty? Haven't noticed." He lifted his glasses and shot her a quick look. "I prefer brunettes."

Sure, you do.

"I think that's enough for now," Asher said and dropped his leg to the floor and stood. "Don't want to overload you."

"Funny." But maybe he was right. What was the point of even getting close to any of these guys when she'd never see them again after a few days?

God, she couldn't handle much longer than a couple days, and surely her brother and family would begin looking for her soon. "Um, could you find out something for me?" Since she was on the topic . . . "I know you guys are busy, but maybe you could check to make sure my family is still okay, and that they aren't checking the hospitals for me."

"I overheard Luke getting an update from Jessica this morning, actually. He's on top of it—your family is good."

Relief struck her. "Thank you, and uh, thanks for watching out for me. I'm sure you'd prefer to be in the other room."

He scrunched his nose and mouth together. "Nah, I hate intelligence shit. I'm more into the action."

"I highly doubt that's the only reason you're doing this job."

He smiled. "This isn't a job, sweetheart. It's more of a calling."

"Right." She stood. "I guess I'm gonna hit the shower."

"Do me a favor. Keep the door unlocked in case you slip and fall."

"I'm a civilian, not an idiot. And don't come barging in on me. If Luke were to walk in and think—"

"I told you I like to fight." He pushed away from the terrace wall he'd been leaning against and strode toward her, stopping only inches away.

"Yeah. A 'worthy opponent.'"

He smoothed a hand over his beard. "My buddies happen to be the best fighters I know. How do you think I practice and keep in such good shape?"

"Well, I'd prefer Luke and you not throw down. Not over me, at least."

"You're quite confident you'd provoke such a strong reaction from him, aren't you?"

She tensed. "Um."

"Relax." He leaned in closer to her. "We don't mess around with each other's women."

"I'm not *his* woman."

"I'm not so sure about that."

"Yeah? And how about his sister—is she off-limits for you?" She'd been reaching, but . . . it shut the SEAL up.

* * *

"THANK YOU," JESSICA WHISPERED TO EVA A FEW MINUTES after she and Asher had joined the room with the rest of the team later that evening. "I heard what you made Asher do today."

Eva tucked her hair behind her ears and smiled. "He told you?"

Jessica's attention snapped to where he stood by the window for a brief moment. "No, he texted Knox, complaining." She gave a gentle squeeze to Eva's shoulder. "French films with English subtitles . . . thank you, thank you, thank you."

Maybe they really did hate each other? "Anytime."

A grin met Jessica's lips before she walked back into the pit, to the area crowded by computers and SEALs.

Eva took a seat next to Knox, the only one without a gadget in his hand. "So, you think Malik knows we're here?"

"I'm sure. It's what he wanted, but we didn't have a tail when we left the airport in Nice," Knox answered.

"And we didn't have one, either," Luke added. He dragged his gaze slowly up and met her stare from across the room. "But he's anticipating our moves."

Eva had gone back and forth between regret and confidence in her decision to turn him down last night.

And the way his blue eyes, like the color of the sky on a clear night, held hers right now . . . it created the hard sting of desire once again.

"Six weeks ago," Owen nearly shouted, cutting thoughts of sex from Eva's mind and pulling her back to the situation at hand.

"And?" Luke asked.

Owen pounded a fist into an open palm and smiled. "I

finally placed Malik and his brother in the same city together. Guess where."

"Here," Luke said, his brows stitching tight as if putting the pieces together.

"Well, Nice—but I'm betting the safe is somewhere close by here," Owen answered.

"Would Malik really take the chance of having us in the same city as the safe?" Jessica eyed her brother.

"Maybe he figured he wouldn't have time to get to it if he were farther away," Owen said.

"Which means he's confident he'll get the code from us." Jessica held up a finger all of a sudden. "One sec." She reached into her pocket and held her phone. "Yeah?"

Luke lifted the computer off his lap and set it on a table before approaching his sister. His hands rested on his hips as he eyed her.

Jessica nodded a few times as if the caller could see her, and then said, "Okay, thanks for the update."

"Well?" Owen pushed away from the desk, the wheels of the chair rolling across the gold carpet.

"It doesn't look like Ender will wake. The doc thinks he'll stay in a coma." She frowned.

Luke's hand plummeted to his side like a ton of bricks cutting through the air, then he started for the door.

"Where are you going?"

"To speak with Malik. With this news, I don't want to waste time."

"Whoa. Wait a second." Jessica crossed the room and grabbed his arm, urging him to look at her. "Are you out of your mind?"

"He's not going to do anything to me in this hotel for the same reason we're not making a move on him. So, why the hell not have a friendly heart-to-heart? Maybe it's about time."

"He's not in his room, remember?" Owen stole Luke's attention. "He's in the casino with three of his guys, playing poker. We have two men covering him now."

"Who the hell plays cards at a time like this?" Luke cursed beneath his breath. "I'll have to go through metal detectors, then." He bent down, lifted his pant leg and unsnapped a pistol from a hidden holster.

"You'll need a blazer," Knox noted and quirked a brow. "There's a dress code for the private gaming area he's in."

"Are you really doing this?" Jessica faced the room as if seeking help from the group, but they simultaneously looked away from her, not wanting to tell her *no*, apparently—but also, not wanting to say *yes*.

"Any of the shops still open? I didn't exactly bring evening wear," Luke said with a hint of a smile that fell away when he looked at Eva. "And don't let her out of your sight while I'm gone."

"Bring me with you," Eva sputtered before she had a chance to think her words through first.

Luke stalked toward her, his brows lowering with an uncompromising look in his eyes. "Why?"

She fought the tremble in her bottom lip and said, "He wants us both. If you're going to face him, let him know you had the guts to bring me, too."

"Not a bad idea," Knox said.

Eva resisted looking at Knox; she couldn't lose sight of Luke. She needed him to know she was serious.

"I won't put you in danger," he said sharply.

"If you're safe, shouldn't I be, too?" She crossed her arms.

He lifted his chin, his gaze narrowing, but he kept his lips tight.

"It'll confirm that we're both here and we didn't fall for his trap. It puts us on an even playing field."

"We don't want an 'even playing field.' We want an advantage." He started to turn, but she caught his arm.

"Of course, but we let him think that."

"Malik doesn't know whether Ender's alive," Knox interjected. "It could be a smart play to rattle him by having her show up with you at the casino. It's a move he won't expect."

"I don't like it," Luke said, his jaw tightening.

"You'll be by my side," Eva noted.

"She should go," Jessica said.

Luke's shoulders squared back, and he pulled his arm free. "Fine," he hissed. "I'll have to get you something to wear downstairs."

Triumph spread throughout her body. "You don't know my size, remember?"

His blues traveled the length of her from head to toe. He leaned forward, and his breath touched her ear. "I've seen you naked, sweetheart. I've got your digits memorized now."

Goose bumps scattered across her skin at such an inopportune time, and a soft kiss of air left her lips when he stood erect, ignoring the weight of the stares from the room.

"I want this wrapped up," he said while straightening, and a huskiness bled through his command.

She wondered if his sense of urgency also had to do with a sudden need to get away from her.

CHAPTER SEVENTEEN

WHEN EVA HAD EXITED THE HOTEL ROOM, WEARING THE black fitted dress he'd picked out for her, he'd nearly thrown her over his shoulder and locked her back in the room.

And hell, maybe he should have.

Inside the elevator now, her attention was on the ground, which suited him fine. It afforded him the chance to study her, to take in every curve and beautiful line of her body.

Eva officially looked the part of Everly Reed—from the dress to the makeup.

"You look stunning." He toyed with his collar and popped the top button. He'd refused the tie, but the blazer and black dress shirt made him feel like he'd been sprayed in starch and a hot iron had scorched the material to his body.

"And you look"—her gaze briefly flicked up to meet his eyes—"lethal."

"Is that a compliment?" He smiled.

"I'm not sure yet." She tucked her long, silky strands behind her ear, exposing a diamond stud. Jessica had given her the earrings to wear before they'd left.

The elevator doors parted, and he pressed his hand to his ear. "What's the target's position?"

"He's still in the same spot," Owen said into his comm.

"Copy that."

Eva glanced back at him as they walked through the lobby. There was something in the look of her eyes that had his stomach dropping.

It wasn't fear he saw, but he wasn't sure what the hell it was, either.

After crossing the plaza and reaching the main casino, he placed his hand on the small of her back as the doors were opened for them.

A tiny shudder moved beneath his palm, and he wondered if his touch had the same effect on her as it was having on him right now.

"You said you've been to Monaco before. Vacation or . . .?" he asked as they worked their way past the gaming tables and through the aisles of slot machines, the clinking sounds taking a back seat to the thumping of his heart.

"My dad was filming a racing movie here five years ago. He insisted I come."

"Must've been fun." He eyed Knox at the roulette table off to his right and Asher at his nine o'clock.

"There's the room." Luke tipped his head to the back corner. "Are you nervous?" He stopped walking and faced her. "You can back out."

She kept her eyes on the two closed doors. "I want this over."

God, he hated this. He reached for her hand. "Best to make it look like we're a couple."

"Okay." She allowed him to tighten his grasp, and a buzz pulsed up his arm.

"Any seats open?" he asked the suited man guarding the private gaming room.

"Ten thousand euro buy-in." The guy's snake tattoo wrapped around his thick neck, the tongue extending up the jawline.

"Not an issue." Luke tucked a hand in his pocket and started to reach for the wad of cash Jessica had supplied him, but he stopped when the man held up his palm.

"There's a wait. What's your name?" He held a phone now, and Luke offered him the alias, Cross. "She's not playing, too, right?"

"What? I can't play cards because I'm a woman?" She folded her arms, a flash of defiance settling across her face.

"Are you playing?" the man asked, his tone deepening to borderline offensive.

Eva's lips rolled inward, and her cheeks deepened in color. "No, I'm not."

The guy sniggered and pointed to the bar behind them. "Wait there. It shouldn't be too long."

Luke thanked him and motioned to two empty stools at the bar.

"So, now we wait." Eva crossed one long leg over the other, and the skirt of her dress edged higher up her thighs.

He nodded and drummed his fingers on the counter.

"Lethal in a good way," she said, catching him off guard. "You stole everyone's breath when we walked into the room."

He stabbed a finger at his chest. "Me?" He swept an exaggerated gaze from left to right. "Honey, they're all looking at you."

"No." She swirled a finger in the air, and he wanted to snatch her wrist and press her palm to his heart so she could feel how fast it beat around her. But he wasn't romantic, and he shouldn't keep wanting her, so . . .

"Do you not have any idea how beautiful you are?"

"I don't care about that stuff." She blushed. "Well, your beautiful package caught my eye, at first—"

He tipped his head back and laughed. "'Package'?"

"You know what I mean. You're hot." She slapped his arm and slowly pulled her hand away. "I'm not insecure, by the way. But one of the perks of being Eva is I no longer have to try and impress anyone with how I look."

He swallowed back the untimely lust that continued to gather inside of him like a storm that was about to surge. The appearance of the bartender saved him from saying anything ridiculous. "What do you want to drink?" He let go of a hard breath.

"Oh, how about champagne?"

Luke looked at the bartender and ordered, "Le champagne et l'eau minéral." He scooted his chair a touch closer to hers, fighting the impulse to rest a hand on her thigh, even though it seemed like the natural thing to do.

"No alcohol?"

"I don't drink on an op." He smiled. "Usually."

"So back at the house in Pennsylvania—"

"Was different."

Her long lashes lowered, hiding her gaze as she focused on her lap. Her nerves were clearly pulling her apart, even if she didn't want to admit it.

"So . . ." He cleared his throat. "Was there one defining moment that made you up and leave your old life behind?"

Her focus moved to his face, and it had his leg muscles tensing.

Any time this woman looked at him—really looked at him—his insides thawed and set him on fire.

"Not really." She lifted her shoulders. "At first, it was

about freedom from the spotlight. But once I got a taste of it, I didn't want to go back."

"But you missed writing?" He looked at the bartender as he served the drinks. "Merci."

"Merci," she said and took a quick sip from the flute. "Yeah, I decided I wanted to try my hand at screenplay writing as Eva, not Everly. I wanted to see if I was really good—or if it was my name that had carried me."

"Hm." He gulped half his glass of water to cool off. "And what'd you discover?"

"I landed my current gig all on my own merits, so—"

"So you rocked it anyway."

Owen's voice sounded unexpectedly in his ear. "God, you have it bad for this woman."

Shit. He'd forgotten Owen could hear everything. "Turning you off until I'm with Malik." Luke fidgeted with the comm and then sighed. "Okay, now we can talk."

"Since when do you want to talk?"

She had him there, but . . .

"Oh," she said. "Are you trying to distract me again?" She took a sip of her drink when he nodded. "Does that mean you'll answer some questions for me? We could take turns."

"What, are we in high school? Are we going to play the twenty-questions game?"

She chuckled. "What's that?"

He waved a hand in the air, made eye contact with Knox and Asher, and then looked back at her. "Just ask a question."

"When did you know you wanted to be in the military?"

He didn't even hesitate. "I was three."

"Three?" She edged closer, her hand falling to his knee, and she looked up at him. "Really?"

He blinked twice, trying to rein in his thoughts. "Yeah, I used to wear my dad's dog tags and run around the house shooting bad guys. My bedtime stories at night were about his missions."

"Aww." She hiccupped and pressed a hand to her mouth. "One more from me, and then it's your turn." She scooted a little farther to the edge of her seat, her knees bumping his. "How do you do it?"

"Do what?"

"I figured out who you really are," she whispered. "Asher thought I was watching movies all day, but really, I was working through theories in my head."

"Oh, yeah?"

She nodded. "I'm curious about how you stay in the shadows and no one connects the real you to *this* you."

He glanced around, checking to ensure no one was within earshot. "I'm not two people. That's you."

She hiccupped again and shook her head. "We're different; you're right. I said *goodbye* to my old life. You, on the other hand, live two simultaneously. Has anyone ever found you out?"

"Not until you, Hollywood." He sucked down the rest of his water.

"Your sister is a cyber guru, huh?"

He wasn't all that surprised Eva had figured him out—well, he assumed she hadn't worked out every detail in her head, but still . . . "Jessica deleted my digital footprint a long time ago, but if anyone ever makes the connection between 'this me'"—he dropped his voice to emphasize her wording —"and the real me, it could prove dangerous for anyone close to me."

"I get that." She sighed. "I hope it never happens, for your sake. And I hope, someday, you get to step out of the shadows."

His stomach dropped and he closed his eyes, trying to

prevent all hell from breaking loose on the inside.

A quiet moment passed between them, and a smile touched her pink lips. "You didn't get to ask your question."

"Oh, that's easy." He smiled. "Best kiss?"

Her fingers rested on her collarbone, and then slowly sank to her plunging neckline. "You should know the answer to that." She tensed. "Yours?"

He leaned back and closed one eye. "High school girlfriend." His tongue darted between his teeth as he fought back the laugh trying to break free at the sight of her scrunched-up nose. "Kidding." Unable to stop himself, even knowing his buddies had eyes on him, he dropped his head so her lips were within reach.

"Me?" she whispered, staring at his mouth instead of his eyes.

"Unfortunately," he whispered, easing back into his seat and allowing another sweeping silence to settle between them for a few minutes.

"This is crazy, isn't it?" she asked after finishing her drink. "We're sitting here in Monaco, listening to this woman sing a cover of a Taylor Swift song, acting like—"

"There's someone singing?" He craned his neck around to find the woman on stage with a microphone in hand. "Shit, I didn't even notice."

"Aren't you supposed to notice everything?"

He scratched at his jaw. "There's a certain someone who makes it hard for me to do that."

"I see why you have your rules." She squeezed her eyes closed as if she hadn't meant to voice her thoughts. "Knox sort of mentioned . . ." Her eyelids fluttered open.

Before he could speak, a hand wrapped over his shoulder.

"Cross, your table is ready."

He stood and held out his hand to help her balance in her high heels.

Bright fucking pink heels to go with her lipstick. He should've gone with a subtle look when shopping for her tonight, and not something that'd draw the attention of everyone with a pulse.

"You ready?" he asked.

"As ready as I'll ever be," she murmured and took his hand.

He turned his comm back on as they followed the man to the poker room.

There was only one table in play. Nine seats were occupied, and an open seat was directly across from Malik Yilmaz.

Three men were seated at an empty table behind him, and Luke had to assume they were his guys.

Luke grabbed a chair from another table and positioned it behind him for Eva. When he set the euros on the table, he finally drew Malik's eyes, and Malik's hand stilled atop the poker chips he'd been casually shuffling.

"Welcome, Mr. Cross." The dealer exchanged his cash for multicolored poker chips, all with the casino monogram of a crown on them. "You're small blind."

Luke placed his bid and glanced at Eva, ensuring she was okay.

She didn't look the least bit intimidated, which would've surprised him last week, but now he knew better. Maybe she considered herself to be playing a role, and acting came easy to her.

"How's everyone tonight?" Luke addressed the table when Malik touched his cards, a slight tremble in his fingers.

"Ace over here's been on a winning streak." A guy with a

heavy Texas drawl jerked his thumb to the man to his right. "Maybe you can help tip the scales."

"I'll do my best." Luke smiled at the old timer and checked his cards. They were shit, but as long as Malik was in the hand, he'd remain in. He figured he could study his tells and use that to his advantage once they were alone together—whenever the hell that'd be. Hopefully, sooner rather than later. He didn't want Eva in the eye of the storm anymore.

"You're American, yes?" Malik quadrupled the big blind, sliding a stack of chips to the center of the table, and kept his eyes pinned to Luke's.

"Yeah. Are you Turkish?"

Malik nodded and his lips thinned, pressing tight into one hard line.

"İyi akşamlar," Luke said to him, curious as to how he'd react.

"Good evening to you as well."

Luke matched Malik's bet and watched the rest of the players bow out.

"Where in the U.S.? I'm from Texas," Old Timer asked, joining the conversation.

Luke watched a four of clubs fall on the turn, which gave him an unexpected straight draw. "We're from Chicago." He checked the turn, waiting to see what Malik would do. It was no longer about cards at this point. They were both prepared to go head-to-head to see who'd blink first.

"Ahh, the windy city." Old Timer scooted his chair back. "Do you like it there?" he asked Eva, and Luke focused on Malik.

"All in," Malik announced, his eyes twitching ever so slightly.

If Luke won, he'd know Malik's twitchy eyes meant he'd been bluffing. "Call."

Malik's pulse pricked in his neck, and Luke's own heart did the opposite and slowed to a steady beat. This was a game of cards, and so the stakes were low—but once they left the table . . .

Without looking at the river card, Luke flipped his hand face up, never losing sight of Malik's face.

"I guess you win, Mr. Cross." Malik's lips twisted into an almost smile, and he stood. "That'll be all for me tonight."

Luke stiffened. He'd need an excuse to get up, as well.

"Honey, I don't feel so good," Eva quickly said.

Maybe he'd been right to bring her, after all. "Looks like a quick night for me. Sorry." He stood, tipped the dealer, and cashed out. "Come on."

Malik had already left the room, but they wouldn't be too far behind.

Asher cocked his head to the right.

"I'm on the move," Luke told Owen through his earpiece.

"The target's heading toward the main exit," Owen said. "Bravo Five has him in his sights," he added, referring to Knox.

Luke gently gripped Eva's elbow, leading her toward the lobby.

"The valet's getting his car. You need to step on it," Owen said.

"Can you speed walk in those things?" He eyed Eva as they picked up the pace.

"Of course."

"A black Suburban just rolled up. Want me to have Bravo Five make a move?" Owen asked.

"No. I'm almost there." A bad feeling carved out a

hollowness in his stomach as he eyed Eva from over his shoulder.

Not waiting for the staff to open the doors, he yanked hard on the handle, prepared to yell Malik's name, but he nearly halted in surprise at the sight before him.

Malik was leaning against the exterior of the vehicle with folded arms, his head cocked to the side, and his brown eyes pinned to his. "We need to talk."

Luke spotted Knox holding a phone to his ear twenty paces up the circular drive, in position in case he needed backup. And he knew Asher had been at his heels on his way out. None of them were carrying, though, because of the security.

He doubted Malik would pull a gun on him now. But, at this point, who the hell knew what might happen?

He ate up the distance between them in five quick strides, keeping Eva at his side.

"I started to grow worried you wouldn't come." Three of Malik's men flanked his sides, but he motioned them back to the SUV with a flick of his wrist. His finger tucked under the collar of his dress shirt, yanking it away from his throat. "You are the man who has Ender and his men, are you not?" He stepped away from the vehicle, dropping his voice to add, "Is my nephew still alive?" Dots of sweat coated his forehead along the line of his scalp, despite the cooler temperature.

"You know who I am. Let's not play games," Luke said, his voice terse.

"I'm not, I assure you. Please, tell me: is he alive?" His voice nearly cracked, emotion breaking through, his pulse spiking at the side of his neck.

"He's in a coma."

Malik's hands turned to fists at his sides, but Luke didn't take it as a threat, so much as a sign of worry from the man.

"Do you care to make an exchange?" Luke scoped out the positions of his teammates, peered back at Eva, and then settled his attention on Malik.

"If only it were that easy," Malik said.

"Actually, it is. You give me what I want, and I'll be happy to turn Ender over to you." Well, he'd track Malik down afterward, but he'd save that conversation for another day.

"You know this idea is not possible, or you would've taken him back in Istanbul." His voice lowered. "You are the man he spotted in Turkey, right? The man who killed the CIA agent in Berlin?"

"Ender texted you my picture."

"If I knew what you looked like, I would have checked every hotel room until I found you. I am short on time. Lives are on the line."

Irritation snapped up Luke's spine, and he inched closer to try and read him to see if he was bluffing as he had been back at the table; his eyes didn't twitch. "Care to enlighten me?"

Malik's gaze flitted from left to right. "Not here."

"My room would be fine with me." Luke's jaw tightened.

Malik shook his head. "I need to know I can trust you first. I need to know you're not working with the agent who killed my brother."

Luke poked his chest with his free hand. "Why would I kill him if I was on his side?"

"People stab each other in the back all the time." Sorrow filled his eyes, throwing Luke for another loop.

"True. You're the one who hired the agent to kill your brother," Luke said. "Or, are you going to tell me—"

"I didn't do it." His thick brows rose, his eyes glancing at the sky. "But you have no reason to believe me. I can understand your hesitations, given what my nephew tried to do to you last week, but there has been a misunderstanding. I did not show my face here to trap you. I showed my face because I need your help."

"What?" Eva spoke up for the first time.

"But—"

"You don't trust me," Luke finished for Malik. "And I'm not exactly prepared to trust a terrorist, so, we're in a shit situation." Luke connected his eyes with Knox off to the right again and then felt the need to look at Eva, despite the warmth of her hand within his.

"I'll call in two hours and leave a message with the hotel for the name Cross. I'll provide an address. But, I need to know you won't show up and blow up the place or kill me, and so—"

"I need you, remember? Why would I do that?" Luke reminded him.

"In case your government has decided they'd rather end my life than find the safe . . ."

"You're planning on handing over the safe?" Luke's shoulders rolled back, his spine straightening. This conversation wasn't going how he'd expected.

"I'm prepared to make a deal, yes." The SUV started up, and one of Malik's men came around the vehicle. "But, I need an insurance policy." His eyes landed on Eva. "She comes with me, and no one follows us, or we have no deal. All you have to do is show me some good faith."

"Fuck your good faith," Luke rasped, drawing the eyes of people both exiting and entering the casino.

"Don't make a scene, or security will be on your ass any second," Owen said in his ear.

"I will not hurt her. You have my word."

"The word of a terrorist? You're out of your mind," Luke said, his heartbeat picking up.

"I'm not a terrorist," he responded, a tremble to his tone. "I am not my brother or my nephew."

His words had Luke taking a step back, tugging Eva against his side. "You can take me instead."

"I'm sorry, but I cannot take the risk. You seem like a man willing to die for what you believe in, but not someone who will let anything happen to her." Malik drew in a long breath and opened the car door.

"I'll do it." Eva stepped around him and toward the door, but he pulled her back.

"Hell no." He caught sight of his teammates closing in on the vehicle out of his peripheral vision.

Eva looked at him with pleading eyes. "I messed everything up. Let me fix it."

Was she out of her mind? He'd never let her go.

"It's me, or we have no deal," Luke said firmly.

Eva swooped before him and grabbed hold of his cheek with her free hand. She stared intently into his eyes and then crushed her mouth to his, kissing him with such a fierce intensity he nearly became dizzy, losing focus on what the hell was going on. Her mouth found his ear, and she whispered, "I trust you."

His heart plummeted as she attempted to pull free from his grasp, even offering her other hand to the enemy. "Let go," she cried.

One of Malik's men wrapped his arms around her hips as Malik held her other hand, pulling her toward the vehicle.

He had to let go of her hand to get a better hold on her body. But when he did, someone from behind tried to jerk him back.

"What the fuck are you doing?" he roared, betrayal cutting through his tone at the sight of Asher and Knox there.

Luke lurched toward the vehicle, pulling his teammates with him, only to have the door slam shut in his face, and he lost sight of Eva behind the tinted window.

"Get a car and follow her," he commanded and began to chase the SUV once it was on the move.

He ran as far as he could but stopped once he'd lost sight of the vehicle. He took shallow breaths and whirled around to see Asher and Knox behind him.

He charged at them, punching Asher clean across the jaw. "Why are you here instead of following her? You fucking did this. You let her get taken!"

"They were following my orders," Jessica said into his ear as Luke's fist connected with Knox's cheek next, rage consuming him.

Knox stepped back and surrendered, his palms in the air. "We'll get her."

"Get to the room," Jessica hollered. "I'm sorry about this, but Eva knew what might happen, and I had to make the call. Blame me, not the guys."

"Eva knew? What do you mean?"

Jessica remained quiet, and so he bolted across the plaza and to the hotel, not wanting to waste time.

The second he was inside the suite, he yelled, "Tell me what you know, and right this goddamn minute."

"First, get ahold of yourself." Jessica raised her hands between them.

"Get ahold of myself?" A broken attempt of laughter left his lips. "This is why I have rules. I broke my own fucking rules," he muttered under his breath, staring at the floor as his eyes burned.

Maybe he was losing his mind.

Jessica's hand rested on his back, and he heard her whisper to the room, "Can you give us a minute?"

He jerked away from his sister's grasp and advanced across the room and slammed both palms against the windows, feeling the glass pane vibrate against his hands. "Tell me you have a tracking device in those diamonds you gave her," he said, his tone gritty and sharp.

"Of course. You know I always have contingency plans."

He spun around and eyed the computer she now held. "We're already tracking her location, and I have someone en-route."

He looked up and expelled a breath. The news didn't change things, but at least they knew where she was. "I need to go."

"Do you want them to kill her?"

He circled his sister so he could view the screen. The little blue moving dot held his eye, and his stomach tucked in.

"We have to wait. Besides, Eva didn't just volunteer to get into his car tonight—it was her idea."

He stared at his sister. Her eyes were like frosted glass. Where was her emotion? How could she remain so cool when the woman he cared about was with Malik Yilmaz?

"Explain," he said as he tried to slow his heartbeat.

She moved away from him and set the laptop on the coffee table. "When you were shopping, Eva asked to speak to me alone. She proposed the idea of helping us get the safe without directly breaking Will's orders."

He gripped his temples, his stomach growing queasy by the minute.

"Swap her life for the code, then follow him to the safe, like we've wanted to do from day one. She asked that if the opportunity arose for her to get taken by Malik—"

"No!" He roared out the word and then blew past her and into the bathroom.

He'd never thrown up on a mission before, but he'd never had feelings like this, and *shit* . . . His palms bore down on the bathroom counter, and he splashed water on his face, trying to get a grip.

What's happening to me?

"You okay?" she asked from behind.

"What the hell do you think?" He caught her eyes in the mirror before patting his face dry. "How could you go behind my back like this?"

"We knew you wouldn't go for it. Besides, we had no idea if the situation would present itself."

"Are you trying to tell me we lucked out with her being taken tonight?" He pounded his fist onto the granite counter. "Malik doesn't even want the safe, apparently," he said, fighting to control the anger inside of him. "So, what in the hell is it he wants?"

"I don't know, but he hinted that we've misunderstood everything."

"We're in the dark. Fucking perfect." He shoved past his sister. "I'm going after her."

"Not yet. If he doesn't leave a message with the hotel in two hours, then yeah, we go in for an extract. I have an armed team on standby."

"Why would she risk her life like this?" His expression softened when he looked at her. "She's a civilian."

Her shoulders sagged. "Give her more credit than that. She deserves it."

"Yeah, and if she dies? What the hell happens then?"

* * *

Two hours had dragged by, the minutes on the hotel clock moving excruciatingly slow.

When Luke had checked with the front desk there'd been no message.

Malik had been one minute late. That one minute had felt longer than the two hours.

"I'm in position. I have five heat signatures in total. Two at the exterior of the structure," Owen reported. "Both men outside are armed. Small handguns. No AKs or M-17s that I can see."

"He had three men with him. Malik plus Eva makes a total of five," Knox said.

"It could be the terrorists who were after Odem that are inside, and Malik is handing us over to them on a silver platter," Luke said as they stopped a block away from the address Malik had provided.

"It matches Eva's tracker, though," Knox reminded him. "Unless, of course, Malik made her lose the jewelry, anticipating our move."

"Thanks for that." Jessica shifted in the front passenger seat to look at Luke, sitting next to Knox.

"Keeping it real; what can I say?" Knox rested the Sig Sauer P226 on his lap and shrugged.

"If something happens to her, I will kill you." Luke glared at Knox.

"Sure you will." He held his palms in the air. "But, we'll get her out. Relax."

"Relax?" He leaned in closer, his chin jutting forward. "Tell me to relax when this is all over, and I'm sucking down gin on the beach. Don't even think about saying that to me now. Got it?"

Knox's attention swept to Jessica. "Damn. Have you ever seen him like this before?"

"I swear to God . . ." Luke tightened his hand around his own Sig.

"You're up, Bravo Three," Jessica announced through her comm.

"Roger that," Asher said.

"And don't get killed," she added.

"You worried about me, Peaches?" Asher was on his way to Malik's home to make first contact.

Luke had wanted to do it, but if things went sideways and Malik opened fire right away, he wouldn't be able to save Eva if he wound up with a bullet in his head.

He didn't want that to happen to Asher, of course, but someone had to do it, and Asher had insisted, probably as his way of apologizing for pulling him off Eva earlier.

Luke's trigger finger itched, and he sealed his eyes as he prepared himself to face Malik—praying that Eva would be unharmed when he walked into the house.

She had to be okay. He couldn't handle any other outcome.

"Just do your job," Jessica shot back.

"Will do, Peaches."

CHAPTER EIGHTEEN

"COFFEE OR TEA WHILE WE WAIT?" MALIK CHECKED his watch.

"Sure, so you can lace it with arsenic?" Her hands tightened on her lap, nervous energy causing her limbs to tingle.

"This isn't Hollywood."

"Are you sure you don't know who I am?"

He ignored her and asked, "Are you comfortable?"

"For a kidnapping."

"You volunteered to come." He took a seat next to her, and she scooted to the other end of the couch, her gaze catching the armed man standing close to the front door, twenty feet away.

"Like I had a choice?"

A long sigh fell from his lips as his eyes cut over to hers. "I'm not going to hurt you."

Her heart squeezed. "I'm supposed to believe a terrorist?"

With a pinch to his brows, he shifted on the couch and smoothed a palm over his stubbly cheek. "I told you I'm not a terrorist. My brother and nephew may have been criminals, but I'm not one."

"So, I can have the location to the safe and be on my way then?" She stood, but the guard strode across the room, his finger slipping to the trigger of his weapon. She dropped back onto the couch. "That's what I thought."

"You don't seem frightened. Why is that?"

"You said you wouldn't hurt me, right? I'm just super damn trusting."

He pointed a finger at her, his eyes drawing closer together. "You're one of those women who shield their true feelings with quips and sarcasm, aren't you?"

She looked away from him and toward the front door again, her heart kicking into her throat as she prayed Luke would arrive soon, and she hadn't made a huge mistake.

What if he never forgave her for tonight? Or worse—what if her plan got Luke killed?

She'd been surprised Jessica had agreed to her idea; and then, her stomach had done somersaults the entire time at the bar when she'd been talking to Luke. Guilt had carved away pieces of her, and she'd come close to telling him the truth. But . . . she'd known Luke would yank her back up to the hotel room.

"You know nothing about me," she said softly.

"Mm. I don't know. You remind me a lot of my daughter."

Before she had a chance to gather a response, a hard knock at the door had her core fluttering, and goose bumps covered her skin.

"It's not him," the guard said while peeking out the window.

"Open it." Malik stood but motioned for her to remain seated.

Asher was on the other side of the door, and he found her eyes right away.

"Where's your friend?" Malik asked.

Asher touched his ear. "You're good to move in," he said, and she assumed he was talking to Luke.

Her fingers threaded together as she fought to maintain her composure.

The guard motioned for Asher to lift his hands. "Easy with the pat down. Don't get too touchy-feely. I don't swing that way. No offense," he said and winked at Eva from over his shoulder when he faced the hall wall.

Another guard came in from outside a minute later with Luke and Knox. "They're clean. No weapons," the man announced.

And then, it was as if everything were happening in slow motion as he stepped inside and diverted his gaze to her, relief in his eyes.

She leaped off the couch, meeting him halfway, and flung her arms around him, burying her face against his chest as he held her tight.

"Are you okay?" He pulled back and brushed his thumb over her cheek as if assessing for damage.

She nodded and whispered, "I'm sorry."

He grabbed her and fastened his arms around her again. He cupped the back of her head, and his heartbeat raced like a lullaby.

"She's okay, as you can see. Not a hair out of place," Malik said.

Luke stepped out of their embrace and faced Malik, but he wrapped his arm around her, holding her tight at his side.

She scanned the room, observing everyone. Jessica, Owen, and a few other of Luke's men she knew weren't present. She assumed they were outside and would, of course, have a plan.

"I don't have much time." Malik pointed to the TV on the wall, and one of his guards holding an iPad cast something onto the screen.

"What am I watching?" Luke stared at the TV, but she could still feel his racing pulse in the palm curved around her hip.

"That's the security feed inside the home I was hiding out in." Malik pointed to the TV now and added in a shaky voice, "Those men work for Ender, and they kidnapped my wife and daughter ten days ago."

"Ender did this?" Luke asked, disbelief etched in his voice. "Why?"

"For my code and the location of the safe." Malik wiped at the sweat on his brow with a handkerchief he'd taken from his pocket. "My brother couldn't convince Ender to turn himself into the U.S. with him. He wanted to protect him, but Ender saw him as a traitor."

"I'm listening," Luke said, but he tightened his hold on Eva.

Eva couldn't stop staring at the replay of the security footage that continued: a girl with dark hair, probably sixteen, screaming as two men dragged her out of a bedroom.

She sank her teeth into her lip, trying to control tears for a man who may or may not be a terrorist.

"Odem contacted me six weeks ago, asking me to meet him here. He'd been shot and was on the run from al Jawali, a criminal organization from Pakistan responsible for most of the illegal poppy sales that—"

"I'm familiar with them," Luke interrupted.

"I convinced Odem to turn himself into the U.S. in exchange for protection. I've never been privy to what he's done over the years because ignorance is bliss. Of course, I knew he wasn't a good man, but he was my brother." He swallowed. "But, when he showed me everything he'd compiled—a trove of blackmail—I knew the information could be dangerous in the wrong hands."

"So, you're trying to tell me you're the reason he cut a deal?" Luke asked. "Why the theatrics with the codes and safe?"

"He would only agree as long as I'd help him. He was worried if he handed over the code and safe the U.S. wouldn't stick to their end of the bargain."

"You were his backup plan in case things went south," Luke said. "Did Ender arrange for his father to be killed by the CIA agent?"

Malik's hands went into prayer pose beneath his chin. "No. He watched the failed exchange and followed the man to Berlin to try and get his father's code."

"But I showed up."

The guard finally paused the security video, and Eva clutched her stomach, her nerves tightening into a hard knot.

"My brother must've been scared and said my name in an attempt to save his life, but now there's a target on my family." He took a moment to breathe as if to gather his thoughts. If the man was acting, he'd win an Oscar. "Ender called to inform me my brother had been murdered and to tell me to hide because people would be coming after me."

Luke edged closer to Malik, and two of his guards skirted Luke's sides. "What are you asking of me?"

He kept hold of Eva when he moved, but part of her wanted to fade away into the dark at that moment.

"You can have the safe. I don't want it. I never did. I just want my wife and daughter," he said, a rattle to his voice.

"Why should I believe you? Ender's in a coma. How do I know you're not fabricating all of this?" Luke asked.

Malik opened his palms. "Ender didn't just kidnap my wife and daughter." His guard changed the TV screen to another video feed, one that showed Malik being forced to the ground, with his hands tied behind his back. "Ender brought me to a different location; he was prepared to torture me for the code and safe. I gave him the code to try and save their lives."

"Not the safe?"

He shook his head. "It was my way of trying to keep my family alive longer. I knew he needed Odem's code, which you had, before it'd matter, anyway. I promised him the safe once he released my daughter and wife."

"Why was he in Istanbul a week ago?"

"That is when he saw you, yes?"

Luke nodded.

"I believe he was meeting with a member of al Jawali—making a deal. I can't be certain, though, because I only heard bits and pieces of his conversation while I was being held."

"Ender was never taking me to you in New York?" he asked. "So, you want me to find your family?"

"Yes, and I also want you to take down al Jawali and find the men responsible for killing my brother. I have to assume the CIA agent was not working alone."

"A tall order." Luke released a deep breath.

Eva's heart skipped into her throat as Malik pointed to her.

"You care about this woman more than whatever is in that safe, which says to me you're an honest man."

Luke was quiet for a moment. "And where's the safe?"

"My family first. I am sorry, but with Ender not awake to

tell the location, who knows what his men have done with my wife and daughter?"

"How'd you escape, and why'd you come here?" Luke asked, mirroring Eva's own questions.

"These men were loyal to my brother, not Ender. They helped me get away when Ender never returned the night he went after you. Unfortunately, Ender never disclosed my family's location to them," he said as if his spirit had dried up inside him. "I decided the best chance to save my family was to find the man who had the code . . ." He tipped his head toward Luke.

"Big gamble," Luke said dryly. "You're lucky it's us who saw your face outside the French Embassy and not someone else."

"Worth the risk. Wouldn't you do the same for the ones you loved?" he responded.

"We'll need those videos, and I need to head back to the hotel. I'm keeping two men here to babysit while I'm gone."

"How will you find them?" Malik asked, his voice breaking as he moved in closer to him.

"We have the best facial recognition software in the world. If you're telling the truth, we'll find them." He reached for Eva's hand. "Asher. Knox. You stay."

Eva couldn't help but wonder if he was punishing them for what had happened back at the casino. She'd seen the look in Luke's eyes when Asher and Knox had pulled him away from her. She hoped he'd forgive them. It was her fault, after all.

Luke started for the door, tightening his grasp on her hand as they moved. "One thing." He paused and pivoted to face Malik. "You saw the contents of the safe, right?"

"Yes."

"Did your brother have anything in there other than intel to blackmail criminals and terrorists?"

Malik's brows drew tight. "Yes, blackmail on some Americans."

* * *

JESSICA TIGHTENED HER PONYTAIL BEFORE HER HANDS landed on the desk, and she dropped her head. "Are we really believing this guy?"

They were in the room Eva had been staying in instead of the suite with the rest of the SEALs.

Eva's attention flitted to Luke. With his back against the window and his arms crossed, he looked . . . well, irritated, to put it mildly.

"I think I believe him. It makes sense, actually," Luke said.

Jessica continued his line of thought. "It's why Odem didn't give Ender his code. Plus, we assumed Ender worked for Malik because the CIA made it look like Malik was Odem's partner. The CIA led us to believe Ender and Malik had Odem murdered."

"There has to be something in the safe about someone in the CIA, something they don't want anyone to know," he noted.

"It could've just been Reggie. Maybe he'd crossed paths with Odem before, and when he heard of the exchange, he finagled his way into the mission to—"

"Reggie would've ended his career by killing Odem, anyway," Luke said, cutting off his sister. "He had to have killed him for more than that." He heaved out a breath. "Not to mention, he's dead. And I'm betting whoever's feeding us intel was working with him."

"That's easy to figure out then, right?" Eva asked. "Who's giving you your intel?"

"I wish I knew. We don't work directly with the agency," Jessica said softly and turned to face them both. "Do you think Will would tell us?"

"What if he accidentally tips whoever it is off?" Luke shook his head. "We can't risk letting Will know what happened tonight, not until we have more to go on. You didn't brief him on what went down with Malik, did you?"

"You asked me not to, and I may not like the idea, but I'm trying to make amends for pissing you off." She held up an index finger. "I'm giving you until sunrise, though."

"That's not a lot of time." He squeezed his eyes tight. "Will's not going to like the deal we cut with Malik."

"Once he knows the truth, he'll change his tune. He's not as bad as you always paint him out to be."

"Do you think you can find Malik's family by sunrise?" Eva asked.

"I've already uploaded the kidnappers' images into my program. One guy's in the morgue; he was with Ender when he took you two. So, hopefully, we can get a match on the other man and see where he's been recently." Jessica looked at her brother, his eyes still closed. "Why don't I give you guys a moment to talk? Come join us when you're done."

This must've gotten his attention, because Luke dragged a palm down his face and opened his eyes as Jessica strode past him, leaving the room.

"So." Eva released a quick breath.

He arched a brow. "So."

She tensed. "Are you angry at me?"

It'd been their first chance alone, and honestly, she didn't even know how to begin the conversation. A million thoughts pounded in her mind, giving her a headache, but she didn't want to unleash a flurry of broken sentences that wouldn't make any sense.

"You shouldn't have done that," he said, his voice toe-curling deep. "You could've gotten yourself killed."

"Nothing happened to me. I'm fine."

"It could've gone very differently. We got lucky, and I don't like relying on luck." His chest lifted and fell as he sucked in sharp breaths.

She placed a hand on his chest, trying to find the courage to speak. But before she could say anything, he grabbed hold of her hips and kissed her.

She stumbled back, hitting the wall, and he swooped her arms up and held her wrists within his one hand, pinning her against him. "I'm mad at you," he said against her lips and kissed her again.

"Why," she rasped mid-kiss, "are you kissing me then?"

He tightened his grasp on her hands. "You want me to stop?" His words vibrated against her lips.

She tipped her chin, relishing in the way his body felt against hers. "No," she cried.

His tongue swept into her mouth, stealing her breath, and the fingertips of his free hand skirted up her dress. A soft caress of her skin left a trail of fire behind, and she angled her head, breaking their kiss to allow his lips to roam over the sensitive part of her neck.

He released his caged hold of her arms, and she brought her hands beneath his shirt to feel his abs. She moaned as he slipped the dress strap off her shoulder to palm her breast. With her back still against the wall, he ravished her like a starving man.

A pool of heat gathered between her legs as her thighs tightened, and it was as if Luke knew what she needed, because he helped her all the way out of her dress to access her sweet spot.

Her head tipped back as her eyes blurred. She was alive—alive to experience the moment. A moment she had sworn to herself she wouldn't give in to. But how could she resist experiencing another chance to connect with him?

"I want you," he said gruffly into her ear before lifting her, and she eagerly wrapped her legs around his hips, allowing him to carry her into the bedroom.

He set her down and raked both hands through his hair, staring at her with nearly glossy blue eyes.

His eyes narrowed, and a twitch to his lips hinted at a smile, which had her even more desperate for his touch.

He stepped closer to the bed, studying her.

"Luke." She rose, and he placed a closed hand beneath her chin, guiding her to his eyes. "I know what you're thinking, but we can pencil that conversation in for another day"—she cracked a smile—"because right now, all I want is for you to be buried deep inside of me, and I don't even care if your friends hear us from next door."

This induced a crinkling of his eyes and the temptation of a grin. "How bad do you want me?" He cocked a brow and smoothed his thumb over her cheek.

She squeezed one eye. "On a scale of one to ten, you know—maybe a four point five."

He laughed this time, and the sound had her nipples hardening and her skin flushing. "What do I have to do to earn a ten?"

"You're a SEAL. An overachiever." She bit her lip. "I'm guessing you can get creative."

"I do love a challenge." He shoved off his pants and boxers.

She freed herself of her panties, and stood before him as

his arms flexed, the biceps popping as he took off his tee. She reveled beneath his stare, her skin like satin beneath her own touch as she tapped her fingers up her chest.

The muscles in his jaw tightened as he pulled her closer, allowing her to forget everything that had happened tonight. "Be with me," she said against his mouth. "Be with me like tonight's our last night."

Because it is, isn't it?

His gaze darkened before he gently nudged her onto her back on the bed. He braced himself on top of her, and she shimmied against him, loving the feel of him against her already soaked center.

She wanted to feel this man in every possible way, but she needed it to happen before she came undone from the pulses of desire pricking her skin.

His hips rotated slightly, his strong body not crushing her as he held his frame above her, while still being close enough so she could feel his warm skin.

"Please," she whispered.

He squeezed his eyes tight as if torn, but then he guided himself to her opening, and she bucked against him as the heat of his cock filled her as deep as humanly possible.

Her eyes nearly rolled in the back of her head as she gripped the cut of his muscular arms and held him tight as he rocked inside her, slowly at first as they found each other's rhythm.

And then he lowered his chest even closer to hers, smashing her breasts against his muscles, and he reached for her hands and threaded their fingers above her head as they made love.

Her eyes flashed closed as a glimpse of the future caught her mind—of her in a pale blue dress with a baby bump.

Emotion punished her, and she was certain that when she opened her eyes she'd be crying.

"Eva," he said, his voice raw. "Everly."

He slowed his movements, and she snapped her gaze open, worried he'd stop. "Yeah?"

"You okay?"

She nodded, fighting the tears, and lifted her head to find his mouth. A mewl escaped her lips as he guided his tongue inside, deepening the kiss.

She grew light-headed from the impending orgasm as it swelled inside of her.

Their lips broke and his forehead rested upon hers as he grunted and came along with her—both finding bliss and hiding from the truth of tomorrow.

She'd been caught in the clash of a dangerous mission, but her heart and soul got swept along for the ride, and she knew in that moment there'd be no turning back.

CHAPTER NINETEEN

L YING NAKED ATOP L UKE WAS ABOUT THE BEST POSITION IN the world, she decided. With her ear to his chest, the strong command of his heartbeat like music; she could easily fall asleep like that.

His fingers combed through her locks before stroking her back. They'd lain there like that for at least thirty minutes after he'd come, all without saying a word.

"Do near-death experiences turn you on?" he asked.

She lifted her head to find his eyes, a smile dancing in his blues. "Funny."

"Just calling it like I see it."

She lowered her head back to the hard planes of his body and felt the stir of his cock against her, and it had her pelvic muscles tightening with need. "And what's your excuse?"

"Oh, that's easy. You."

"I'm your kryptonite?"

His heartbeat crept up, and his hand stilled on her back. "You're so much more than that to me."

"You—" A knock on the bedroom door cut her off.

"Get dressed. I have news," Jessica said through the door.

"Be over in five," Luke replied.

She started to stand, but he caught her wrist and dragged her back to him. "Jessica must know about us."

His gaze tightened. "I don't care." He kept his eyes on her, a slight crease in his brow. "Are you going to be okay?"

She stiffened. They needed a hell of a lot more than five minutes to have a conversation about their feelings. So, she said, "Of course." She forced an innocent smile and rolled off him and stood, but his large hand swept to her hip bone and slipped to the curve of her bottom before he squeezed.

"I could look at this view all day."

She peeked back at him and wiggled her hips. His hand found her center beneath her ass cheeks, and he slid a finger inside of her.

"What are you doing?" she asked as he started to rub her clit with his deft fingers, drawing the breath from her.

"I want you one last time."

One last time.

It was so final.

It was so . . .

She slowly faced him, which forced him to drop his hand. "We only have five minutes, and she must need you, so—"

"But I need you," he said, his voice laced with a sexy grit.

He was hers.

Well, for five more minutes.

Five minutes of memories she could at least remember forever.

And so, she straddled him without wasting a breath or time. She sank down onto his length and leaned back to brace his thighs.

"Five minutes," she mouthed as he stretched her with every inch, and his Adam's apple moved as their eyes locked.

Time stood still for those five minutes.

And when they were both dressed and standing in a room full of suspecting SEALs, heat crawled up her cheeks; she was sure her skin matched the pink of the sweater she now wore.

"So." Ladies' Man Liam coughed into a closed fist.

"Did you find Malik's family?" Luke approached the desk and held on to the top of the chair and studied the computer.

Owen pointed to something on the screen, but from Eva's vantage point, she couldn't see anything.

She scanned the room and noticed that most of the guys continued to observe her with curiosity in their eyes.

Jessica, though, she was focused. A woman in control.

"I got a match on a grocery store security camera of our guy as he exited," Owen said. "This image was taken two hours ago. We switched to the parking lot cameras, but the camera angle wasn't great, so I couldn't get a plate, but I got a vehicle description."

Luke nodded. "Where is that, and what's in the area?"

"It's a small town north of Binghamton, New York," Owen answered.

"I pulled one of our guys off babysitting Ender, but I can't send him alone." Jessica folded her arms as Luke faced her.

"Will won't like it," Luke said, and Eva wasn't sure what he was talking about now.

Jessica shrugged. "We can't ask for a government assist on this, so what choice do we have?"

"What's wrong?" Eva asked. A few of the SEALs she wasn't on a first-name, or any-name, basis with looked right at her as if she were suddenly an enemy in the room.

Luke caught the eyes of his teammates and breathed out of his nose as if coming to a monumental decision. "We can trust her. She already knows almost everything, anyway."

"He's right. She did put her life on the line earlier," Jessica said.

Does that mean I'm in?

"Your guess about me was fairly spot on," Luke said. "We work off the grid for the government on missions such as these. But no one knows about us, aside from a handful of high-ups." He scratched at his jaw, his body growing stiffer. "Our alias is a company called Scott & Scott Securities." He crossed the room and stood before her. "I'm Luke Scott."

It was the first time she'd heard his full name.

Wow, she'd had sex with someone and hadn't even known his last name. She shook away her thoughts, realizing that wasn't important right now.

"Oh" was all she could get out of her mouth.

"We're all still technically active-duty SEALs. But retired SEALs work with us at our security company," he explained. "They don't know about these off-the-books jobs, though."

"Isn't it hard keeping it from them?" Eva asked and looked around the room.

Everyone looked to Luke for an answer, and so, he said, "Very. Especially now when we need their help."

It had to be hard for him to live such a double life. Maybe she knew a thing or two about it—but she was pretty sure his was a hell of a lot more complicated, not to mention dangerous.

Luke eyed his sister. "Who isn't working a job right now? We probably need to send three guys to Binghamton."

"I already made a list. I was waiting for your thoughts before I called," Jessica said.

"Just tell them it's a kidnapping case and no Feds can be involved. They won't ask questions," Luke responded.

"It should take three hours for them to get there. In the

meantime, we'll narrow down the search perimeter and try to get a plate number," she said.

It was three in the morning, and they were already running on fumes. Would they really be able to rescue Malik's family by sun-up?

"Can you push the call to Will until nine?" Luke asked, a mirror of Eva's thoughts.

Jessica checked her watch. "If we don't have them by nine, I won't have a choice but to call him, and you know that. I can't keep lying to him to buy us time."

"Why won't he be okay with your plan?" Eva asked, and she heard a few guys grumble.

"He won't trust Malik's word." Luke rubbed at the whiskers on his jaw, the stubble growing thicker, and the memory of it tickling her inner thighs warmed her heart. It was a shit time to remember such a moment, though.

"Oh." She tensed and fought against the pull of heat gathering up her throat and into her cheeks, yet again. "What do we do now?" She clasped her hands together, suddenly nervous in the overcrowded room of badasses.

"You sleep. Let us handle this," he said like a command.

"I doubt I can fall asleep," she said lightly.

He placed a hand on her shoulder and found her eyes. "You can trust me, remember?"

She knew she could trust him with her life, but could she trust him with her heart?

CHAPTER TWENTY

"WE'RE SURE IT'S THIS LOCATION?" LUKE TUCKED HIS HANDS beneath his armpits, eying the property on the screen.

"The boys are an hour out. They'll be able to confirm once there," Owen stated, cracking his knuckles before drinking his gasoline-colored coffee. They all needed a pick-me-up after having barely slept since their arrival in Monaco. "What're the rules of engagement?"

"Try and keep everyone alive so we can find out for sure if Ender was working with al Jawali, since the son of a bitch probably won't ever wake," Luke said.

"'Kay."

He whistled a breath between his lips and peeked at Jessica on the couch, her dark-rimmed glasses on as she swiped at her iPad. "Anything from Harper?" he asked her.

"Not yet," she replied.

"Our asses are gonna be toast," Owen said. "Eva, Harper, and now our other crew are being brought in on this."

"It'll be on me." Luke was prepared to handle whatever verbal lashing Will threw his way. He knew the guy wouldn't fire him. Well, not as long as he came through with this mission, at least.

He took a moment to allow the idea of getting fired to sit with him, to let the ideas of a future play out without having such a classified life—all he saw was Eva. And yet, a gut-agonizing pain ripped through him at the idea of not being on his team anymore.

How could he choose between the love for his country and the love for . . .? He shook his head; he needed his thoughts to fall through the cracks of his mind so he could focus.

He vaguely heard the sound of a ringing phone as he stifled a yawn—because yawning at such a moment didn't feel right. Of course, having sex with Eva twice earlier hadn't been exactly the right fucking time, either. But he hadn't been able to stop himself.

Knowing the sacrifice she'd made for the mission had nearly severed his heart. And, had he not taken her in his arms then and there, he would've bled all over the expensive hotel rugs.

They couldn't be together; they both knew that. Even now that she had privileged information about his team, it didn't change anything. He'd have to wipe any connection she had to him to keep her safe. He couldn't risk anyone ever coming after her to get to him, could he?

Jessica snapped her fingers in front of his face. "Did you hear me?" She removed her glasses and clutched them in her palm.

"No. Did you say something?" How long had he zoned out? *Christ.* Eva on this mission was like a stun gun to the mind.

"Harper called. She said her handler at the CIA found out she'd been looking into Reggie's old files. She had to tell

Will, so he could cover for her since he was the one who'd pulled her from her assignment to help us."

"How much does Will know about why we're looking into Reggie?" he asked.

"Only as much as she does, which isn't a lot," she said.

"There's only one reason Will isn't calling to rip us a new asshole right now." Luke's arms tensed.

"He wants to do it in person," Jessica said.

"What did you report out to Will in your last message?" Luke asked.

"I told him we'd tracked Malik to a location outside of Monte Carlo, and we were prepping to move in."

"Harper doesn't know we made contact with Malik, which means Will doesn't know we lied to him," Owen said.

"He'll sure as hell figure it out when he shows up," Jessica snapped.

"We should have time to wrap this up before his plane even lands in Nice, but I'd like to know how much time we're working with. Find out what flight he's on," Luke instructed.

"Do you think we can pull off a miracle before he gets here?" Jessica asked.

"If your intel is right about the location of Malik's family, then yeah, I think so."

"Well, that's good, because I've never been wrong," she said, confidence blooming in her eyes once again.

* * *

EVA WAS STILL ASLEEP, AND LUKE HAD NO INTENTION OF waking her, not with his men a few minutes from infiltrating the home where Malik's wife and daughter were hopefully being held.

"Asher says they're five minutes out," Owen reported.

"Let's hope his family is alive for him to FaceTime with, and that this isn't a trap." Jessica's fists bore down atop the desk as they all waited with bated breath.

"Where's Harper? I thought she'd be here by now," Luke asked.

"Shit." Jessica checked the time. "She *should* be here by now."

Luke looked to Liam. "Get her on the phone. Make sure she's okay." He strode to the window and parted the blinds, watching the sun rise above the sea.

"Her phone's not connecting," Liam said a minute later, and his words had Luke pivoting to face him. "I called the CIA safe house, too. No answer."

"When was the last time we heard from her?" Luke asked his sister.

"An hour ago when she said she was leaving to come here," Jessica answered.

"It's only a twenty-minute drive." Worry climbed up into his throat. "Liam."

Liam grabbed his Sig off the table. "On it."

"They're in position," Owen said, grabbing Luke's attention after Liam had left the room.

"It's a go," Luke commanded and crossed his arms as he waited—as the entire room waited—to see what the hell would happen.

He hated being behind the scenes, but he knew he couldn't control everything, and he trusted his men to get the job done.

But still, it never felt right putting any of his people on the line if his own life wasn't on the line right there with them.

A knock at the door sent a chill down his spine, and he hoped it was Harper, but surely Liam would've run into her on the way down to the lobby, which meant it was either Eva, or Knox and Asher with Malik.

"It's me," Eva announced.

He opened the door, and she stared at him with her big hazel eyes, so full of life and a million other things he couldn't quite place right now.

"I couldn't sleep. I've been tossing and turning for hours. Is there news?"

"Come in." He stepped back so she could walk in, but before he closed the door, he heard the chime of the elevators. "Just in time," he said when he saw his guys with Malik.

Dark bags were beneath Malik's eyes, and his brow was damp with sweat. No twitch of the eyes, though—no bluffing. "Have they found my wife and daughter yet?"

"We're hoping they're about to," Luke said and closed the door, still unable to look Asher and Knox in the eyes. He'd forgiven Jessica for allowing Eva to put herself in the line of fire, so why was he still so pissed at his friends?

Maybe it was because he couldn't get the memory of them pulling him off of her out of his mind. They clearly didn't understand what it was like to care about a woman so much.

But, he'd made sure of that with his rules, hadn't he? He'd all but created a team of men who were only capable of meaningless relationships and one-night stands. Had he been wrong?

No, it's to keep everyone safe . . .

A tightness in his chest had him gripping his hand over his heart. "What's the status?"

Malik remained standing with clenched fists at his sides, overlooking Owen's computer at the desk.

"They confirmed it's the house, but then I lost contact. Someone opened fire, and I'm not sure if it was our guys or not." Owen steepled his fingers beneath his chin and stared at the open call with the team.

Static. Shouts in Turkish. And more rounds pelting the air.

A voice buzzed through the pops of noise: "He's at your nine o'clock." And then a half-dozen bangs ripped through the line.

Luke wasn't sure if any of Ender's men would make it out alive, but as long as his guys did, he was fine with that.

"No sight of the hostages, but there's a locked basement," Eddie, from Scott & Scott Securities, announced once the bullets ceased.

"Are you all okay?" Jessica asked.

"All good on our end, boss," Eddie said.

"Baba!" A voice shrieked out the word for *father* in Turkish a minute later. "Baba?"

Malik fell to his knees and covered his face at the sound of his daughter's voice over the speaker.

"They're okay," Eddie said. "What do you want me to do now?"

"There's a location I want you to take them to for today." Luke gave him the address to the home he'd stayed at with Eva in the Poconos only last weekend—days that felt like an eternity ago.

"Can I talk to them?" Malik pushed upright, and Luke nodded the *okay* to Owen.

Malik stood before the computer and spoke in Turkish to his family. Luke only caught about every other word, but most of it was apologies for his brother and nephew.

Luke glanced at Eva. She swiped tears from her cheeks and regarded him with heavy-lidded eyes.

"You promise to keep my family safe? I don't care what you do with me, but them—"

"You have my word," Luke said, hoping to hell Will didn't snap his word in half later that day.

"Then we go back to where we were last night. The safe is hidden there," Malik said.

"Knox, stay with Eva," Luke said.

"I'd like to come." She lifted her long, wet lashes, killing him with her beautiful eyes.

"I'm sorry. I need you to stay here." He swallowed the distance between them in two quick strides and palmed her cheek, forgetting about everyone in the room, and brushed his thumb over her warm skin. "This is almost over."

CHAPTER TWENTY-ONE

"The safe house is locked. No response," Liam told Luke over the phone, as the SUV rolled to a stop in the driveway of Malik's home. "I did a perimeter sweep. No one is here."

"Did you see any cars off the road on your way there?" Luke leaned against his car and placed the call on speaker so his sister and Asher could hear. The rest of the crew was inside Malik's home, waiting to open the safe.

"*Off the road* pretty much equates to winding up in the French Riviera," Liam said dryly. "I'll retrace all possible routes, though."

"Touch base with Knox and update him. If someone got ahold of Harper, they could be coming to the hotel next."

He should've left more than one guard with Eva. He looked to Asher and said, "Head to the hotel. Grab two of our guys from inside the house and bring them with you."

"Sure thing," Asher said.

"Liam, I'm going to send someone to meet up with you also," Luke said. "I'll have them phone you for a location once they're on the road."

Jessica cursed under her breath and crossed her arms, looking off at the sea behind Malik's home.

"Hurry," Luke said to Asher and ended the call.

A bad feeling twisted in his gut, and maybe it was because he was afraid if something did happen to Eva this time, he wouldn't be able to save her. But he couldn't allow himself to think like that. He also didn't know for certain that something had happened to Harper.

"How much time do we have until Will's flight lands?" Luke asked his sister as they walked toward the house to meet up with everyone inside.

"Two hours," she said. "At least we'll have the safe when he's here."

"But trying to explain to him why we don't want him to hand the contents over to the CIA until we know if someone was working with Reggie will be tough for him to digest," Luke noted.

"Right," she said as they walked through the front door.

Malik approached Luke and Jessica, his face muscles more relaxed now that he knew his family was safe. "You ready?"

Luke nodded.

"Then, let's go." Malik motioned for Jessica and Luke to follow him.

They walked to the end of a hallway and stopped before the last door. Malik tapped at a keypad and entered a code.

Nothing inside the room but a bookshelf. Malik thumbed the spines before pulling the fourth book on the fourth shelf down. The walls parted, which led them to another empty room.

"You have your code, right?" Malik asked as they approached what appeared to be a closet door with a keypad on it.

Luke arched a brow, silently saying, *are you kidding?*

"Enter your code at the exact same time as I enter mine."

"If I'm off, will this thing really explode?"

"No. My brother told that to your government to try and buy him some time when he realized he'd been lied to."

Of course.

"Now," Malik commanded.

Luke tapped at the keys, and a second later, the door clicked, and Malik pushed it open.

Luke stepped inside the small room the size of a decent-sized walk-in closet. Documents and photos were taped to every inch of the walls, and he nearly tripped over boxes in the center of the room.

"My brother was old school. He didn't keep any electronic records. These files go back to before the fall of the Berlin Wall. We're talking over thirty years. He said he kept moving the intel from place to place over the years to keep anyone from finding it."

Luke scratched at the base of his throat. "We need to get everything off the walls and packed up—and fast. Can you handle it? I want to call Liam back and check on Eva."

Jessica placed her hand on his shoulder. "You have a bad feeling?"

"Yeah," he said as calmly as possible.

"Okay. We'll get this done."

Malik followed him out of the safe and caught up with him. "What will happen to me?"

Luke halted to face him. "I believe you were trying to do the right thing, but it won't be up to me to decide your fate. But I'll put in a good word for you."

"Thank you. I'm so grateful you were the man chosen for this job. I can't ever thank you enough for saving my family."

Luke nodded, not sure what else to say, then went outside

to make his call, desperate to hear the sound of Eva's voice, but before he could phone her, his cell began buzzing.

It was Liam. "Harper's been shot," he said straight away. "I found her body near an abandoned car. She was left for dead, but she's still got a pulse."

He dropped his head.

"I'm in the back of an ambulance with her right now. Tell our guys to get to the hotel."

"Already on it. They should be there any minute. Let me call and warn them. Did she get a chance to say anything to you?"

"No. She's lucky to even be alive. I just hope she stays alive."

"'Kay. Let me—" Another call was coming in. "That's Knox." He switched lines before Liam had a chance to respond. "You may be in trouble."

"I'm so sorry," Knox said quickly, his breathing labored.

"What's wrong?"

"She's gone. Eva's fucking gone."

CHAPTER TWENTY-TWO

FIVE MINUTES EARLIER

"I TAKE BACK WHAT I SAID." KNOX LIFTED HIS SHADES AND found Eva's eyes.

She lowered her coffee mug to the terrace table. "What are you talking about?"

"I told you to forget about whatever happened between you and Luke."

"What are you trying to say?"

"You've changed him. In a good way, I mean. He's always been rough around the edges, but aside from his team, he never made room for anyone else in his life." He smiled and slipped his sunglasses back in place.

"Yeah, you mentioned the rules." A lump started to claim her throat, emotions punctuating each second that lapsed until he talked again.

"But man, you should've seen him when you got into Malik's car. Hell, he clobbered Asher and me. He was ready to kill us."

"Sorry about that." She rubbed her hands against her thighs, hoping to slow her pitter-pattering heart.

"I think the man is falling in love with you."

"What? He doesn't love me. We don't love each other, I mean. We've known each other a week."

He shrugged. "My mom fell for my dad in twenty-four hours."

"He's rich," she teased.

"Before he had money." He smiled back.

"Well, we're not in love. I don't know him well enough to even dance around the idea." Her stomach tucked in at the words that left her lips. "You can believe in the possibility of love, but it takes time to truly know if someone is the one."

"Maybe. Maybe not. All I'm saying is you could be the one to break his rules, and maybe that wouldn't be such a bad idea."

"Why? Are you bored of playing the field? Do you want to settle down without quitting?"

"This isn't about me. This is about what I think is best for my boss. For my friend." The sincerity of his words blew through her and warmed her heart. "Anyway, I gotta take a piss." He stood and patted her on the shoulder.

And that killed it, she thought, lightly chuckling.

She eyed the untouched mimosa next to her coffee. "Why not?" She started to reach for it but stopped when a shadow fell over the table.

Her gaze swept up to a man connected to a rope with a gun pointed at her head.

Too shocked to move, to think, to do anything—she only stared at him as he dropped beside her.

All black from head to toe. She could only see the pale green of his eyes. "Scream, and I put a bullet in your head," he whispered, his gaze darting to the open door. "Where are they?"

"Not here," she rushed out.

"You're lying." His finger slipped to the trigger, and the muzzle of the gun touched her forehead.

She lifted her hands in the air in surrender, tears building in her eyes. "They're gone. They went somewhere."

"Where? To get the safe?"

Oh, God . . . "Yes," she cried.

"You're coming with me." The guy pointed to the terrace wall. "Climb up. We're jumping."

She looked at the rope looped around his waist and lifted her gaze, trying to locate its point of attachment.

"I won't let you go. You'll have to trust me." He flicked the gun again, urging her to hurry.

She knew if they didn't leave soon, Knox would appear, and the masked man could get a shot off before Knox had a chance to draw his weapon.

"Okay." She shook as she hoisted herself up the three-foot wall to stand on the cement ledge, only a few inches in width.

"Wrap your arms around my waist," he said once he stood next to her.

Knox would be there any second. She didn't want him to die, and so she did as he'd said.

"Jump," he yelled, just as she caught sight of Knox before they went over the ledge.

* * *

SHE SCREAMED, BUT IT WAS A WASTE OF BREATH AGAINST THE duct tape over her mouth. Her hands and feet were bound, and her body jerked from side to side, rolling with every bump in the road as the vehicle raced down the road.

The trunk was small, and her knees were pinned to her chest.

She'd tried to calculate in her head how many seconds had passed since they'd left the hotel.

Seconds had turned to minutes.

And now she'd lost count.

Knox had peered down at them after she'd landed on the sidewalk, a hard slap to her bare feet. The guy had held a gun to her temple as a warning to Knox not to fire, and then he'd hissed, "You did lie," as he forced her to run toward a bank of palm trees.

Now the car came to an abrupt stop, and she pounded her bound fists at the roof.

Hope climbed into her chest at the memory of the diamonds Jessica had given her to keep her safe if anything had gone sideways last night.

She lifted her shoulder to her earlobe, then remembered she'd already given them back. "No," she bellowed, tears streaking her face, a harsh sob fighting against her taped lips.

The engine died, and a door slammed shut.

He was coming for her, and he'd want the location of the safe.

But she'd die before saying a word.

CHAPTER TWENTY-THREE

"Knox checked the hotel surveillance," Luke told Jessica and Owen as soon as he ended the call. "The guy broke into the suite above ours and dropped down onto the terrace by rope. He tried to catch up with them on foot, but they'd disappeared before he even made it downstairs."

"Shit." Owen rushed a hand through his blond hair.

Why'd she have to take off those damn earrings? Luke tucked a fist inside the palm of his hand as he bowed his head, trying to figure out what the hell to do. "Whoever took her won't go far, not if they think the safe is nearby and they're looking to use her as their bargaining chip."

"The guys will find—" Owen started.

"I should be the one looking!" Luke pointed to his chest.

They were still at Malik's home, waiting for the safe to be packed up, but how could he sit around when Eva was out there?

"We need you here to help strategize." Jessica placed her hand on his forearm as if she could calm down his racing heart.

"It had to have been a pro hit," Owen said. "Dropping in

214

by rope . . . Other than us and MacGyver, who the hell does that?"

"It's gotta be someone with the CIA, probably former military." Luke's nostrils flared. "Maybe even a CIA asset, not necessarily an agent."

"No one outside the agency knew of the safe house, and only a select few knew Harper was there," Jessica reminded them.

"We need names of anyone stationed within a hundred-mile radius of our location, someone who could get to Harper fast enough to stop her from coming our way," Luke snapped.

"Will should be able to give us a name, but he's still in the air," Jessica replied.

"We don't have time to wait," Luke was quick to say. "Something is in the safe that will tell us who the hell wants that information buried—something to reveal this prick's identity."

"We'll find it." Owen gave a quick nod. "We'll get Eva back."

"Can you hack the CIA?" Luke peered at his sister, knowing he was asking her to break a dozen laws.

"Luke," Owen grit out. "You can't ask her to do that, man."

"Eva could die, probably *will* die, if we don't do something." He paused to take a breath; he couldn't let thoughts of her being tortured enter his head, or he'd completely lose all control. "This guy will offer her as an exchange, and you and I both know shit will go belly-up. This isn't like last night."

"I have friends in the agency. People I can trust. I'll make some calls," Jessica said.

"What if you put a target on their head, like Harper's?"

Owen countered, which had Luke gripping his teammate's shoulder.

"The mission is now about Eva. It's about her survival, you got it? We do whatever it takes to bring her back safe." He shook his head, realizing he'd gone over the edge or was sure as hell about to.

He staggered back, his black boots rubbing against the tiled floor. He couldn't think straight, not with Eva in danger. His heart beat furiously in his chest, and he wanted to claw out the damn organ that was making him feel so much right now.

"There're only four people outside of our team who know what we really do. How would anyone else know of the hotel, and that we're there?" Owen asked after he'd given Luke a minute to cool down.

"Someone could've been watching Harper, and when they realized she'd been looking into Reggie, they pressed the gas on their plans," Jessica rationalized.

Owen held his palms face up as if to say *hear me out*. "Or, it's one of the big four who don't want the contents of the safe exposed. Who better to clean up the mess than a team that doesn't exist. Let's say, for argument's sake, it's CIA Director Rutherford. He forced Reggie to take out Odem—"

"Why send me to Berlin to get the USB, though?" Luke interrupted.

"Maybe Reggie was the fall guy all along, and the plan had always been for us to complete the mission. Pin everything on Reggie and Malik, and no one would be the wiser," Owen pitched. "I mean, how the hell did they find out Reggie's specific location in Berlin so fast? Not to mention the fact Reggie wasn't in the city, but on the outskirts of town in some place where no one would witness your shoot-out."

"I didn't have orders to kill," Luke reminded him.

"Maybe a sniper was in position from higher ground, prepared to put a bullet in Reggie's head after you got the USB," Jessica said.

"I don't believe it. The director's a good man." Luke pressed a fist to the bar top counter.

"You were the only one commissioned to go after Reggie in Berlin. Will said the director didn't want to draw attention from German officials or anyone in the CIA by sending too many people," Owen added. "Had more of us been with you, we'd have prevented Ender from shooting you, and we could have spotted a sniper in the wings."

He couldn't digest this. He couldn't stomach the idea of such betrayal from someone he'd trusted with his life. "It's not uncommon for us to be sent individually to protect the integrity of the mission or to prevent compromising our team."

"I don't want to believe it, either," Owen said. "But, we have to consider the possibility that someone from our side is—"

"Excuse me," Malik interrupted, standing at the edge of the hall. "One of your guys sent me to grab you ASAP."

They hurried to the safe, and Luke rushed out, "Did you find something?" He knelt alongside one of his crew who was on his knees, holding a set of images.

His teammate flicked his finger at an image of two SEALs with guns in hand, standing before a dead woman and child. "That's Reggie, right?" he asked. "It's a side view, but I have a few more shots—some of them actually shooting the unarmed woman and child. I can see why he'd rather shoot Odem than risk these pictures seeing the light of day."

"Reggie was a SEAL? He killed those people in Afghanistan?" Jessica whispered and snatched another image.

"It was the start of the war over there after 9/11. Shit

must've gotten hairy, but that's sure as hell no excuse—" Owen began.

"Is that who I think it is next to him?" Jessica cut him off, her voice grave.

Luke's throat tightened, and he nodded. "Yeah, the fucking *Ghost*."

* * *

No calls. Nothing from the man who took Eva.

Two hours had passed, and not a damn word, but Luke was pretty sure he knew why.

"Will's here. Knox spotted him in the lobby," Jessica announced. "He's taking the elevator now."

Luke looked around at his remaining crew in the hotel room: Asher, Owen, and his sister. The rest of his team waited in position at Malik's home, and Liam was still at the hospital with Harper while she was in surgery.

"We ready for this?" Owen huffed out a breath.

"I'm always fucking ready." Asher tipped up his chin and made eye contact with Jessica. "How about you, Peaches?"

Jessica rolled her eyes and checked the ammo in her piece before strapping it to her ankle beneath her pant leg. "I still can't believe this is happening, or that there's not some other explanation."

A knock on the door had Luke's muscles tensing.

"It's me," Will called out.

Luke buried his anger the best he could and let him in. "You could've told us you were hopping on a flight over here."

"I was in a hurry." Will walked in and directed his focus on Jessica. "It was a pleasant surprise to get off the plane and find out you've completed the mission." A tight grin met his lips. "Where's Malik now?"

Jessica's gaze skated to Luke's as he stood behind Will. "He's being held by some of our team."

"I'm surprised you got him to hand everything over without a fight," Will noted.

"It took some arm-twisting," Luke said.

"Well, I talked to POTUS on my way here." Will twisted his neck to the side to catch sight of Luke. "He's pleased. Says *good job*."

"Unfortunately, what Jessica left out of her text was that we've encountered a new problem," Luke said. "Eva, the woman who got mixed up in all of this, was abducted this morning from the hotel. We believe someone else is after the safe, and they're looking to make a switch."

Will crossed his arms and fully faced him, a pinch of irritation on his face. He swiped a hand through his dark hair as his eyes fell to the floor. "Did you get some sort of ransom request?"

"Not yet."

"If this man is working with the men who were originally after Odem Yilmaz, it could prove highly problematic. We can't let them get access to the safe," Will said.

"Agreed," Luke said. "So, we've come up with a plan."

Will raised a brow. "And?"

"We swap both codes and the location of the safe for Eva," Luke replied.

Will's green eyes narrowed. "What?"

"We've already removed the contents of the safe and placed them in a secure location, but Eva's captors won't know that."

"You opened the safe?" Will scratched at his jaw. "Did you get a chance to look at anything?"

"No time. It was all hard copies. Nothing electronic. We put everything in boxes for now," Jessica interjected.

"Where's the intel being kept?" Will asked.

"The fewer who know about it the better, so none of us would be tempted to make a deal with Eva's kidnapper. Particularly this guy," Jessica said, jerking her thumb toward Luke. "Two of our men took the boxes outside of Monaco. They're with them as we speak, and we'll radio our guys once Eva's safe and her captors have been taken out."

"Smart." Will tucked his hands in his pockets.

Jessica nodded. "So, now we wait for her abductor to call, so we can make the exchange. We have men in position to grab her kidnapper when he shows up at Malik's residence to access the safe," she explained.

"Do you think this man is working with anyone over here?" Will asked.

"The same man who grabbed Eva also took down Harper. We believe he acted alone, but he probably has a team on standby to go after the safe. He'll suspect we'll have men in place to try and stop him at Malik's." Jessica's gaze softened.

"What the hell happened to Harper?" Will's mouth tightened.

"She was shot; her body was abandoned on the way here." There was a tight strain to Luke's words as he reeled back his desire to unleash his anger.

"Christ." Will touched the platinum wedding band on his ring finger. He still wore it, even though his wife had died in combat in 2003.

Grief burrowed into the pit of Luke's stomach as a wave of emotions crashed to the surface. *I can't lose Eva. She can't go out like this, not because of me.*

"I have a hard time believing he'll trade Eva without

confirming the contents of the safe first," Asher said from behind. "She could get killed if anyone opens fire."

Three, two, one . . .

Will released a heavy sigh. "I can't believe I'm saying this, but—call your people, tell them we'll arrange a meet if the abductor calls. Explain you've already emptied the safe and can show them the files only if Eva's safe."

Luke feigned surprise, his mouth agape. "You'd be willing to risk the files getting in the hands of an enemy to save her?"

Will cupped a hand over his mouth.

What a fucking actor . . .

"I trust you guys to get the files back once we've secured Eva. When he runs, you'll find him in time. It's what you do."

Luke's forearms tightened at his sides. "You're right," he said in a low voice. "We always get our man."

CHAPTER TWENTY-FOUR

"Your people have arranged for a swap." The harsh grit of his voice plucked Eva out of her daze.

He grabbed her off the cement floor she'd been curled up on, and held her by the arm as he forced her to move.

Once outside, the daylight pierced her eyes, and she dropped her lids closed.

She swallowed the last drop of fear swirling around inside of her as he tossed her into the trunk as if she were trash.

She wasn't sure how long she'd been on the floor in that room—maybe three hours. She'd already sped through her gamut of emotions at hyper speed while waiting for the masked man to reappear.

Anger had paralyzed each of her limbs at first, before sadness had spilled like a rush of hot water over her skin. And now, she didn't know what to think or feel.

Her masked abductor hadn't said a word to her after he'd unceremoniously chucked her into the dark room before slamming the door. She'd screamed against the tape, tears had smattered her skin, and the memories of her past had blanketed her mind.

Memories from childhood, mostly: the moments she'd said goodbye to when she'd closed the door on her old life. A flicker of regret had started to burn in the pit of her stomach as she had lain on the damp floor.

The memories gnawed at her: from the first time she'd seen her mother win an Oscar, to her sister's big audition for a major Paramount film—to the time her dad had let her yell *Cut!* on set of one of his movies at age seven.

And then her mind circled back to last week. She'd spent the last hour trying to understand her feelings for a man she barely knew, and how it was possible to have such emotions so fast.

She had cut through Luke's impenetrable walls and found the beautiful soul he'd been keeping shielded from the world, but after all of this was said and done, what would happen?

Her eyes opened at the feel of the car rolling to a stop maybe ten minutes later.

She broke her quiet resignation and screamed, a desperate attempt with the tape on her lips, sounding more like a pair of screeching brakes.

Her shoulders relaxed and the back of her throat squeezed as the anticipation of what was to come rose to the surface, and so, she stopped yelling.

A door opened and closed.

A few heavy steps progressed closer to her, and then her captor opened the trunk. "Ready?"

She nodded, and he reached between her ankles and cut the zip tie.

He held on to her elbow and helped her out.

Once on her feet, she adjusted her gaze, close to tears yet again as she eagerly searched for Luke while being escorted to the front of the car.

A bright yellow sports car appeared in the distance, with

an SUV following behind it. The sea served as a backdrop to her rescuers.

The man kept his arm looped around hers, holding her tight against him. He glanced to the left then right, and she surveyed his gaze.

He had masked men crouched on higher ground. Rifles in position and aimed toward the road. Four men in total that she could see.

Would Luke be able to spot them from his vantage point? Maybe not until they got closer, and by then, it could be too late.

But Luke was a SEAL—he would prepare for every scenario, she tried to reassure herself.

The man reached behind his back. With a gun in hand now, he rested it against his chest with the muzzle fixated toward her chin.

Liquid welled in her eyes again, but she fought to hold her ground and not wilt to her feet.

Luke's Lamborghini slowed a hundred feet away before stopping. Even at such a distance, she could see Luke's eyes right on her, and not up above at the snipers. She was throwing him off, wasn't she? Was she leading him to his potential death?

Luke exited the vehicle, and a man she didn't recognize remained in the passenger seat.

Asher, Knox, and Owen stepped out of the SUV behind Luke's car and positioned themselves alongside Luke with rifles in hand. The guys looked up, noting the snipers in the wings, and directed their weapons toward the masked men.

Luke held his palms up as he started to walk.

Each step closer had her heart breaking into shards.

"I need to verify the intel before I hand her over, and

clearly you've noticed my men"—the man tipped his chin to the left and right—"waiting in case shit goes south."

"Get me the boxes," Luke said, already halfway to her. His gaze drifted to the snipers in waiting before drawing her back in with his blues. "You okay?" He mouthed the question as if the man holding her couldn't read lips.

She tightened her lids closed and mustered a nod and a quick prayer before looking at him again.

"Don't come any closer," the man said once Luke was within ten feet.

Luke halted, but a dark shadow of anger brushed across his face. "Four boxes of hard copies. No electronic files."

"I'm aware of Yilmaz's recordkeeping," the man said.

"Guessing you don't work for al Jawali, given your lack of an accent. Friends of Reggie, huh?" Luke said, his voice deepening a couple dozen octaves.

Eva's shoulders shrank at the sight of Asher and Knox carrying the boxes toward her.

"I'm friends with whoever writes the biggest check," the guy answered dryly.

"Mercenary? Former Spec Ops?" Luke asked, as the guys dropped the boxes before the man, and both looked at Eva when the cardboard boxes thudded against the ground.

"Doesn't matter, brother. All that matters is we both walk away with what we want, right?" His fingers curled tighter around her bicep.

"You can let her go then," Luke demanded.

Her captor jerked his head to the left, and two men stood, guns still in hand as they came down to the road.

One of the masked men popped the top lid off one of the boxes and reached inside. He thumbed through some of the pages, closed the lid, and began doing the same with the rest of the boxes.

"Where's Malik?" her abductor asked while waiting for his asshole colleague to verify the documents—documents Eva knew Luke couldn't possibly hand over, so he had to have a plan.

"Dead," Luke said.

"Saves me the trouble." The guy snickered.

"Looks good, boss." The masked sniper lifted one of the boxes and placed it in the trunk where she'd been previously stashed.

"If I find out you made any copies," the guy in charge started, "I'll hunt this bitch down like a deer and keyhole her. You got it? And then, I'll come for you."

Luke's jaw set in a hard line, and Eva hoped to hell he wouldn't lose his temper.

He was a SEAL, she reminded herself, yet again; he'd keep it together.

"You have my word. Now, you have what you want. Let her go." Luke's low, almost too calm voice, had a chill creeping up the back of her neck.

"My men will be waiting until I'm a safe distance. So, if you don't want to risk a shoot-out, I suggest you don't follow," the guy answered.

She gasped when he shoved her in Luke's direction.

Luke swallowed the distance between them in three quick strides and wrapped his arms around her before pulling her behind him to shield her.

She wanted to be relieved, but it wasn't over yet.

When she watched the man drive in the other direction a moment later, she lifted her gaze to the snipers who still had their guns trained on them. But, Asher and the other guys had their weapons positioned on the masked men, as well.

Luke reached for a gun he had tucked at his back. He held

it tight as he walked them backward, keeping his eyes on the snipers.

"She comes with me," he hollered to the guy in the Lamborghini she didn't recognize.

The man locked eyes with her before stepping out and heading to the SUV behind the sports car.

Once they were in the Lamborghini, Luke set his gun on his lap and removed the tape from her lips.

"I'm so fucking sorry," he said, his voice hoarse as he slipped a blade between the zip ties at her wrists and tears cascaded over her cheeks. He cupped her face between his palms, and she braced his forearms. "Are you sure you're okay?" The emotion caught in his throat.

"I don't know," she whispered.

He swallowed as his pupils constricted, and he let out a deep breath. "We need to get out of here."

She glanced out the windows at the snipers who remained in position. "You shouldn't have done this for me." She shook her head as the wheels screeched, the smell of burning rubber flitting to her nose as he made a quick U-turn.

"You wanted to stay with that asshole?"

"The safe, though. The intel . . ."

"It'll be okay. Don't worry."

"You always get your guy, huh?" She swiped at her tears, a touch of relief settling inside her with the snipers out of sight.

"I already got him," he said in a calm voice. "He just doesn't know it yet."

CHAPTER TWENTY-FIVE

"You were right. It's Davies and his men: former Delta guys turned hired mercenaries. They've been working out of France, mostly," Jessica said over the speaker as Luke raced down the road along the Riviera. "Five men in total, right?"

"Yeah," Luke said. "Did you confirm payment?"

"It took some digging, but I tracked it to an offshore account. I had no idea Will had that kind of money stashed away."

"Saving for a rainy fucking day," Luke rasped.

"Yeah, like needing a team in a hurry to get to Harper and Eva," Jessica replied. "Well, we're tracking them. Echo Team is waiting for our command to take them out."

"I'm almost to Malik's now. I'll call and give you the word soon."

"Okay, be careful."

"Always." Luke ended the call and peered at Eva.

"Echo Team? Delta? What's going on?" Her fingers fused in her lap, a tight band of nervousness stretching her thin.

"You're familiar with the Bravo guys—Owen, Asher, Knox, Liam, and myself. Echo is the other group."

"Oh. And the Delta mercenary people? Who are they?"

"The man who took you is former Special Forces. When he got out, he became a private contractor for hire. He started taking jobs for anyone, regardless of their side of the law, a couple years back. He was probably a convenient choice since he and his guys live nearby."

"And your team is going to get the intel back?" Her hand touched her chest, waiting for the moment when he said *yes*, so she could breathe again.

"Sort of. Only the top twenty or so documents were legit. The rest of the pages were a bunch of Wikipedia documents we printed out. We assumed they wouldn't take the time to look at everything."

"Thank God."

She was alive.

Luke was alive.

The bad guys would lose.

"That CIA guy, Reggie, is dead. So, who hired them?" she asked as Luke parked outside Malik's home.

"You're about to meet him."

* * *

LUKE STROKED HIS STUBBLY JAW AND LEANED AGAINST THE Roman-like post in the middle of Malik's living room.

Malik wasn't in sight, and Eva had no clue where he was. Luke had motioned for her to sit on the couch between Asher and Knox, and she felt tiny between the men.

Where was Liam, though? She glanced around the room, nervously rubbing her hands up and down her thighs as she tried to figure out what was about to happen.

Owen sat at the bar counter with his palm resting atop his sidearm, his eyes drilling straight at the mystery man standing before Luke.

"You look nervous, Will." Luke pushed away from the column and crossed his arms before the man.

Will? Didn't Jessica mention his name on the phone in the car?

"Yeah, of course, I am. I have to call POTUS and tell him we lost the intel." He slipped his hand in his jeans pocket.

"No, you don't," Luke said.

"What do you mean?"

Luke tipped his chin toward the hallway. "The intel's still in the safe. It hasn't been removed."

Will's head jerked back as if he'd been slapped. "Are you shitting me? Why didn't you let me know you gave those men false documents? Wasn't that a bit risky with her life on the line?"

"Why do you seem so upset?" The muscle in Luke's jaw squeezed.

"I'm not. This is good news."

Luke's hand went behind his back, and Eva's eyes widened when he curled it around the butt of his gun. "The guys who made the swap for Eva—it's crazy how easily they believed us, don't you think? I mean, sure, they had the show of the snipers, but it's almost like someone told them to trust the intel was good. You know, someone who would think the boxes truly had the right content in them." Luke took one long stride closer to Will.

"What are you trying to say?"

"How could you do it, man?" A touch of anger sliced through Luke's words.

"Do what?" Will's gaze tightened, suspicion crossing over his face.

"For starters, why have those assholes try and kill Harper and take Eva?"

"What the fuck are you talking about?" Will snapped.

"How long has Yilmaz been blackmailing you? Since the day he sent you the images of you and Reggie murdering innocent people in Afghanistan? Or, did he stumble upon those photos later and only begin to blackmail you recently?"

Will's mouth fell ajar, and before Eva had a chance to react, Will stretched his arm out, aiming a gun straight at Luke.

Luke's weapon was pointed right back at him, his shoulders squared, the tension evident in the pinch of his muscles.

Asher, Knox, and Owen were on their feet, sidearms in hand as well.

"So, you did look at the intel," Will said through gritted teeth.

The fact that Luke brought Eva there meant he knew what he was doing, and so she attempted to allow that detail to comfort her, despite the fact there were five drawn weapons in the room.

"Why'd you kill that woman and child? Why spend fifteen years trying to cover it up?" Luke's voice dipped lower with a rasp of betrayal.

"It was an accident," Will said, eying Owen from over his shoulder. "Put your guns down. We don't need to do this."

"Put your piece down first," Luke said as if he knew Will would never do it. "Denise had just died. Your wife was killed overseas by some asshole radical insurgent, and I'm guessing you unleashed hell for revenge."

Eva's stomach tightened as she listened to the exchange; images of what Luke said filled her mind.

"It was a mistake," Will said.

"And it would've ended your career. But, I'm betting you didn't know anyone had seen what you'd done—we were in the middle of war," Luke said, dragging out his words slowly as if stretching them through the muck.

"I'm not going to let some photos destroy everything I've worked for," he yelled.

"When you learned Yilmaz was turning himself in, you made sure it was Reggie on the op. He probably didn't even know about the blackmail photos until then—you were the big fish for Yilmaz. The main guy worth blackmailing. How'd you get Reggie to do it? Either way, he was screwed, so . . ."

Will remained quiet, and she spotted a slight tremble in his hand.

"You promised him safety and money if he did it, right?" Luke continued. "But Reggie had no idea you were going to have us show up for the USB in Berlin. He thought he was meeting with you." Luke kept his gun steady but turned his head enough to catch sight of Eva out of his peripheral view. "You were there to take the shot after we left, but with Ender showing up, I took care of your dirty work for you."

Owen stepped closer, his green eyes tightening as he stared at Will. "You always planned to use us, didn't you? We'd get the safe, you'd grab what you need, then turn it over to POTUS and become a hero. But with Harper poking around, you got worried we'd connect the dots between you and Reggie and look at what was in the safe."

"Harper's going to live, by the way," Asher spoke up. "And clearly, your contingency plan to take Eva failed." A puff of anger filled out his muscular chest. "How many fucking missions have we been on to clean up your messes? I sure as hell know you don't have enough money to pay off Yilmaz, so what deals did you make with him?"

"Answer him," Luke snapped, anger curling around his words like a tight ribbon squeezing out the life.

"Fuck you." Will tipped his chin. "I'm a good man. I've done what's best for this country; I never assigned you to anything that didn't merit it. That pig has been getting away with crimes for years. It was time he was brought down."

"You don't hold the scales of justice, man. We're servants to justice," Luke said.

Nausea overcame her as she digested everything happening, hating that Luke and his team were facing such betrayal. Her palm rested flat on her abdomen as her lip moved between her teeth, desperate to shut her eyes and wake up tomorrow.

"I won't go down for this," Will said, his voice settling somewhere on the frequency of somberness—acceptance of death.

"I know what you're trying to do, but it won't work. I won't kill you." Luke's words cut through the air, and she tensed as trepidation filled her.

"I'll put a bullet in you. I won't hesitate." Will's hand trembled slightly.

"Put the gun down," Luke said slowly, a plea to his voice.

The blood pumping from her heart went to her ears as Will slowly pivoted, pointing the gun at her. "Can you take the risk with her?"

"You won't do it," Luke said.

"Guess we'll find out."

She instinctively covered her face, and a gunshot popped in the air a second later.

"Asshole." Asher's voice sang in her ears.

She slowly dropped her hands.

"You fucking shot me in the arm!" Will lay curled on the

floor, clutching his bleeding arm, the liquid soaking the carpet.

"Better than your face," Luke said dryly, pain cutting through his words. "You're gonna rot in prison for what you've done." He tucked his gun into the back of his pants and kicked Will's weapon away from his reach.

She covered her mouth, blinking rapidly as she assessed what had gone down.

"Are you okay?" Luke grabbed her hand and helped her stand, as Knox created a tourniquet around Will's arm.

"I think so," she whispered.

"I'm sorry you had to see that, but I didn't have time to bring you anywhere else first." He pulled her in for an embrace, tucking her safely in his arms, and she sniffled against his shirt, trying to keep herself together.

Only thirty minutes had passed since he'd saved her from the masked man, but that felt like an eternity ago.

He stepped back and held her cheeks. "Do you want to get out of here?"

She nodded.

He wrapped an arm around her waist, and they started for the door. "I'll meet you guys back at the hotel after you're finished with him. And don't fuck him up, Asher. I know what you're thinking."

CHAPTER TWENTY-SIX

"Is it all finally over?" Eva asked, her fingers fisting the blanket to her chest.

"Almost," Jessica answered for Luke because he couldn't get his mouth to move.

He couldn't believe everything that had happened today —everything that could have happened to Eva.

Her life had been in jeopardy because of him. It solidified why he couldn't ever be with someone. It was too damn dangerous.

But, with Will's betrayal, did he even have a job anymore?

"We, uh,"—he coughed into his closed hand—"still need to wrap up a few loose ends with the bad guys who were after the safe in the first place."

"Oh." Her chest lifted and fell with a sobering breath. "What does that mean for me?"

"We'll take you back to the States." Jessica sat next to her on the bed. She wrapped a hand over her shoulder as if she were trying to be sisterly, but on Jessica it looked awkward and forced.

Eva's long lashes lifted as she viewed Jessica.

Jessica cleared her throat. "We should keep an eye on her until it's clear. If Ender mentioned anything to al Jawali about her in the truck before the accident . . ."

Luke's arms tightened across his chest as he leaned against the wall opposite them, digesting the situation. "I doubt he said anything, but it's not a chance I'm willing to take." He wouldn't be able to watch her again though. The commander in chief was expecting his arrival and a briefing tomorrow at Camp David.

"My work starts in ten days. Will I be back in time?" she softly asked.

Luke looked to Jessica for a brief moment. "I hope so. We won't be sent in to take out al Jawali, but—"

"Why not?" Eva's brows raised, a flicker of relief in her hazel irises.

"That kind of stuff will be handled by DEVGRU, or a combination of spec ops guys. We do the stuff that's more behind the scenes," he explained.

"And never get credit for it." She wet her lips, a slight tremble there. "But you don't do this for credit," she noted before he had to say it.

"Ender's been handed over to the Feds. I doubt he'll ever wake, but he's not our responsibility anymore." Jessica stood.

"What will happen to Malik and his family?" Eva asked, allowing the blanket to fall to her lap. Traces of goose bumps scattered across her forearms.

"He has diplomatic immunity, which if POTUS wanted to he could probably get around, but I made the case this morning for his return to Turkey. I think it's best for him and his family to stay low-key for a while," Jessica answered.

It was Luke's first time hearing the news, but he was in agreement.

He should've listened to his gut from the beginning about the case, but then again, he'd never have suspected his superior to be involved in twisting all of the intel up to mask the true mark: himself.

"I'm going to go wrap things up with the guys in the other suite. We head to the airport in an hour, if you want to freshen up first," Jessica said.

Luke waited for them to be alone, and then he sat on the bed and found her hand. "If you hadn't shown up at the cabin, none of this would've happened."

Her lips twitched at the edges. "I know."

"No, I mean we would've handed over Malik and Ender as traitors, and Will would've gotten away with everything." He tensed at the thought.

How many ops had he been sent on to do Will's personal bidding? He was only supposed to be the point of contact, so hopefully, this had been the first time. He couldn't think any other way, or guilt would rip him apart.

"So, my almost dying a few times wound up being a good thing." She smiled as he shifted to better face her and guided his hand up, brushing the pad of his thumb beneath her mascara-streaked eye.

"No," he finally said. "But what happened to you proves how dangerous knowing me is." His chest constricted as he stood.

"You could've died because of me," she said, catching him by surprise as he braced the back of his neck with both hands. "You might have sacrificed your mission and turned over the safe to save me." She shoved the blanket to the side and stood.

He held his breath as he waited for her words, wondering if she'd be the one to sever the—well, whatever it was—

between them. Maybe she'd save him from having to do it himself?

"I get why you don't want your men to be married and have kids. I know SEALs have families, but what you do is different, I guess." Her gaze dropped to the floor, and her hands knotted at her sides. "And I assume you lost someone from your team, and he was married, right? So, there's that, too."

Memories of his best friend with a hood over his head two years ago came to mind. "So, you agree with me?"

She reached for his forearms and stepped in closer to him, lifting her chin to meet his gaze. "We're a danger for each other," she whispered, her eyes filling with tears.

"We are," he rasped.

"And it's scary. It's terrifying, actually." She closed her eyes, and the first few drops of liquid rolled down her cheeks. "But fear is what keeps us going. Fear isn't the enemy, right?"

Shit. He stepped away from her and out of reach. "Don't do this, please. This isn't one of your movies where we get to write the ending and everything works out. This is real life." He dragged a palm down his jaw, his body tight with the pull of indecision, even if he knew what needed to be done in his head—his heart was trying to guide him another way.

"Don't talk to me like I'm some child. Some lover of fantasy with no grasp on reality. I deserve more than that." She opened her eyes, the color deepening as if she'd been wounded. She brushed past him and headed toward the en-suite bathroom.

"Eva, wait. I didn't mean—" He cut himself off when she slammed the bathroom door in his face. He rattled the knob, but it was locked. The sound of running water had him pressing his palms to the door. "Everly," he said this time, hoping to catch her attention.

"Go away. It's what you want, right? We'll go back to the States and back to our lives of living in the shadows."

"Open the door," he commanded, his voice dropping as frustration gnawed at him. He didn't want to hurt her; it was the last thing he wanted—but that's what would happen if they tried to see where their relationship could go. After losing her twice within twenty-four hours, he couldn't risk a third time in the future. A third time could kill her.

"Leave. I'm naked now, and I have nothing left to say."

"Open the door," he said, softer this time. "And I've seen you naked before."

"Clearly, that won't be happening again."

"Don't do this. I don't want it to end like this." He curled his hands into fists and pressed them against the wood, his knuckles whitening.

"As long as it ends, what does it matter?"

"You knew this day would come. You knew how impossible it would be for us."

"And then you made love to me and screwed me all up again." She smacked her hand, or something, against the door. "And now I am acting immature and crazy. Thanks for that."

What the hell could he say at this point?

Could he tell her he'd love to take her to dinner, to try and have a normal life, and to see what could happen between them—that he'd love to play cards and lounge around with her on a rainy afternoon, and then have sex in every room of his home in Nashville?

Her life was more important than what he wanted, though. And he couldn't forget that his head hadn't been focused on the mission with her around. Of course, she wouldn't be on future ops with him, but . . .

No, he was trying to convince himself it could work, and he couldn't do that.

"Please, let me in." He lowered his forehead to the door, bracing the frame as his heart and mind raced in different directions.

"Why? Our relationship started through a door, so maybe it should end through one."

She was crying, and the sounds of her broken sobs would destroy him. "I need to see you. I need a chance to—"

"Say *goodbye*?"

He lifted his head and pushed away from the door.

"If I see you, I'll want you to kiss me. And I can't handle the touch of your lips, knowing it'll be for the last time." She grew quiet, only the sounds of the water in the back to lull him into a state of uncertainty.

"You're leaving before me with Owen. I need to see you—"

"No," she said and hiccupped. "Thank you for saving me. I'm sorry for everything that happened with your team, but let's just end this here. If you don't have any plans on changing your mind, I don't have any plans on opening this door."

He cursed under his breath, and rolled his head skyward as if the answers were above him. "Don't do this."

"I can be as stubborn as you."

He almost smiled.

She was damn stubborn, and it was a quality that had had him tripping all over his words and actions ever since she'd made the decision to show up at the cabin a week ago.

"You drive me nuts," he whispered, not sure if she could even hear him, or if he'd meant for her to.

"Ditto."

He pulled at the tight skin on his throat and expelled a long breath. He allowed the silence to sweep between them, trapping them in the moment.

"I care about you," he finally said after a few minutes. "I hope you find what you're looking for in life." His hand hovered before the door, and he resisted the impulse to shake the knob to try and see her again. "Goodbye."

He turned on his heel and rushed from the room before he gave her a chance to respond.

"Can you stay in the room with her until she heads to the airport?" he asked Jessica once he joined some of the team.

"Yeah. Do I need to pick up the pieces of a broken heart when I go in there?"

"Like you'd know how," he grumbled.

She rolled her eyes. "Liam's on his way back, by the way. Harper's doing much better. She'll make a full recovery."

"Thank God for something."

She touched his chest, and his sister's normally icy stare dissolved. "Are you okay? I mean, Will's betrayal, plus—"

"It's a lot, but I'm always okay, aren't I?" he asked.

"Yeah . . . but I'm worried this time might be different."

CHAPTER TWENTY-SEVEN

"Is this your first time at Camp David?" President Rydell handed Luke a Scotch and offered Jessica a drink before sitting in the leather armchair across from them.

"Yes, Mr. President." The aged drink kicked up in the back of his throat but went smooth into his chest. It was what he needed, plus maybe five more. The last twenty-four hours had been a whirlwind.

From his anger at Will to his gut-wrenching ire at himself for the way things had ended with Eva—he'd become a tightly wound bottle of rage, and he was near ready to explode.

"It was a shock to all of us about Will Hobbs. We have a team investigating all of his actions, dating back to 2003." He took a sip of his drink and crossed his ankle over his knee. "He'll pay for what he's done."

Luke nodded, not sure what to say. He was waiting for the moment when the president would announce the disbandment of his group. The idea made his lips twitch, so he took another drink.

"What happens to us, Mr. President?" Jessica bit the bullet.

"After talking to the CIA director this morning, we've decided not to make any changes. The intel alone you recovered from the safe is going to take down a half a dozen operational terrorist cells. If you consider everything you've done in the past five years, we can't afford to lose you." He released a long sigh. "But, we've decided to eliminate one position. Well, more so alter it. We'd like you two to be the point of contact for future missions. Will was a middleman, and maybe that was the problem. We'd like to work directly with you."

Luke leaned back into the couch and took a moment to consider his words.

"It'd be an honor, Mr. President." Jessica looked to Luke for a response.

He blinked a couple of times as he thought about what this meant—any hope he'd clung to that he could be with Eva in the near future had gone out the window.

"Yes, of course," he finally said and stood. "Thank you, Mr. President." He extended his palm, and Jessica followed suit.

After they chatted for a few minutes, Jessica and Luke made their way to the chopper outside. "That was unexpected," she said, her words competing with the blades. "It's what you want, right?"

"Yeah." But he also wanted Eva, even though he'd said goodbye to her.

He couldn't have both, he reminded himself.

"The teams will be happy," she hollered over the noise once they'd strapped in.

He squeezed the emotions down his throat, emotions that had been foreign to him up until the moment Eva had come crashing into his life with her "Clark Kent" glasses and her beautiful smile.

His gut tightened, and he tipped his head back and listened to the sounds of the familiar helo blades, which afforded him the safety of what he knew—being a SEAL.

He'd been born and raised for this life.

But part of him didn't want to go at it alone anymore.

"Are you sure you're okay?" His sister squeezed his arm, taking him by surprise.

Without opening his eyes, he nodded, not wanting her to see the thread of emotions slip through his eyes. He'd also promised her he wouldn't lie.

And hell, he was anything but okay right now.

CHAPTER TWENTY-EIGHT

Eva took a shaky breath and pressed both hands to her cheeks as she stared at the last page of her finished script. The words had poured straight from the heart during the last five days she'd been tucked away in Charleston with Owen.

"I'm done." Emotion squeezed in her throat, and she swiped at the tears on her cheeks.

Owen sat in front of his laptop at the bar counter of the pub he owned. She'd learned he was a man with a lot of skills, apparently; one of which included making ridiculously delicious cocktails.

The pub was closed down in the winter, so they'd been staying in an apartment he had on the second floor. Luke hadn't been too concerned about a threat, but he'd wanted her with one of his people until everything blew over. Well, that's what Owen had said on their drive from D.C. to Charleston.

"You really banged out an entire script from start to finish in five days?" He came next to her and brushed a strand of blond hair from his face. He had the whole Charlie Hunnam look going for him. Intimidating, but super sexy. Of course, he wasn't Luke, and she highly doubted any man would ever measure up to him.

"It's amazing what you can do when you've almost died." She closed her laptop and sniffled, trying to stifle the tears.

"You didn't write about what happened, did you?"

Amusement spread through her, warming her cheeks at the sudden nervous look on his face.

"No one would believe that story."

"You're probably right."

"I scrapped the movie I'd been writing before I met you guys, though. Inspiration sort of seized hold of me when we got here."

"This place can do that," he said, his eyes now focused on the wall at her side, and she followed his gaze to see what had captured his attention.

It was an old framed photo of two people, but how could she not have made the connection sooner . . .? "Is that you? You're so young." A smile found her lips, and she faced him again.

"Yeah," he said, his voice flat.

"Who's the guy next to you?" Concern had her skin breaking out into goose bumps, and she crossed her arms.

"My brother." He cleared his throat and blinked as if ushering away whatever thoughts were on his mind.

"Oh?" Relief swelled in her chest. "It's hard for me to imagine you running this place alone, while working at Scott & Scott, as well as doing your other job. Does he help out?"

"He's dead, so no."

Her fingertips pressed to her lips, shock spiraling through her at fifty beats per second. "I'm so sorry."

"It was a long time ago. He was military."

"Was that before or after you joined?" She couldn't seem to stop herself from asking questions—it was second nature to her—but the way his mouth tightened, she worried it'd been a mistake.

"Let's talk about you instead." And it was as if a switch had been flipped, and his lips curved at the edges into a smile. Forced, but still. "Who are you gonna have star in this film? Do you need me to help cast the female leads? I'd be happy to assist."

It took her longer than him to pull her thoughts out of the darkness, but when she finally did, she said with a chuckle, "Because you don't already have your plate full."

"You won't forget us little people when you're . . ." He let his words go, as a puff of air left his nostrils. "Shit, you're already famous, right? So maybe I should ask, are you gonna go back to that life?"

"Well, I—"

"Hold that thought."

He grabbed his phone from his pocket and answered. "Yeah?" A pause. "Okay, great. I'll tell her."

Her heart sped up. She knew Luke's team hadn't been sent to take down the terrorists, but the thought of his voice being on the other end of the line, knowing he was okay, it had a quiver of hope darting up her spine.

She understood his reasons for letting her go, but it didn't make it any easier to accept.

"You're free," Owen said after he ended the call, which snapped her out of her Luke-induced state of mind.

"Oh. Was that—"

"Jess," he said, and a moment of disappointment washed over her. "So, where would you like me to take you? Your place in New York?"

Her gaze flicked to her laptop, to the memory of her finished script. "Actually, I think I'd like to go home."

He tucked his phone in his jeans pocket. "I thought New York was home."

She smiled. "I mean my other home."

* * *

"You really can't tell us what happened?" her mom asked.

"I'm sorry." Eva glanced around the room swelling with family members she hadn't talked to in a while; they'd all gathered at a moment's notice when she'd put in the request.

She was fortunate to have them.

Her older brother, Harrison, had his back to everyone, his palm resting on the mantle above the lit fireplace in her father's office. "People will find out you're here. The real you. It's probably not a good idea to stay much longer."

"That's okay," she said softly, letting them know for the first time her decision to return to her old life. "I'm done hiding. I thought it was what I wanted, but"—she stretched her arms, palms up—"I miss you guys. I miss being part of this family."

"Are you serious?" Her mom was on her feet and striding to her. She wrapped her arms around her. "Finally."

Harrison faced her now. "What about your show?"

"I spoke with everyone yesterday and let them in on my secret." She smiled when she pulled back from her mom. "The director figured me out a few months after I started, but he assumed I had wanted my privacy." She'd been in shock when he'd dropped that bomb on her, but also relieved that her lie of a life had been paper thin. "I'm going to keep working on the show for as long as they'll have me, but I'll need to do a better job of safeguarding my life from now on."

"We're happy to have you back, sweetheart," her dad said

from behind his desk. He was never a man for hugs and big emotions, but she loved him for who he was.

Her mom clapped her hands together before glancing at her dad's fourth wife. "Well, I think this is cause for celebration. Let's have a party this weekend."

"I'm not really up for that right now," Eva said and looked to her older brother for support.

"Yeah, she's had a stressful few weeks, apparently; let's just be glad we have her home," Harrison said.

"It's up to you." Her mom smiled.

"Could I have a word with Dad alone?" Eva glanced around the room, and her family scattered. She waited for the doors to close before she went to her bag resting against one of the bookshelves that lined the wall.

Her gaze lifted as she reached inside, catching the spine of a Tolstoy novel on the shelf, and her heart shriveled in her chest.

"Are you okay?"

Shoving thoughts of Luke from her mind, she stood upright with the printed screenplay in hand and slowly approached her father's desk, terrified of losing her nerve.

He reached for his glasses and slipped them on when she placed the pages in front of him.

"Crossfire?" He read the title aloud.

She tucked her hands in her khaki pants pockets, not sure what to do with her cold fingers as she fought the nerves tangling in her throat. "It's about a man caught in the moment of indecision—love or career. He thinks he can only have one choice, not realizing he can have the world if he only wants it bad enough."

"Is there any action?" He started flipping through the pages.

"Of course." She looked skyward for a moment,

corralling her thoughts so she could string together the right words. "I want to make a movie with you, Dad. It's been my dream, and I'm so proud of this script. I couldn't get myself to hand it over to anyone else first without at least seeing if you wanted it."

He removed his glasses, his green eyes narrowing. "Sweetheart, I've been waiting a lifetime for you to ask me."

"But I don't want you to say *yes* because I'm your daughter." She placed a palm on his desk for support. "I needed to know I had what it takes to be in this business—"

"I get it. I did the same thing when I was your age."

His words had her taken aback. "What do you mean?"

He motioned to the armchair in front of the desk, and so she took a seat.

"I was in my late twenties, and your grandfather was this famous producer, as you know—but I always feared I'd be living in his shadow. So, I changed my name and went out on my own for a few years, which is when I met your mother." He smiled. "She fell in love with me without knowing I was a Reed."

"And then what happened?" she asked, surprised that she'd never known of the story.

"I was failing miserably on my own, and so she convinced me to go back and be who I was born to be." He laughed. "Basically, I needed my name to make it anywhere in the industry."

"But you're incredible. That's not true."

He shrugged. "Maybe that's the case now, but when I was young, I swear I didn't know my left from my right sometimes. I realized I needed to be in my dad's shadow to learn enough so I could cast my very own someday." He stood and scratched at his white beard. "I never wanted to eclipse your light, though. And I never could. You shine so damn bright. You know that, don't you?"

Eva was on her feet, wiping the tears from her face yet again as he came around and reached for her arm. She'd never heard such words from her father, and maybe she never knew she had needed them until now.

"What I'm trying to say is I want nothing more in the world than to make a movie with you." He looked into her eyes, his experience obvious, not so much from the wrinkles, but from the depth of his green irises.

"If it's shit, you'll tell me, though, right?"

He laughed. "I've always been honest with you. This time will be no different."

She nodded and smiled. "Okay." A tiny bit of happiness filled her heart when her dad hugged her—something he hadn't done in years. "Let's do this."

When she left his embrace, his gaze softened even more. "Why is it you still don't look happy?"

She wished she could tell him in figuring out who she truly wanted to be, she'd fallen for someone she could never have.

He pointed to the script. "Is your story about a certain someone who may be the cause of whatever's eating at you right now?"

She gave an innocent lift to her shoulders. "Maybe."

"Tell me, then . . . how does the story end?"

CHAPTER TWENTY-NINE

"PEOPLE ARE TREATING ME DIFFERENTLY. I DON'T LIKE IT."

Jayme nudged Eva in the arm and stared off at the ocean. "What'd you expect to happen when you came out?"

"They're being super nice to me. And the guys who didn't give me the time of day before have been asking me out." Eva slouched back into her chair on the dock, waiting for the cast to wrap up with hair and makeup before they began shooting.

"Well, it may have more to do with your change of clothes and makeup. You look a little more alive, don't you think?"

Luke saw me for me without all of that. She allowed the thought to slip to the front of her mind before scolding herself for it.

Almost a month had gone by since she'd seen him.

It had been four weeks of sulking while simultaneously being excited about her future film with her dad. Harrison's studio would be supporting the project, and they had an expected release date for 2020.

She'd spent three years hiding only to end up right back

where she'd started, but maybe she'd needed that time away to figure out who she was and who she wanted to be.

"Are you ever going to tell me what happened when we were on break that led to"—she waved her hand in the air —"the new you?" She smirked. "I mean, the old you?"

"Don't you need to be with the crew getting dressed?" Eva arched a brow, hoping her friend would back off.

"I'm not filming today, and you know that, brat. By the way, I know all of your secrets. What is it that you're keeping from me?" Her arms crossed, as if she could intimidate her.

Yeah, well, she'd been surrounded by Navy SEALs and men who wanted to kill her, so an actress wouldn't be knocking her off her game anytime soon.

"Nothing happened." She blew a loose strand of hair off her face and lifted her sunglasses for a brief moment to catch Jayme's eyes. It was cool outside, but still sunny.

They had started filming at Virginia Beach last week, trying to keep the show as authentic as possible. The U.S. Naval Special Warfare Command was located at Dam Neck, one mile from where Eva sat. Being so close to real SEALs was a harsh reminder of the SEAL she missed.

"Of course something happened." Her fingernails tapped at her pink lips. "At least tell me when you're bringing me to California so I can see Harrison."

"Harrison doesn't date actresses. Even wonderful ones like you."

"Dumb rule."

"Keeps him honest," she said and grinned. "Now—"

"Holy shit. Who is that guy talking to the guard?" Jayme's mouth fell open as she shielded her eyes like a visor. "Did we hire a new guy for the show? He sure as hell looks the part. He has the look of a SEAL." A flash of excitement buzzed in her eyes. A new conquest.

Eva looked over her shoulder, and her heart stuttered in her chest.

Luke.

My Luke.

What the hell?

A tremor of fear shot down her spine. If he was there, did that mean she was in danger again? Why else would he be on set? She hadn't seen him since she'd slammed the bathroom door in his face in Monaco—a regret that filled her every day because she hated how things had ended.

Maybe she had a second chance to say goodbye now?

Goodbye: such a painstakingly horrible word.

He was wearing shades, but she could still feel his gaze burning straight toward her as his lips stopped moving.

God, he looked so sexy in his jeans and dark brown leather jacket.

"He's mine. I have dibs," Jayme announced as Luke headed toward them.

Eva turned back toward her friend and slipped off her sunglasses. Her heart was a slow drum beat now. It was amazing how everything seemed to slow in a moment like this—a moment when your world spins and you can't tell which way is up.

"He says he knows you," the guard said from behind.

"Oh yeah, he knows me," Jayme said with a hint of sexy curled around every one of her words. She played with her blonde tendrils and sunk her teeth into her lip.

"Eva," the guard responded, and Jayme's eyes flicked to her, widening in astonishment.

I can do this. She tightened her hand around her glasses at her side as she stood and turned. "Yeah, I know him." She tried to hide the breathy tone of surprise in her voice.

"Next time, Eva, let me know if we'll be getting a

visitor." The guard eyed Luke and then shook his head and walked away.

"I'm Jayme."

Luke kept his focus on Eva despite Jayme's extended hand.

"Is something wrong?" Eva cut straight to the point, her heart rate now increasing with Luke only two feet away.

His gaze moved to Jayme, and he said, "Can we have a minute?"

"Oh, sure. You know where to find me if you need me."

Luke removed his sunglasses and held them at his side, and she crossed her arms as if she could shield herself from the heat of his stare. "What are you doing here? How'd you know I was in Virginia?"

"We need to talk." The pinch of his brows and the set of his jaw had her taking a step back.

"Am I in danger?"

His mouth tightened and he shook his head.

"Is someone I know in trouble?"

"No."

"Then I can't think of anything we have to talk about." She wanted to look away. Hell, she wanted to run away. But she couldn't seem to get herself to move. She'd been fantasizing about this moment as if her life were a movie.

But, as he loved to point out to her, this was real life, and in real life, not everyone got their happily ever after.

"We need to talk."

Her shoulders slumped forward. "Fine, but not here." She couldn't stop herself from giving in. "We're about to start shooting. My rental? Seven?"

He gave a stiff nod. "That works."

"I assume you know where I'm staying since you found me here?"

The gentle curve of his lips into a smile had her stomach dropping.

"Okay, then. You, uh, should go."

He stayed before her, quietly holding her eyes, creating a strong ache in her chest—a tight grip around her heart.

"Goodbye," she said, hating her use of the word, but still too confused to know what to do.

"See you soon." He finally turned, stealing one last glimpse at her before exiting, and it took all her strength not to buckle to her knees.

"Holy mother of all things—"

"Jayme." Eva pivoted at the sound of her voice and clutched her friend's arms for balance. "You're not supposed to be here."

"I was hanging around. I couldn't miss an epic kiss." She huffed. "Uh, why wasn't there an epic kiss?"

Her eyelids tightened at the memory of Luke's mouth on hers. "Because there never can be. We can't be together."

"But you want to be, don't you?"

"I-I don't know."

CHAPTER THIRTY

HE SWALLOWED HIS HEART, WHICH HAD FOUND ITS WAY INTO his throat at the sound of Eva's front door opening. He rose, tucking his hands in his pockets like a nervous kid, like the time he'd asked a girl to junior prom.

"When I said seven, I meant you could meet me outside." Her brows rose and fell as she tossed her keys on the kitchen counter and moved with slow steps farther inside. "I'd ask you how you got in here," she said softly while stopping a few feet away, "but I should know better than to waste such a question." Her lips twitched at the edges, as if she wanted to smile, but resisted.

"Sorry to bust in here on you, but I didn't want to take a chance that a door would come between us this time."

She peeled off her jacket and flung it onto the little two-person kitchen table off to the side. "And what is it that you came here to say?" Arms crossed her chest as she attempted to hold her ground, but he knew her legs had the same tremble as her bottom lip. "Is it a coincidence we're in Virginia together?"

"No. I would've come sooner, but I've been out of the country."

"Oh. Another mission?"

"Yeah." He filled his cheeks with air. He'd come all this way and spent the last ten hours finding the right words, only to lose them all. "You're Everly again, huh?" he asked, ditching his script.

"I still go by Eva. Always have." Her gaze flicked up for a moment in thought. "But yeah, I'm me again."

"Well, if you're happy—"

"Oh yeah, I'm like the cherry on top of a sundae. I'm perfect. Really happy." Her voice strained as her chest slowly lifted and fell.

"Good." He removed his hands from his denim pockets. "So, uh, did I ever say *thank you*—you know, for everything you did? Most people wouldn't have handled the situation how you did. It takes a lot of courage and—"

"That's why you're here?" She crossed the short space between them and elevated her chin, her arms falling like weights at her sides. "You're here to give me a pat on the back and a job-well-done speech?" A lash of anger bit into her words, but he could take it.

He deserved it, in his mind.

"Why wait a month to tell me this? Why not just send an email?" She started to turn, but he captured her wrist and spun her around.

Her eyes dropped to his fingers wrapped over the silk of her sleeve, and he could feel her body heat beneath his palm despite the material. She slowly dragged her hazel irises up to find his, and he knew she'd see what he felt on the inside.

"What do you really want?" The velvety rasp from her lips had his muscles tensing.

"I can't stop thinking about you," he admitted, not letting go of her arm because he'd craved nothing else for the last four weeks but being near her.

She turned her cheek, her eyes falling to the carpet. "Has anything changed? No. You're still you." Her eyes darkened when they touched his. "And now to make it worse, I'm me again. I'm in the spotlight, and so—"

"I know, and now I hold even more responsibility at work."

She faked a quick laugh and attempted to pull away from him, but damned if he would lose his hold of her.

"Luke," she seethed, and he finally released his grasp. She whirled around and stalked toward the sliding glass doors that looked out onto the beach.

"I was hoping to take you out for a cup of coffee. If you don't hate me when your drink is done, we can upgrade to dinner. That's how first dates go these days, right? I'm out of practice."

Her palms landed on the door, and she bowed her head, touching the glass. "Why are you doing this? Haven't you done enough? Have you really come here to hurt me?"

"I'm not here to hurt you."

She lifted her head and looked back at him. "But that's what will happen when you leave, when you disappear from my life," she said, emotion cracking through now.

He rubbed at the ache in his chest. "Ninety percent."

"What?"

He angled his head and swallowed a gulp of air. "That's the divorce rate for first marriages as a SEAL, especially guys from DEVGRU. Well, according to Google."

"And were you part of Team Six?" Her eyes thinned, the familiar curiosity he loved about her bubbling there.

He took a hesitant step her way and gave a quick lift of the chin to say *yes*.

"It's like the spouses are serving, too, I guess," she whispered.

A fist tightened in his core.

"If you have the guts to do what you do, then you have to let the people in your life decide if they have what it takes, too."

He dropped his head but remained quiet.

"If they understand the risks and the challenges, you need to let them make the choice for themselves. You can't make it for them. And that's what you've done with your rule, not just for you, but for your men."

"I know." He swallowed. "My life has been classified for as long as I can remember, and I've never been able to share who I am with anyone not in the same boat as me."

"So why are you doing it now?"

"Because you're not just anyone."

Her eyes fell shut, her lower lip quivering.

"But . . ." He needed her to know the gritty details before he could continue. He knew Eva understood the dangers for her—but did she fully grasp everything? "When my teammate died two years ago—the only married guy—his wife witnessed his beheading online. I felt responsible for his death because I'd sent him alone on the op."

It'd been Will's call, but what if Luke had said *no*? Now that he knew Will was a traitor, it had him second-guessing every op he'd ever been on.

"We buried an empty casket. Never recovered the body. Still haven't found his killer. His wife, well, I'm not sure if she'll ever be able to move on, and that's on me."

She opened her eyes and reached for his forearm, the

gesture causing his lids to lower lazily toward her polished nails. "That's not your fault."

"Asher was his replacement. I think it's put a chip on his shoulder, knowing he had to fill one of my best friends' shoes. What I'm trying to say is what we do is hard. Really fucking hard, but I think it's harder on the people we care about." He looked up.

Her mouth rounded, but she didn't say anything.

"Would you come outside with me?"

"On the beach?"

"Yeah."

"Um, okay." She pointed to the glass door. "We can go out that way."

"I know." He shook his head. "How do you think I got in?" He grabbed her coat and helped her slide it on before opening the door. "You need to upgrade your security while you're here."

"It's a rental."

"And it's your life," he said while shrugging on his jacket and stepping back to let her exit first.

"And it's a nice place, by the way." He reached for her hand once they stepped out onto the sand, and she took it, which dispelled some of the concern he had that she'd forgive him.

"A perk of being Everly again." She peered at him and smiled, and he tightened his grasp on her palm, guiding her closer to the beach.

"The water always calms me. Same for a lot of my buddies. Maybe it's because we've had to learn to operate in it—I don't know, but something about it helps me think."

"Yeah? You have a lot on your mind?"

"Just one thing." They edged closer, the crest of the waves drawing his eye.

"And what's that?"

"I'm thinking you already know." He shifted to face her, repositioning their bodies so he could maintain his grasp on her hand.

"Maybe a girl needs to hear the words."

He gulped. "You *want* to hear them?"

"More than anything."

He squeezed her hand. "I have seven days off before I go back to work, and I was kind of hoping we could spend that time together to help you decide if I'm someone you possibly—"

"I don't need seven days to know." She reached for his cheek and brushed the back of her hand over his clean-shaven jaw. "I'm afraid of losing you though. So, I need to know you're not going to disappear on me again." A light smile touched her lips. "Aside from missions to save the world, of course." Liquid pooled at the corners of her eyes.

He shifted his face so his lips could brush against the back of her hand. "I'll make the promise under one condition."

"Yeah?"

"Did you bring any fuzzy socks with you to Virginia?"

She arched a questioning brow.

"I've been dying to see you dance around in them. Hell, I haven't been able to get the thought out of my head since you mentioned it."

She cry-laughed. "Really?"

"Well, yeah, but I'd prefer you to be in the socks and nothing else."

"What happened to the coffee?"

He clenched his teeth, fighting the desire to grab hold of her and kiss her. "If you insist, but I'd really like to—"

Her lips swallowed his words, and the sweet taste of her

tongue in his mouth had him groaning as he lifted her into his arms.

"Thank you," she cried against his lips a moment later.

"For what?" He kept his hold on her but leaned back to find her eyes.

"For not being an idiot and making me wait until I was old and gray to come to your senses."

He laughed and brushed his lips over her cheek and found her ear. "You make me crazy; you know that, right?"

She arched against him as if in desperate need, mirroring his own desires.

"What made you come to your senses?" She ran her fingers through his hair, and he slowly guided her feet to the sand.

"All this time I had worried that caring and worrying about you would take my mind off missions and put my guys at risk, but in the last four weeks I discovered the opposite. Missing you is so much more dangerous. I couldn't think straight this last month."

Her arms looped around his neck, and she pulled herself against him. "I've actually been able to write a lot with you gone."

"Really? So, you want me to leave?"

"Don't you know writers tend to get creative inspiration from heartache?" She pressed a quick kiss to his lips.

"So, which would you prefer?"

"Mm. No competition." Her lip wedged between her teeth, and he wanted to taste the flavor of her gloss again. "Happiness all day long."

"Are you sure?"

Her mouth swept close to his, and he could feel her soft breath dance across his skin. "I'm prepared to show you just how sure I am." She smiled and he kissed the crook of her lips.

"And are you really going to throw out your rules for me?"

"Honey, the second we met, they went out the fucking window; I just didn't know it yet."

She laughed. "What do we do now, Skywalker?"

"Socks, and only socks, Hollywood."

Her gaze darted to the sand as if a moment of indecision had seized her, and it had his heart folding.

"What's wrong?"

"I'm going to be shooting a movie with my dad, and now that I'm Everly—what does that mean for you . . . for us?"

Relief struck him. *This* he could handle. "I'd be happy to take on an alias. How about Luke Cross?"

"You can't be Luke Scott when you're with me, I get that, but—"

"It's only a name." He pressed a palm to her chest, feeling the rapid beating of her heart. "Names don't define us. As long as I get to be with you, you can call me Mary Poppins for all I care."

A deep belly laugh came out of her, and she gripped her stomach. "I think I could fall in love with you."

He braced both her cheeks, pulling her in with his eyes. "Well, I fell for you the moment you tried to shoot me with a rifle in New York."

"You did not, and I wouldn't have shot you." She playfully rolled her eyes.

"Okay, maybe it was when you mentioned the socks." He looked down at her tall brown boots. "Speaking of which . . ."

"Mm. Yes, sir." She stepped back and saluted him. "Maybe I could get used to taking orders from you. Well, as long as it involves orgasms."

"Is there any other way?" He lifted his brows a few quick times to tease.

"What kind of missions have you been running?" She laughed.

He shook his head. "I'm going to count to ten, and if you're not back inside and naked by then I'll be forced to take matters into my own hands."

She backed up, almost into the water. "You wouldn't dare."

"You want to try me?" He grabbed hold of her thighs so fast she hadn't had a chance to react and tossed her over his shoulder.

"What happened to *ten*?" she laughingly cried as he trekked up the sand toward her rental.

"Got impatient." He slapped her ass. "We have time to make up for."

"And whose fault is that?"

"All a clever disguise to give you more content for your scripts."

She slapped his back as he carried her. "I will knock the smile off your face. Those muscles of yours don't scare me, you know."

"You don't even know I'm smiling!"

"Trust me, I know."

He dropped her onto her bed a few seconds later and stared at her. Disbelief echoed throughout him—that he'd found someone like her. "Are you sure?" He had to ask one more time. "It's not an easy life. The secrets. Even some of my best friends who are SEALs think I'm retired. I lie to them, and it sucks, but—"

"I have you. And Jessica. And the guys. And hey, maybe they'll even get a chance to fall for someone now, so then there will be more women in the group." She stood and held his hand, bringing their clasped palms between them to press her lips to his knuckles, holding his eyes the entire time. "We have each other."

His eyes thinned, the weight of the world lightening a touch on his shoulders. "We have each other," he repeated, knowing he'd finally found his mark: *her*.

EPILOGUE

SIX WEEKS LATER
  Charleston, SC

"EVERYONE'S REALLY IN THERE?" EVA POINTED TO OWEN'S
pub and turned toward Luke.

He held her wrists, brought the backs of her hands to his
mouth, and pressed his lips against her skin. "They're my
family. Well, my military family. I want you to get to know
them more, so you know you don't have to go at this alone."

She rolled her lips inward and slipped her hands free to
palm his cheeks. "I'm not alone."

"When I'm on ops, I mean. It'll make it easier on you to
have people in your corner back home when I'm not around."
He'd rather take an acid bath than leave Eva . . . but knowing
he had her to come home to made his missions so much more
worth it somehow.

"I have people."

"I'm talking about people who know what I do. We're a

tight-knit group, and now you're part of it. There may not be many wives, but—"

"Who's married?" She smiled as her hands traveled to the back of his head and her fingers threaded through his short hair. "Is Marcus's wife here?"

He lowered his hands to her hips and braced her as she secured her arms loosely around his neck. "No, she couldn't make it, but she's still part of the family. We all still look after her."

His stomach roiled as he thought about Marcus who had been killed two years ago; it was a painful reminder of what could happen to Eva if he died on an op, too.

Eva was all in, though. She'd been stubborn, and now— well, now, he'd never let her go.

"So, who's inside who's married? Did one of your pals go to Vegas and have a *Hangover* moment?" She snapped her fingers and closed one eye. "Liam, right?"

He laughed. "No. Noah and his wife are here. I've been wanting you to meet them."

Noah was one of his long-time best friends since day one of the SEALs, and he'd retired from the Navy not too long ago to be with his daughter. He ended up falling in love with Jessica's best friend, Grace.

"I thought just the team was inside—you know, people who know your deep, dark secrets."

Luke released a sigh and tipped his chin toward the moonlit sky. "Yeah, well, I told Noah the truth in New York last week."

"What? Really? How'd he take it? Doesn't he work jobs every once in a while at the security company? I also thought you didn't want him to know the truth since he's a dad." She stepped back and pressed a hand to her abdomen.

"Which question do you want me to answer first?" He grinned.

"Go in order," she said with a smile in her eyes.

"Noah said he already knew, or"—he lifted his shoulders —"suspected something. He wasn't pissed. And, since I've been breaking rules ever since you and I met—*and*, since I'm going to be a dad, too, thanks to my super SEAL swimmers—"

"Did you really just say that?" She smiled for only a second before her lips flattened. "I feel like you're not telling me something. What are you leaving out?"

"Always with the questions." He angled his head and narrowed his eyes. "Noah and Grace live near your loft in New York, and I'd feel more comfortable knowing you had not only Jessica but them to help whenever I'm away. And I couldn't ask Noah to be a godparent tonight with the lie of what I really do between us."

"We're asking him to be a godparent?"

"Well, I thought you could choose someone on your side, and I'd ask someone close to me. They could flip a coin to decide who gets our baby if something happens to us."

She slapped his chest. "Luke!"

He shrugged. "What? I can't ask anyone else I know because they're doing the same crazy shit as me. Plus, Noah's a great father, and so—"

"Nothing is going to happen to either of us." She grabbed his forearm and held his eyes. "Got it?"

"Contingency plans. I always have them," he said, and she huffed out a rough breath.

"Fine." She shook her head.

His lips quirked into a grin as he dropped his gaze to her stomach. "I still can't believe we're having a baby."

"Like you said, your super SEAL swimmers managed to disarm my birth control defenses."

"Damn straight." He pulled her against him and dropped his mouth over hers for a kiss.

"It's unexpected," she said when they started for the pub, "but nothing has really gone as planned since I met you."

"I wouldn't have it any other way," he said before they entered Owen's place.

He caught sight of most of the guys huddled around the bar as Owen and Jessica made drinks. But it was Noah and Grace whom he wanted to chat with first, and they were at a booth off to the side of the bar.

Owen mock-saluted him as he held Eva's hand and strode through the army of empty tables.

"About damn time," Noah said. He stood to greet him, giving him a quick one-armed hug before doing the same with Eva. "I was beginning to worry this guy made you up."

"I'm very much real." She shook Grace's hand and smiled. "Nice to meet you guys. I've heard—well . . . you know Luke . . . he doesn't talk much about anyone or anything."

Grace laughed. "Sounds about right. But, we're so glad he found you."

"Where are the kids?" Luke asked.

"Lily's with her mom, and the twins are with my sister," Noah answered.

"Well," Luke began while placing his palms together, "there's something we wanted to ask you."

"We should probably make the announcement first, right?" Eva asked.

Luke reached for her hand and peered at his buddies toasting with shot glasses behind him. "Good point."

"Shit, man, you're making me nervous." Noah stood on the other side of him when Eva and Luke faced the room.

"Yeah, well, you're about to hear why," he muttered under his breath. Being a father was going to be a lifetime op —one he could never screw up. He'd already bought every book in the store about how to raise kids. It was . . . overwhelming to say the least.

Noah cupped his hands to his mouth and yelled, "Hey!"

The guys from Echo and Bravo Teams turned and eyed them, most still with drinks in hand.

"They have something to say." Noah wrapped a hand over Luke's shoulder.

"Well, why the hell did you bring us down here? Are you getting hitched?" Asher lifted a brow, and Jessica smacked the back of his head.

"Christ, woman," Asher rasped.

"How about you do it?" Eva asked.

"Are you sure?"

"Yes, please," she mouthed back to him.

"I'm going to be a dad," he sputtered fast without a second thought. "So don't get me fucking killed on any ops."

"That's a direct order," Eva added in all seriousness before breaking into a smile.

* * *

"I'M GLAD NOAH SAID YES TO BEING A GODPARENT. I REALLY like him and Grace." She sighed. "Did you see the look on Jessica's face tonight, though? We definitely shocked her."

Luke looked up to find Eva's eyes. "Honey, we just made love, and I'm still busy touching you—maybe we could talk about my sister later?"

She smirked. "What? You know I can never turn off my brain."

"Even during sex?" He buried his face against her soft skin again and trailed his lips up her stomach.

"Well, no. I'm only thinking about you then," she said while stroking his hair.

He cupped her breasts and gently squeezed. "Your tits are already getting bigger."

"Ow. They're sensitive, too." She laughed and he scooted up to kiss her lips.

"Sorry, sweetheart, but you're irresistible, and I'm in heaven right now." He rolled over to his side and pulled the sheet loosely over his body. "I never realized I could have it all. You. A baby. My work."

"If you don't ask, you won't receive."

He shifted on the bed slightly and slowly said, "Marry me, then?"

Her lips parted, and she sucked in a sharp breath. "But you said we can't. Your real name can't be connected to me, and—"

He found her hand and clasped it between their bodies. "It doesn't have to be legal right now, but it could be . . . you know, something just for us. I know we're doing everything backward, but—"

"Yes," she rushed out.

His heart slowed to a steady beat, and he pulled her into his arms and held her, knowing no matter what happened in the future, he'd made the right choice.

He had everything he could ever want, and he'd spend his days continuing to try and make the world a better place for Eva and his child.

"I love you," she said, her words like smooth silk.

"I love you, too, Hollywood."

"Mm. Skywalker and Hollywood. I think we're a perfect fit."

He touched her stomach. "But what will we name the little guy?"

"'Guy'?" She turned so her body partially draped his, her fingernail running lazily up and down his chest.

"We're having a boy." He coughed into a closed fist. "I'm not gonna go to jail because I lose my shit over some guy making out with my daughter in the back seat of a car."

She chuckled. "Or in a bedroom. Or at a school dance. Or a locker room."

He pinched her nipple. "Gotta have all boys. There are too many possible scenarios I may not be able to account for otherwise."

"I'm sure you can come up with plenty of contingency plans."

He grabbed hold of her and flipped her beneath him so his palms were on each side of her. He stared down into her eyes, nearly losing himself in that moment.

"Read my lips, sweetheart." His eyes tightened, but his lips crooked into a smile. "Boys."

"So they can turn out like you?" She paused for a moment, her brows drawing together and a beautiful sincerity touched her eyes. "Of course . . . having a few more heroes in the world might not be such a bad thing," she whispered then kissed him.

STEALTH OPS BONUS SCENES

Want more Bravo Team?

Stealth Ops Bonus Scene # 1 is now available for newsletter subscribers - or available to download on my website.

Bonus Scenes #2 - *A Stealth Ops Christmas* features mini-stories for Bravo Team. *It's recommended you read *Finding Justice,* as well as the prologue for *Finding the Fight* (at the end of *Finding Justice)* before reading *A Stealth Ops Christmas.*

All bonus scenes are listed and available on my website.

Coming 2-20-2020 Stealth Ops: Echo Team

Chasing the Knight - Wyatt Pierson (Echo One)

* * *

Harrison Reed joins the Dublin Nights series -> *The Real Deal*

* * *

A Stealth Ops World Guide is now available on my website, which features more information about the team, character muses, and SEAL lingo.

ALSO BY BRITTNEY SAHIN

A Stealth Ops World Guide is now available on my website, which features more information about the team, character muses, and SEAL lingo.

Hidden Truths

The Safe Bet – Begin the series with the Man-of-Steel lookalike Michael Maddox.

Beyond the Chase - Fall for the sexy Irishman, Aiden O'Connor, in this romantic suspense.

The Hard Truth – Read Connor Matthews' story in this second-chance romantic suspense novel.

Surviving the Fall – Jake Summers loses the last 12 years of his life in this action-packed romantic thriller.

The Final Goodbye - Friends-to-lovers romantic mystery

Stealth Ops Series: Bravo Team

√*Finding His Mark* - Luke & Eva

⁌ *Finding Justice* - Owen & Samantha

• *Finding the Fight* - Asher & Jessica

• *Finding Her Chance* - Liam & Emily

Finding the Way Back - Knox & Adriana

Stealth Ops: Echo Team

Chasing the Knight - Wyatt Pierson (2-20-2020)

Becoming Us:

These two books take place in that "5-yr gap" between the prologue and chapter one of Finding His Mark.

Someone Like You - A former Navy SEAL. A father. And off-limits. (Noah & Grace's story.)

My Every Breath - A sizzling and suspenseful romance. Businessman Cade King has fallen for the wrong woman. She's the daughter of a hitman - and he's the target.

Dublin Nights

On the Edge - Travel to Dublin and get swept up in this romantic suspense starring an Irish businessman by day…and fighter by night.

On the Line - a novella

The Real Deal (guest stars Harrison Reed)

Stand-alone (with a connection to *On the Edge*):

The Story of Us– Sports columnist Maggie Lane has 1 rule: never fall for a player. One mistaken kiss with Italian soccer star Marco Valenti changes everything…

CONNECT

Thank you for reading Luke and Eva's story. If you don't mind taking a minute to leave a short review, I would greatly appreciate it. Reviews are incredibly helpful to us authors! Thank you! Learn more at BrittneySahin.com.

www.brittneysahin.com
brittneysahin@emkomedia.net
FB Reader Group - Brittney's Book Babes
Stealth Ops Spoiler Room
Bonus Content

Made in United States
North Haven, CT
14 August 2023

40276435R00171